DEAL KILLER

Neal Sanders

The Hardington Press

Deal Killer is a work of fiction. While certain locales and organizations are rooted in fact, the people and events described are entirely the product of the author's imagination.

Also by Neal Sanders

Murder Imperfect (2010)
The Garden Club Gang (2011)
The Accidental Spy (2011)

Liz Phillips and Detective John Flynn mysteries:
A Murder in the Garden Club (2012)
Murder for a Worthy Cause (2012)

For Beverly Sanders Archer
because sisters are forever

DEAL KILLER

Prologue

From the Boston Globe, Thursday, September 13

Pericles Will Acquire Struggling
SoftRidge in $200 Million Deal

Nashua-based SoftRidge Inc. agreed yesterday to accept a $200 million offer from Boston's Pericles Corp. in a deal that analysts say will cement Pericles' dominance in what was once a highly competitive market.

SoftRidge has struggled since the death of its founder last year, and faced an uncertain future with dwindling cash. In April, SoftRidge announced it had retained Highsmith & Co. to explore the sale of the company. SoftRidge stock, which traded at more that $40 per share as recently as 2007, dipped below $7 earlier this month. Pericles will pay $9.50 per share, a 10% premium to SoftRidge's Wednesday's closing price of $8.60.

"We believe that an acquisition by Pericles represents the best reasonable outcome for shareholders, employees and vendors," SoftRidge Chairman and interim CEO Lawrence Driscoll said in a prepared statement. "We evaluated multiple offers; the one from Pericles was both financially satisfactory and represented a certainty of closing within the time frame set by the Board."

Pericles Chairman and CEO Ross Maynard called the acquisition "a natural consolidation that benefits the served market."

"For more than a year, SoftRidge customers have not known whether the products they ordered would be delivered," Maynard said in a telephone interview. "I admire those customers' loyalty to SoftRidge, but the company's options were increasingly restricted by its finances."

Founded by Peter Kincaid in 1983, SoftRidge was once touted as southern New Hampshire's answer to Route 128. Analyst Jim Borgmann of Goldman Sachs notes that as recently as 2002, Pericles and SoftRidge were of comparable size, competing vigorously for the same customers.

"Kincaid made a number of acquisitions that didn't pan out," Borgmann said. "The company went into the recession with an inadequate cash reserve. Their technology has always been first-rate, but customers demanded a strong balance sheet. Pericles' sales force pounded on SoftRidge's financial weakness at every opportunity. Eventually, suppliers got frightened."

Maynard said he expects to close the acquisition quickly. "Absent any deal killers, we expect to complete the transaction prior to the end of our third quarter."

1.

Monday, September 17

Lynn stared at the plate of donuts in the semidarkness of the room. Especially at the chocolate one. Its dark brown glaze dripping down the side glistened over the deep, rich cocoa-colored base.

She could ignore the jelly-filled fat pills, the mushy donuts with pink frosting, and the ultra-sweet ones covered with shredded coconut. Plain crullers were more alluring, though she had the will power to resist their temptation. But chocolate glazed ones were her regular antidote to boredom. The chocolate one was going to be a problem.

A voice droned on from the head of the conference table. The number of sales offices. The aggregate square footage of those sales offices. The territories served by those sales offices and their staffing levels. *The guy is reading his PowerPoint slide*, Lynn thought. *No commentary, no personal asides. Not a scintilla of new information. He's just reading the damned thing in little more than a monotone. He's wasting everyone's time.*

It was a waste of time because all of the data he was citing was in the Information Memorandum – called the 'IM' in shorthand – given to Lynn the previous Friday and in front of everyone right now. It was the job of each person in the room to have read the document cover to cover. She had read it several times over the weekend. Her copy of the IM was rife with yellow and pink highlighter pen marks, with sticky notes on the three dozen pages that raised the most flags. Lynn came to these meetings well prepared.

The slide changed. The speaker now drilled down into the staffing levels of the sales offices and offered an interesting breakdown between application specialists and quota-carrying salespeople, with a third column for 'admin' people. 'Admins' meant secretaries and receptionists. Lynn did the quick mental calculation based on the figures in the table that the average salary of the 'admins' – 100% of whom would be women – was less than a third of the quota-carrying salespeople – 85% of whom would be men. In her experience, the admins closed at least as many deals as the sales professionals, yet had perhaps a one-in-a-billion shot of moving from behind the computers in their Steelcase cubicles and out into the quota-carrying world where the money was made.

Lynn was giving in to the urge to eat the glazed chocolate donut when a hand reached in front of her in the semi-darkness and eased it out of the pile. The hand headed directly toward a mouth and a third of the donut disappeared in a single bite. The hand and the mouth belonged to one of the attorneys up from Boston. Lynn did some quick guesswork about the lawyer; he looked to be about thirty so he was too young to be a partner. That would make him a senior associate, the equivalent of Andy, her boss. She looked at the hand that held the remnant of the donut and saw a wedding ring. Not that the lawyer would be interested in her even if there wasn't one.

At 10 a.m. on a mid-September morning, Lynn Kowalchuk, a 27-year-old, third-year investment banking associate with the New York firm of Clarenden Brothers, was at the headquarters of SoftRidge, Inc. The facility was a non-descript, single-story structure in an industrial park on the outskirts of Nashua, New Hampshire, a picturesque small city 45 miles northwest of Boston. The building, actually the first bay of a larger structure housing three other tenants, was identifiable as being the home of the corporation only because of a small sign out on Spit Brook Road. SoftRidge did not put its money into self-promotion.

Eighteen people sat around the table in the drab conference room. A strict protocol was being observed because this was the due diligence kick-off meeting intended to lead to the completion of the acquisition of SoftRidge by its much larger rival, Pericles. Those representing Pericles – the investment bankers, accountants and attorneys – sat on one side of the table, those representing SoftRidge on the other. Company management was arrayed on either side nearest the screen so they could stand up and indicate things in the

PowerPoint presentation with their red laser pointers. The senior-most SoftRidge executive at this session occupied the end of the table, a symbolic link between buyer and seller.

Lynn was on the buyer's side of the table. As one of three investment bankers, she sat at the back; the two lawyers were in the middle, the three accountants were up front with the screen looming just a few feet from their faces.

The voice droned on, now segmenting the marketing organization by horizontal and vertical markets served. Lynn's eyes, now better adjusted to the darkness and relieved of temptation, opened the IM to one of her yellow tabs corresponding to vertical markets. The tab had three exclamation marks. She wanted to see if the wording buried in the dry language of the IM was mirrored in the words on the slide.

* * * * *

He looked around the darkened room, judging the situation, looking for things that could upset his plan. The moron Fuller had moved on from sales to marketing, listing 'SWOTs', which he felt compelled to explain – to a room full of MBAs – meant "strengths, weaknesses, opportunities and threats".

All right, then, SWOTs it is, he thought. *Strengths: I'm smarter than anyone in this room and time is on my side. Pericles wants to close the deal by the end of the quarter so they've got less than two weeks for final due diligence and contract signing.*

Weaknesses? The other members of his team, to be sure, but that could also be an opportunity. For years, the Pericles people had made no secret of their disdain for SoftRidge. SoftRidge was simply a thorn in their side. An annoyance. The guys whose products their customers threatened to buy unless Pericles came down in price to meet SoftRidge's quote. The existence of SoftRidge meant Pericles was forced to discount their product by as much as fifteen percent. Following the successful acquisition of SoftRidge, those discounts would disappear and those fifteen percentage points of margin would immediately be added back to Pericles' operating profits.

If Fuller, Morton, and Li have any brains at all, they know they're short-timers the minute the deal gets done, he thought. The other managers were praying for one- and two-year severance packages. They weren't going to get them. His own guess was that Pericles would offer three months plus accrued vacation, period. *That's probably why Fuller is up there droning like a thoroughly defeated hound dog. His options are underwater. He doesn't stand a chance in hell of landing a six-figure sales and marketing executive position anywhere else. Tough break,* he thought.

Opportunities. Oh, yeah, there are opportunities. He would scream with outrage when he was offered three months severance and a consulting option in return for signing a non-compete agreement. He would demand more consideration. He would say that a non-compete agreement was a worthless piece of paper in New Hampshire and that he would be on the phone the next day to three other companies, offering his services to beat Pericles at their own game. And his counterpart from Pericles would smile and say, 'Well, why don't you do that?'

And he would act defeated and swear vengeance. Except that the vengeance would already be complete. Pericles was going to pay him a tax-free $4.2 million bonus, and they didn't know a damn thing about it.

Threats. If there was a threat, it was on the other side of this table. Accountants, lawyers and investment bankers, all hired by Pericles to get through this, the final due diligence. He dismissed the two accountants. Two junior woodchucks from one of the 'big four' firms, neither one older than 25. Their job was to match invoices to purchase orders and check them against the master ledger. Fine. Let them do that. They weren't looking for or going to find what he had done. This was out of their league. When the time came, Pericles would issue checks and wire transfers and he would be home free, a wealthy man.

He looked at the lawyers more carefully. A man in his mid-thirties and a woman in her mid-20s. The guy was a little old for this kind of work. He scanned down the All Hands list in front of him.

Frank Deruda and Fay Collins. Frankie boy was sneaking peeks at his smartphone instead of paying attention to the presentation. The white-shoe New York firm of Ellis and Reid wouldn't spring for a full-blown partner for a lousy $200 million deal, so Frankie boy was probably some kind of a perpetual associate. Cross him off of the threat list. Frank Deruda was probably looking for a job as someone's company counsel because his career as a hot shot lawyer certainly looked like it was going nowhere.

Fay Collins was only slightly more problematical. She seemed to be listening to Fuller's moronic presentation, so she probably had only skimmed the IM, so that was good. But she was taking notes, and that was bad. In theory, the lawyers were there strictly to tie up loose ends. Make certain that distributors had valid contracts and that no employee had planted a side deal in among the human resources files. The lawyers made certain that no customer had been given special consideration as part of a sale, that sort of thing. He had covered his tracks well. He would keep an eye on Fay, but thought the risk low.

Which left the investment bankers. Those on his side of the table were a joke. Two were fresh-faced junior woodchucks without a clue of why they were there, except that they were billing hours and getting their meals paid. Their nominal boss was a blithering idiot named Josh Tilighman who preened in front of every reflective surface. Tilighman had been part of the team that pitched his firm's services to SoftRidge and created the Information Memorandum. He questioned none of the numbers with which he was presented and made not the slightest attempt to grasp the technology.

Pericles' three investment bankers were the single remaining threat. *Andrew Greenglass, Lynn Kowalchuk, and Deborah Fowler,* according to the All Hands list. Andrew Greenglass he dismissed immediately. The guy had been thumbing out text messages since he sat down at the table 45 minutes earlier and was paying absolutely no attention to the presentation. He was the 'partner wannabe' and would likely disappear after this meeting. His next appearance would be at the closing dinner where he would drink too much and tell lewd jokes.

That left the two women. He figured the blonde for Deborah Fowler. Blondes always had names like that. Deborah Fowler looked to be about 26 and seemed intent on making certain her hair was perfect. She played with it constantly, moving it off of her shoulders to achieve just the right alluring balance.

She was strikingly attractive, which meant she had been hired from out of the middle ranks of some second-tier business school by a partner who hoped against hope that Ms. Fowler would hop into bed with him to show her appreciation for being hired by the esteemed New York investment banking firm of Clarenden Brothers. The spine of her Information Memorandum was uncreased, the pad of paper in front of her was untouched.

She had left the top two buttons of her crisp white blouse unbuttoned, the better of show off the lacy bow on the top of her C-cup bra. Deborah Fowler was not going to be a problem. Deborah Fowler was here to posture, probably pouting that she had to spend two weeks in the Nowhere Land that was anywhere outside of New York City.

Which left the Kowalchuk woman. What did that name make her? Polish? Lynn looked to be in her late twenties. Probably three, maybe four years out of B-school if she had gone straight to graduate school with her four-year degree. If there was a threat, she was it. Her IM was filled with yellow stickies and multiple pages were dog-eared. She was filling the second page of her pad with notes, but the notes were from her reading of the memorandum, not from Fuller's ludicrous presentation.

Worst, this Polish princess had to have been hired for her smarts, because it wasn't for looks. She had short, brown hair which fell, limp and styleless, above the collar of a blue Oxford shirt. The roundness of her face left him with the impression she was carrying a few extra pounds. Large, black-framed glasses made her look owlish. She wasn't ugly, she was just... plain. While Deborah Fowler's breasts pushed magnificently against her blouse, creating a little peek-a-boo gap between buttons that added to her allure, Lynn Kowalchuk's blouse showed only an insignificant rounding. While Deborah Fowler sat erect in her chair, Limp-haired Lynn hunched over her notepad.

Investment bankers had no fixed role in this final due diligence, which was itself a problem. In Boston, Ellis and Reid was drafting a final contract that fleshed out the letter of intent that Pericles had offered and SoftRidge had accepted. That final contract would have dozens of attachments, each one in the form of an exhibit.

Most exhibits were lists of things – inventory, customers, accounts receivable – that Pericles was buying or, in some cases, not buying. The lawyers and the accountants assembled and checked the exhibits. The bankers' job was to check the whole package, looking for things that weren't 'right', using whatever sixth sense they possessed to ferret out anything that went against their definition of 'normal'.

That was where the problem lay. His fourteen phantom accounts were owed an aggregate $4.2 million. Unless someone went looking and found a reason to withhold payment, Pericles would write checks or transfer funds when the deal was completed. And with the clock ticking toward the end of the quarter, and an entire day wasted with this kickoff meeting, there would be precious little time for such exploration.

But all the notes she was taking bothered him. Plain, limp-haired Lynn Kowalchuk bothered him. He would have to find things to keep her busy and out of mischief. He would keep a close eye on her. Befriend her, perhaps. Bed her, if necessary. And if she started to get close, if she began asking the wrong questions, he would do whatever was necessary to preserve his tax-free $4.2 million bonus. *Because I deserve that bonus and intend to retire on it*, he thought.

He heard his name being called. The idiot Fuller had gotten through sales and marketing in under an hour. He ought to have taken two. He rose, adjusted his suit jacket, and walked to the front of the room, laser pointer in hand. Ready to do his part to run out the clock.

Ready, if necessary, to kill to get the deal done.

2.

"Of course, management is toast." Andy Greenglass waved his knife in the air for effect. "There's an animosity between Pericles and SoftRidge that goes back two decades, and you better believe that it's personal. Pericles' CEO is on the record that he doesn't want any member of SoftRidge's management around the day after the acquisition. Anyone at SoftRidge who thinks differently is deluding himself."

Lynn poked at her salad, trying to remember what had caused her to order such a disaster. Iceberg lettuce, shredded carrots, and tomatoes that were so preposterously unripe and lacking in flavor that they may as well have been made of cardboard. There had to be fifty thousand garden-ripened tomatoes within a five mile radius of this restaurant. Why couldn't this pathetic restaurant buy one? From the corner of her eye she saw Deb, too, push clumps of lettuce back and forth across her plate, not eating.

Andy stabbed at the air again, skewering a member of SoftRidge's management as he did a piece of his steak. "Ross Maynard didn't even want to pay out accrued vacation. He said the whole company had been on vacation for the past two years. He also wanted to fire the whole work force. Mitch had to talk him through the WARN Act consequences to get him to relent. But mark my words: six months from the acquisition date, every trace of SoftRidge is going to have disappeared. And I'll bet any of you fifty bucks that Maynard drops every member of management to two weeks severance as a last-minute contract demand. And another fifty bucks says that SoftRidge's Board will cave."

Despite the presence of friendly faces, Lynn felt herself beginning to tense up. Day One had been a disaster. SoftRidge had insisted on giving everyone a full corporate presentation and had paraded eight managers through the meeting. The plant tour had consumed two hours because someone decided that 'the team' needed to understand what they were buying. Each step had been explained in excruciating detail.

Then, at 6 p.m., the word had been passed that there would be a group dinner, the better to 'get to know one another'. How well did a bunch of hired hands — none of whom would ever see anyone from SoftRidge again after this assignment — need to get to know the company? The lawyers and accountants had eagerly jumped at the chance for a fancy, free meal. Andy had begged off, which gave Lynn the opportunity to do the same. Left with no one she knew and no one she wanted to get to know better, Deb had also declined.

And so they were here at a chain restaurant that could have been a Bertucci's or an Olive Garden for all the difference it made, eating iceberg lettuce salads topped with tasteless tomatoes.

Lynn longed for the comfort of take-out Chinese in front of her computer or a television in her hotel room. She had never really felt at ease in groups, never cared for the forced camaraderie of a group dinner. She had always been a loner and seemed destined to remain one.

The impersonal nature of investment banking due diligence suited her. She would get an assignment and pack her suitcase, not knowing for certain if she would be gone two weeks or two months. In three years, she had been part of forty-two transactions in seventeen states. Without ever having asked her why it was so, Andy knew that she preferred out-of-town assignments over those in or around New York, and he inquired only whether she would prefer Atlanta or Portland, Denver or San Francisco.

She did not know herself why she was such a loner. Had she subjected the issue to rigorous analysis, she could have written out a page full of points, starting with being an only child who had never been required to socialize with siblings. She had been continually uprooted as her father's department store career progressed, working through a progression of Midwestern cities. Her near-perfect SATs had given her access to almost any elite college in the country, but she chose the anonymity of being one of 3700 incoming freshmen on the 30,000-student campus of U.C. Berkeley.

Only for graduate school did she choose a small school, Dartmouth's highly regarded Amos Tuck School of Business, a hundred miles north of where she now sat. Tuck accepted fewer than 250 students per year. There, for the first time in her life, she felt herself under scrutiny by professors and classmates and was profoundly uncomfortable.

She had never had a social life, never felt a need to be fashionable. She missed these things in a vague sort of way. In an airport or a mall in a far-off city, she would buy romance novels and read them in one sitting, throwing them away in a lobby waste receptacle rather than leaving them for a maid to find in her room.

She lived in a two-bedroom Manhattan apartment with three roommates she barely knew and who loved it that she was seldom home. Her clothes came from Land's End and L.L. Bean catalogs and her wardrobe was little more than a closet full of blue shirts, sweatshirts, and all-season slacks. When she got her hair cut, it was at an inexpensive, impersonal chain in whatever city she was working, and her bob hair style had not varied since her undergraduate days. With such low living expenses, and with the competitive salaries and bonuses paid by investment banking firms, she had already accumulated several hundred thousand dollars in her brokerage account.

She knew she was not beautiful. She knew Deb Fowler was. This morning, she had seen every pair of male eyes in the room appreciatively take in Deb's face and body, just as they had done in the half-dozen projects the two of them had worked on in the preceding eighteen months. If Deb ever tired of investment banking as a career and elect to throw away that top-of-her-class Sloan School of Management education, all she would have to do was simply pick out the wealthiest and best looking man then in the room and become the beautiful, stay-at-home wife of some corporation executive or law firm partner. Deb had never said anything like that, but the look in men's eyes made it depressingly likely. Lynn had seen those same male eyes give her a quick, dismissive glance and then go back for a second helping of Deb's blonde hair, perfect face and wonderful figure.

Lynn had attracted the attention of a handful of men, mostly during her four years at Berkeley. They had seen past her plainness and glimpsed something much more attractive inside. A few of those relationships had evolved to become sexual. But for the most part she had not been ready. By and large she had held men at a distance until they either accepted the role of male buddy or else, frustrated, drifted away.

However, at 27, Lynn felt she was on the cusp of a change. Part of the change was forced on her by time. Clarenden Brothers hired only from top schools and mediocre performers were quickly weeded out of each year's hires. But, as at all investment banking firms, Clarenden Brothers' associates either became vice presidents after four years or else they were invited to seek opportunities elsewhere. It was up or out.

The firm paid very well, but being a 'deal grunt' brought no new business into Clarenden's coffers, and new deals were the lifeblood of the investment banking world. Lynn had earned the highest evaluations possible at each review. Within a year she would be asked to start managing projects or, worse, pitching them to prospective customers, in order to justify her rising salary and year-end bonus.

Part of the change was in herself. She had matured physically and emotionally since getting her MBA three years earlier. She knew her plainness was partly cosmetic, the ten extra pounds a function of too much Chinese takeout in distant cities and towns. On their last deal in Columbia, South Carolina, Deb had lured her into a mall department store's cosmetics area and supervised a 45-minute makeover. The effect was dramatic, if temporary. "You give me an afternoon in a competent salon with a stylist and there could be a whole new you," Deb had said.

But Lynn had bought none of the cosmetics and had demurred on the hair styling. The next morning, she had shown up for due diligence in her trademark blue Oxford shirt and khaki slacks, her hair again covering most of her face.

"Coward," Deb had whispered. And then mercifully said nothing else about the matter. But Lynn had memorized the product names and how they had been applied. She had paid attention. She just wasn't ready. But during the rest of that South Carolina assignment, Lynn had found herself joining Deb every morning in the hotel gym.

The three investment bankers finished their meal sharing the kinds of tales that professionals who have worked together on multiple projects tell one another. Deb dissected the Highsmith & Co. bankers representing SoftRidge, saying they seemed more preoccupied with getting the right sandwiches for lunch than with speedily closing the deal. She rolled her eyes and said that the Highsmith vice president on the deal had spent much of the day leering at her. Lynn voiced her concern that the first day had been a waste of time.

Andy dismissed her caution. "This one's a slam-dunk," he said, confidently. "I say we're out of here in a week, max."

* * * * *

He looked around the table and motioned to the waiter for another two bottles of wine. *Yes, this was the right decision*, he thought. The accountants for both sides were already tipsy. They would be late tomorrow and he would have to put on a display of annoyance at their slow work and inability to focus on the mundane detail work that was needed to get the contract exhibits in order. The idiot Fuller was hitting on the attractive attorney – Fay something – with at least a modicum of success. The male attorney was nodding off.

SoftRidge's three investment bankers were also eyeing the attractive attorney even as they fortified their courage with more wine. The senior-most of them, the twit Tilighman, attempted to impress everyone with tales of his new Porsche and his access to box seats at Red Sox games. He hadn't worried much about his company's choice of investment bankers before today. Based on tonight's performance, he dismissed any lingering doubt that Highsmith & Co. would be a problem.

His concern was that the Clarenden Brothers bankers had begged off. That was a bad sign. Andy Greenglass had told him he could stay for only part of tomorrow. That was good. But the two junior woodchuck bankers had shown increasing impatience with the process as the day progressed. Debby Big Tits has surprised him by interrupting the presentations at multiple points with insightful questions. The Information Memorandum covers may not have been creased, but there was some kind of intuitive understanding of the business.

And Limp-haired Lynn had just kept writing away, making continuing notes from the Memorandum and the draft contract. She had asked no questions because she knew the day-long presentation offered no new information. She was simply using the time to organize her own inquiries. She was going to be trouble, he could tell.

He had a choice to make. He could wait and see if someone raised unusual questions about the names on the accounts and then act, or he could line up assistance now and direct that person to act immediately, even if those questions hadn't yet been raised.

He had never killed anyone and he did not look forward to the experience. It was a task he would prefer to delegate, provided the price was not unreasonable, that he could have some guarantee of results, and be certain that his anonymity was ensured. What he had read in newspapers about hiring hit men was that there was an excellent chance that the person you hired was an undercover police officer. He had perused the internet on the subject the past few weeks – using computers in public places rather than his own – and had gotten some useful ideas. And, the more he thought about it, the more he came to understand that he needed a backup plan.

He now had just such a plan in place, and he was comfortable that he was not dealing with the police or police informants. He had gone to school with Joey Gavrilles, though Joey had likely not graduated. He had even dated Joey's sister for a time. He had gone on to college while Joey embarked on a life of petty crime. He had run into Joey at a Home Depot a month earlier – a serendipitous meeting that had given him confidence that this *thing* was meant to be. Later, over beers, he had asked Joey for the name of someone who might be able to 'take someone out of the picture' in the event of a problem.

He had offered to pay for such information, and Joey had said that he had someone in mind – a middleman who knew lots of people who did such work. But Joey had also said not to ask him for the name of the middleman – and it would be a telephone number and not a specific name – until he knew he needed it. Joey had further advised him to buy one of those disposable cell phones that truckers used because, when he called that number, it had to be untraceable.

The advice had continued: when you pay for that service, it will need to be in cash and in twenty and fifty dollar bills, so he needed to start stockpiling that cash now so as not to arouse suspicion. If and when he contacted Joey, it would not be at home but, rather, through a bar, and he would need to use that same untraceable phone. Joey's fee, payable upon receipt of the phone number, would be a thousand dollars.

He had come away from that chance meeting buoyed by the good fortune that he had not completely distanced himself in school from people like Joey Gavrilles. As Joey began to miss school days, with rumors that the absences were the result of run-ins with the law, the respectable kids began avoiding Joey. But he had stayed friendly. Now, that friendship had paid its greatest dividend.

Around the table, twelve people made fools of themselves, ensuring that the second day of due diligence would be no more productive than the first. He smiled. *With one possible exception, everything is perfect.*

3.

Tuesday, September 18

Lynn sat with Charlie Li, SoftRidge's vice president of engineering. They had quickly found common ground in their UC Berkeley degrees, though Charlie had been nearly a decade ahead of her. It had given the two of them a point of reference that might otherwise have made the conversation purely ask-and-answer, and this was not the way she delved into a company and its people.

"You missed a hell of a dinner last night," Charlie said at one point. "Nashua has about two and a half good restaurants. The wine flowed freely and I think everyone was feeling no pain last night, which means they're feeling plenty of headaches this morning."

Lynn gave him a kind of half-smile. "I'm not much for drinking. Or for large groups."

"Well, it was probably your only chance," he said. "Management is really tight with the dollar. I don't think you'll see another dinner like that around here ever again. Not that there will be a 'here' after the deal."

Lynn thought back to Andy's pronouncement that 'management is toast'. "You don't expect an offer from Pericles?"

Charlie snorted. "Those guys hate us with a passion. They've been trying to put us out of business ever since I got here. We've got fundamentally better technology and products. What they've got is half a billion dollars on their balance sheet. They're buying us for one reason: because we refused to die."

"What happens to your technology?" Lynn asked.

"Oh, it will filter into their next generation of stuff, provided it doesn't wreck their margins. They'll own the patents, and Ross Maynard has a reputation as a 'suer'."

"So what does that mean for you?"

Charlie slumped a little further in his chair, and stared into his cup of coffee rather than looking at Lynn. "It means I see if my skills are transferable. Any idea I've got today becomes the property of Pericles, and any product I develop in the future that can be traced back to things I knew when I worked here are the property of Pericles. Basically, it means I'm screwed."

"No pot of gold at the end of the rainbow?"

"Maybe three or four months of severance and two months of accrued vacation."

"Options?"

"The options were at twelve bucks and up. The deal is at under ten."

"Then why are you guys selling?

Li shrugged, but now he looked up at Lynn. "That was the Board's call. They didn't ask us. But it had to happen: Because of its other businesses, Pericles has the size and the balance sheet we never had, and they used it against us in the market. They scared the bejesus out of our customers with their constant talk of us going out of business."

Lynn took it all in. She had never heard of either company until three days earlier when Andy tossed the Information Memorandum on her desk and told her to be in Boston for a meeting with Pericles on Saturday morning, and then to be in Nashua on Monday morning. Through the IM she had learned that SoftRidge had put itself up for sale six months earlier and that Clarenden Brothers' client, Pericles, had offered a price that the SoftRidge Board of Directors had found acceptable.

As was its usual practice – and one fairly common in business – Pericles had used its own staff to perform due diligence in that first round and came away satisfied. Clarenden's assignment was to oversee the final fact checking and bring together the exhibits and schedules that were the heart of the contract. Andy had told her to pack for two weeks.

She had never gotten emotionally attached to any deal on which she had worked. The fun – and the challenge – was in finding the things that everyone else had missed. Sometimes she was part of the team that was buying, sometimes she represented the seller. She really didn't care which side of the table she sat on. An assignment for the seller was always longer as it meant preparing the IM and meeting multiple potential buyers.

When representing a selling company, someone from the investment banking firm always had to sit through every presentation, regardless of how many were given and over what period of time. The first few times management gave its presentation to prospective buyers, a Clarenden VP or senior VP attended the meeting. By the third or fourth presentation, it was the 'deal grunts' like herself who sat in, making notes on buyer interest and management gaffes and reporting back to Andy what she saw in each meeting. On one memorable deal, she had sat through a marathon of thirty-five presentations over four weeks. By the end, she knew every PowerPoint slide and every joke, and she hoped never to see Austin, Texas, again.

One of the truisms of investment banking, told to her since her first assignment, is that 'management lies' and that it is the banker's job to determine the truth. Management always says the future is always bright and products always work better than those of the competition. Management always says financial reverses are always one-quarter events and legal issues are always 'routine'. In the world of investment banking, the corollary to lying management is that 'only raw numbers tell the truth'.

If an investment banker had the assignment of selling a company, its job was to justify management's statements using outside data. If the banker worked for the prospective buyer, the job was to tear away the fabric of lies and get to the underlying truth, and construct a fair price based on that truth.

And so Lynn's job – at least in her own mind – was to determine how much of the Information Memorandum was a lie, and to what extent management and its investment banking accomplices had shaped its financials to present the best possible picture to potential buyers. A price had already been agreed upon and nothing could raise that final price, but last-minute problems could drive the price of the deal down - sometimes, down significantly. It was the reason why bankers did not get close to management. Friendship made spotting lies harder.

* * * * *

He drummed his fingers impatiently as managers reported due diligence progress – or lack of it – over the course of the morning. His artificial annoyance turned real, however, when he spoke with Charlie Li, and his concern about Limp-haired Lynn grew stronger. He learned from Charlie that she had been waiting in the lobby when he arrived at 7:30. And, rather than observing the protocol of waiting in the lobby for a member of senior management or one of the Highsmith investment bankers to escort her into the building, she had tagged along with Charlie into the building.

She and Charlie Li had spoken for nearly two hours and no one had known about it. Li was sitting in front of him now, telling him the conversation was about nothing; college life, what Pericles expected, and SoftRidge's product superiority. Li was saying she left the meeting in a cheerful frame of mind and asked no probing questions.

His strongly held belief was that all people of Chinese descent were poor judges of people and their intentions. Li could have given away any number of important data points that would lower the purchase price. While he did not especially care about whether Pericles paid $200 million or $100 million, he did not want any interruption in the process. He did not want Pericles demanding concessions that would cause SoftRidge's Board to reconsider their offer. He did not want any regulatory authority looking at the deal other than the perfunctory rubber stamp of approval.

Above all, he did not want any careful examination of certain accounts. Millions of dollars would be flowing out of Pericles to pay SoftRidge vendors and shareholders. On October 3, he intended to be a very wealthy man.

It was important that his dummy accounts not be scrutinized. Ordinarily, there were multiple levels of analysis in these things, but on the day the acquisition was completed, those safeguards would disappear, at least for a brief period. In the days just after Pericles acquired SoftRidge, $200 million would be disbursed to shareholders. More than $60 million of checks and automated payments would be disbursed as the acquired company's debts were cleared, most of those to names that were unfamiliar to those doing the paying.

Pericles' staff would also process a substantial volume of severance checks and other payments associated with the acquisition. In this blizzard of ledger-clearing, his theft – small in the scheme of things but hugely satisfactory to himself – would go unnoticed.

Charlie had to be warned, but warned in such a way not to raise questions.

"You know what the Board's rules are," he said to Charlie. "Absolutely no contact with anyone from Pericles unless one of our bankers is present for the entire conversation. They didn't make any exceptions. Technically, they could fire you for having that conversation."

"Not that it would make any difference," Charlie said, glumly. "On October 1, you, me and everyone else in management is going to be told to clear out their desk."

"Except engineering, Charlie," he said. "They're going to need you and your people. The Pericles people have never understood our technology. That's why they've never matched us in the marketplace. You're going to be golden, Charlie, mark my words."

Charlie Li looked back at him with appreciative eyes. He may not have believed what he was being told, but it was clear that Charlie wanted to believe.

"The rest of us – sure," he continued. "We know what they think of us. It starts with Ross Maynard and permeates the organization. Do you know what their code name was for this deal? 'Soft Underbelly.' I once saw one of the Pericles guys' folder when they were putting together their offer. So do I think I'm out of a job at the end of the month? Sure. But not you, Charlie. They're going to need you."

"So, no more unaccompanied visits with their bankers. Tell them you're sorry, but make them wait like they're supposed to. OK, Charlie? Better yet, Driscoll is here today. Tell him that you got waylaid by one of Clarenden's investment bankers and you're uncomfortable as a result. But make it your idea. Don't tell him we talked. That would make it look bad for you."

Charlie Li gave a short nod, then a more aggressive one. "Yes," Charlie said. "You're right. I'll do that."

As Charlie Li left the room, he thought, *What a dumb son of a bitch. If it wasn't for me, this company would have died a long time ago.*

As he sat back in his chair, he daydreamed of his new life with its added $4.2 million in security. He had already identified a set of fixed-income investments that he felt certain would yield at least six and a half percent. Those investments meant he would see an annual income stream of $273,000, more than enough to finance the lifestyle he had in mind, all by itself. Added to his other investments, and allowing for some immediate, discretionary spending to support his retirement hobbies, he could look forward to the next thirty years as ones free of financial worries.

It strengthened his resolve: nothing would get in the way of his plan. Not some hag of an investment banker, not Charlie Li. Nothing and no one.

4.

Lynn and Deb sat in the SoftRidge lobby, growing angrier by the minute. Andy, of course, had left for the airport before noon with the excuse that he had to be at important meetings in New York. They had already waited here in the lobby for half an hour.

"This is bullshit," Deb said, and took her phone out of her purse. She dialed a number and waited. "I need Ross Maynard," she said into the phone. She held the phone so Lynn could hear the conversation.

"Mr. Maynard's office." A woman's voice, professional and non-committal.

"This is Deborah Fowler from Clarenden Brothers. I'm at SoftRidge working on closing the deal, and the company has clammed up on us. I need Ross's help. Be sure to tell him the name: Deborah Fowler."

"Just a moment, please."

Lynn marveled at the succinctness of the conversation and Deb's expectation that she would get results. Thirty seconds went by.

"Miss Fowler, as I live and breathe. To what do I owe the honor?" It was the gravelly voice of Ross Maynard, Pericles' Chairman and CEO, oozing charm. Lynn had met him just once, at Pericles' offices in Boston four days earlier. To the best of Lynn's knowledge, Deb had met him only the one time as well. Yet, she had gotten through to the CEO of a billion-dollar corporation on the strength of a three-sentence message. She concluded that Deb had caught his eye at the meeting.

"We're getting stonewalled here in Nashua," Deb said. "We're suddenly being told that there has to be someone from Highsmith with us at all times, and the Highsmith people aren't available, so we're just sitting in the lobby, waiting for someone to come out and hold our hand."

"I'd be glad to do that myself, Miss Fowler," Maynard said, not missing a beat. "My acquisitions guy got a call at noon from Larry Driscoll claiming that someone from your shop tackled the engineering VP as he came in the door this morning, stuck to him like bubble gum on his shoe, and grilled him for two-plus hours. Is that true?"

Lynn vehemently shook her head and mouthed the word, 'no'.

"That's not the way it happened, Mr. Maynard…" Deb said.

"Ross," he interrupted. "If you're going to work on any more deals for me, it's got to be Ross."

Lynn closed her eyes and clenched her teeth. *He's making a pass at her, right over the phone.*

"That's not the way it happened, Ross. Lynn Kowalchuk was here early this morning. Their engineering VP came in and invited Lynn to join him. They had a good conversation, but nothing that could conceivably be called 'grilling'."

"Is Miss Kowalchuk there with you?"

"She's right here."

"Ask her if she stepped over the line, even a little."

Lynn shook her head again. "Absolutely not."

"She says she never stepped over the line."

"Then those pains in the ass are over-reacting, as usual. I'll make a call. I want this wrapped up, but I want it done right. You know our deadline, Miss Fowler?"

"I understand, Ross."

"We're going to have a hell of a party here when this closes, irrespective of what Clarenden does by way of a closing dinner. You've got to promise me you'll be here."

"You have my word on it, Ross." She rolled her eyes as she spoke. She pressed a button that ended the call.

"Sounds like you made a conquest," Lynn said.

"He's a dirty old man with one wife, one ex-wife, and four children; two of them daughters our age," Deb replied. "But it will get things moving."

Five minutes later, a tall, angular man in an impeccably tailored suit came out into the lobby. Lynn knew him from photos as Larry Driscoll, SoftRidge's chairman of the board of directors. He was past sixty with thin gray hair, a lean face and frameless bifocals. Driscoll's dominant feature was untrimmed eyebrows that seemed to dance on their own when he spoke.

"I owe you ladies an apology," he said. "Would you come back to my office?"

A minute later, they were in that rarest of amenities at SoftRidge – a private office with a window. Moreover, it was large enough to have a sofa, and coffee table, and two side chairs. Lynn noted that Driscoll's office was mostly bare of ornamentation, an acknowledgement that he spent little time at the facility. A perk that would have gladdened the heart of any manager toiling away in a cubicle was going to waste. What kind of company was this?

An admin brought in coffee unbidden, together with a half dozen cold cans of soda. *This for a meeting of three people*, Lynn thought.

"My apology that I wasn't at the kickoff meeting yesterday," Driscoll said. "But there's not a lot I can add to the discussion, so I thought I'd stay out of the way and let company management handle it. We've made our deal with Pericles' Board. We all want to get it closed by the end of the quarter. I just had Ross Maynard imply to me that we aren't holding up our end of the bargain." He indicated the beverages with his hand. Lynn reached for a Diet Coke.

"I also had a complaint that one of you broke convention and did an unauthorized and unaccompanied interview with our head of engineering." He looked first at Lynn, then at Deb. "Is that true?"

"Charlie Li saw me in the lobby as he came in and invited me back to his office," Lynn said. "There was never any coercion."

"He said he was uncomfortable," Driscoll said.

"I did nothing to make him uncomfortable," Lynn countered.

"Well, let's do this," Driscoll said, pouring himself a cup of coffee. "I understand that the Highsmith guys are spread thin. If you can't find one of the Highsmith people, you see Bill Griffin, Jeff Wright, Sandy Calo, or Frank Kepner. I'm authorizing them to sit in on interviews in Highsmith's place. Ditto any documents. They'll find them for you promptly. Let's get this deal done right, and done on time. And if they can't help you, you come see me. Agreed?"

Not waiting for a response, he rose and held out his hand toward Lynn. She shook it quickly. He then held out his hand for Deb. She took it and he clasped his hand over hers; a two-handed shake. "You let me know if you need anything," he said to Deb.

Lynn said, "I need to see the patent file, if that's reasonable."

Driscoll turned toward Lynn. "Of course." He reluctantly let go of Deb's hand and went to the phone on his desk. He punched an extension and mumbled into the handset.

"And I'd like to start going over distributor contracts," Deb said.

"I'll walk you there myself," Driscoll said. "And we can drop off your companion at the patent file."

* * * * *

Lynn thumbed through the patent files, checking for completeness of the filings and any letters implying infringement on the part of SoftRidge of other companies' patents. But her mind kept going back to the twin conversations with Ross Maynard and Larry Driscoll.

Charlie Li and I just talked a few hours ago, she thought. Charlie Li was at ease. We found the Berkeley connection and it was like I was family. How on earth could he have told Driscoll that he was uncomfortable? Or that I had 'waylaid' him? And how did that get back to Larry Driscoll so quickly?

She began setting up straw men and knocking them down.

Let's try this one: Larry Driscoll wants to scotch the deal, or at least delay it while he looks for a better offer. Not a chance. He just changed the rules to make it easier to get documentation.

OK, SoftRidge has a better offer and they don't want to pay the break-up fee, so they're trying to get Pericles so mad that they walk away. Also a lousy prospect. She knew the next highest offer had been for stock and couldn't close for at least three months because of shareholder approval. SoftRidge doesn't have enough cash to last that long.

Someone wants to slow down due diligence to push the deal close past September 30. Not a possibility because of SoftRidge's lack of cash.

Someone wants us to do half-assed due diligence so we close without having looked closely at everything.

Lynn closed the patent file. The inane, full-day dog-and-pony show. Accountants with hangovers this morning. And an immediate reaction when she showed up early and began engaging management.

Someone is trying to run out the clock. Someone here has something to hide. It fit.

* * * * *

Day Two was coming to an end with virtually no progress having been made in due diligence, which should have suited him just fine. Then something unsettling had happened. Larry Driscoll standing in his doorway. He had asked Larry how everything was going.

"Ross Maynard just put a gun to my head," Driscoll had said. "Ross said, 'you stonewall my people one more time and I'll put out a press release saying we're delaying the close to sometime in December'."

"You know he doesn't mean that," he had told Driscoll. "He needs this deal to get his product pricing up. He pulls the plug – even for ninety days – and we drop our prices by half for anyone who pays cash net ten. That'll get him back to the table."

It was brave talk for a man whose future was tied to a deal closing on September 29 or 30, and who would be ruined – or even in jail – if the deal closed late or failed to close at all.

"Maybe." Driscoll then walked fully into his office and closed the door behind him. Driscoll lowered his voice to just above a whisper. "But Maynard has our internal financials now. He knows how much cash we have and how long we can last without him. That's a game of Russian roulette I don't want to play."

"Here's what I've done," Driscoll continued. "I've given the two Clarenden bankers – they're down to two now – permission to hound you and a couple of other guys any time they need something. Whatever they need, you drop what you're doing and get it for them. Is that clear?"

"Perfectly clear," he had said.

And then he was alone, and thinking.

'Plan A' no longer has an absolute guarantee of success, he thought. *Clarenden has a pipeline to Ross Maynard, and Ross issued exactly the right threat. I can't slow-roll them. I need to get Limp-haired Lynn out of the way.*

With the door to his office still closed, he unlocked his briefcase. Into a manila envelope, he placed a photograph and a sheet of paper. Also from his briefcase, he retrieved the disposable cell phone, acquired and activated for cash, he had purchased after that fateful meeting with Joey Gavrilles, and a small sheet of paper. Three days earlier, he had used the phone for the first time when he had called Joey and obtained the number he now had in his hand.

He dialed the number.

"I need some assistance," he said. "I need to meet you this evening. Joey Gavrilles should have vouched for me."

"You get yourself down here to Boston," the gruff voice at the other end of the phone said. "We're going to meet at a nice, public place. You be out in front of Faneuil Hall with all of the tourists at eight o'clock. You call me again from there and I'll give you further instructions."

5.

Lynn and Deb contentedly ate Moo Shu Chicken and pork fried rice with chopsticks as they absorbed every detail of the patent file. They were still in SoftRidge's offices, though it was well past 7 p.m. As far as she could tell, only a security guard was in the building with them.

Charlie Li has been right. SoftRidge's technology was superb and, while she was no expert on the subject, the company seemed to have a complete technology solution. In a rational world, customers would have flocked to SoftRidge. Instead, their technology edge failed to translate into market share because Pericles had sown such doubts about SoftRidge's financial viability.

And those doubts were real enough. SoftRidge had not made a profit in three years and, consequently, had burned through most of its cash reserves. Raising new equity had been out of the question; investors would not pour more money into a company that consistently posted losses while its competitors turned healthy profits. And banks did not want to lend to a company for the same reasons. Backed into a corner with no solution, SoftRidge had done the right thing in putting itself up for sale.

She kept coming back to her epiphany of earlier in day. *Someone is trying to run out the clock.*

"Deb, what if there's something really rotten inside SoftRidge. What if Pericles' staff missed something big? Something that would be a deal killer if it got uncovered?"

Deb looked up from her file. "Like what?"

Lynn cast about for an example. "A live patent infringement issue."

Deb took a sip of her Diet Sprite. "SoftRidge has to sign a representation that it knows of no patent claims. If one turns up next month and it turns out there's paperwork on it and SoftRidge hid it, the deal unwinds. That's basic reps and warranties."

"I know that," Lynn persisted. "So it isn't a patent claim. What could a company be hiding that enough due diligence could uncover, but that a seller wouldn't have to give a representation to?"

Deb did not answer for more than a minute while she thought. "Something not conveyed," she said at last. "A patent they hold that isn't on the list that someone will sell to the highest bidder. A block of inventory that someone is holding back. A disgruntled customer that's going to return a lot of product after the deal is done and then switch vendors. It's our job to find every patent, verify that all of the inventory is on the list, and talk to every major customer."

Due Diligence 101, Lynn thought. *And there are two of us, and a little over a week to finish the job.*

"And there's always the cute trick of hiding the bomb," Deb said. "The key part that has been obsoleted by its supplier. The letter telling SoftRidge there aren't going to be any more doohickeys is in one of the fifty boxes of stuff in the Data Room, but it's misfiled."

"Here's a theory," Lynn said. "That all-day time-waster yesterday was part of a plan by someone to run out the clock on us. Getting everyone drunk last night so nothing got done today was part of the same game plan. So was keeping us out in the lobby."

"Or not," Deb said. "The company is proud of what it has accomplished. No one is required to drink wine with dinner. That guy, Li, figured out he screwed up by talking to you alone and covered his ass with management."

The rebuke stung Lynn. *Maybe she's right*, she thought. *Maybe I'm just paranoid.*

"But when you tell me something's wrong, I believe you," Deb said. "I've seen you find the 'gotcha' when no one else was bothering to look. And yesterday was just weird. But I'll tell you this: if something is going on, it isn't the entire company that's doing it. Driscoll didn't just apologize: he fixed it so it wouldn't happen again. I'd say you've got one person with something to hide."

* * * * *

At eight o'clock, he had paid an ungodly sum to self-park his car in a safe garage adjacent to Boston's Quincy Market complex. He hated the idea of paying to park. In Nashua, no one paid to park, much less eighteen dollars for two hours – and at night. But neither would he have turned his car over to an attendant who would carelessly throw open his car doors or leave the car where it could be rammed or dented. He hated Boston just as he hated New York.

He positioned himself in front of Faneuil Hall looking at the tourists milling around and, at exactly at eight, he dialed the number. He listened around him to see if anyone's phone rang. He heard no cell phone ring tones.

His call was answered on the third ring.

"Where are you?' he asked. "I thought you said to be in front of Faneuil Hall?"

"Screw you," came the reply. "You want to meet me; you stand out in front of Victoria's Secret and ogle the nighties with all the other guys. I'll find you."

This wasn't the way it was supposed to happen. And he wasn't going to be dictated to. He started back toward his car. He would find someone else.

His phone rang.

"Wrong direction, Bozo. Victoria's Secret is the other way. South Market building. The one on your right."

He stopped, stunned. The person had spotted him. And had his cell number. It was an untraceable phone, but now someone knew the number he was using. Then he thought: *Of course. Caller ID.*

"You want to do this, let's do this," the voice said.

"Since you can apparently see me, why not just come to me?" he said.

"Because two guys talking in front of Victoria's Secret is two guys. Two guys in front of Faneuil Hall talking is two fruits hooking up, and you don't want that kind of attention."

He reviewed his options. If he walked back to his car, the person would follow him and know his license plate number. He could ride the subway for half an hour or take a cab to the airport and back. That would certainly shake the person. But it would get him no closer to his backup plan, and he had only this one name. And that name was not even of the person who would do the work. It was only the middleman.

He started toward the South Market building and Victoria's Secret. He stared at the lingerie for several minutes. The display window's lighting provided him an indistinct reflection of the world around him.

Five minutes later, a man was standing alongside him.

"Joey Gavrilles said you could find someone to do a job for me," he said.

"Pleased to meet you, too," the man said. He was in a leather jacket with the collar turned up and wore too much aftershave. From the poor reflection in the store's plate glass window, he saw only a man slightly taller than himself. He wore a cap pulled down low over his eyes, obscuring much of his face. He spoke with a decided Boston accent.

"Joey said you'd pay the going rate for my services," the man said. "Joey didn't say who you were, and I don't want to know. Tell me your problem."

He went into his rehearsed speech. "There's a woman. Here's her picture and the license plate number of the car she's driving." He pulled out a photo taken earlier that day with his cell phone camera while she was going through files. "She's staying at the Crowne Plaza in Nashua. Her name is Lynn Kowalchuk. She needs to be put out of action, but only if I call you and say that it's necessary. But if I say it's necessary, the person who does this needs to move quickly."

"Christ almighty," the man said. "You want someone to stand around, waiting for your call? That's not the way it works, pal. I mean, are you nervous? Cold feet?"

He shook his head. "I think she has the potential to be a problem. I don't know for certain yet. I'm trying to prepare for that eventuality…"

"Like she might tell your wife or she might not?"

"It's not that."

"It's always that," the man said. "Here's a solution for the squeamish. What if she has an accident. Not a fatal accident. Just something that – what were your words? – 'puts her out of action'? Sends her to the sidelines, like in a football game."

He pondered the suggestion.

"That sounds good," he said, finally.

"I'll check it out and give you a price tomorrow," the man said.

"I thought we'd do that now," he said.

"Now that I know what you need done, I can find the right person. Maybe I can get it done on the cheap," the man said. "You'd like that, I bet."

"When would it get done?" he asked.

"Quick. I call you tomorrow, it gets done right after that. You leave that little phone on so you can hear it, OK?"

He nodded. Then the man in the leather jacket was gone.

6.

Wednesday, September 19

Lynn studied Frank Kepner's fingernails. Grown men don't chew their nails, but Frank Kepner did. Senior executives of corporations didn't wear Aerosmith tee-shirts, but Frank Kepner did. And hiking boots were not on the approved footwear list of men in the management suite. But Frank Kepner wore them, and had them propped up on his desk as he spoke.

"Trying to get vendors to ship you stuff once they know you're up for sale is hard enough," Kepner was saying. "Trying to get them to ship you stuff when the sales guy from Pericles is telling them that the company is one step away from laying off the whole work force is a whole different smoke. Your client is a real son of a bitch."

Lynn nodded. Maybe Pericles engaged in unfair tactics, maybe they didn't. All she wanted was the current bill of materials on half a dozen products.

"I say that because we've had a lot of vendor changes," Kepner said. "Guys we did business with for ten years dropped us as soon as we went public with the announcement that we were 'exploring the sale' of the company. Or else they demanded cash in advance, which we couldn't pay."

"But you were a late payer for nearly a year beforehand," Lynn said.

"They lived with it," Kepner said, shrugging his shoulder. "They always got paid. They figured it into their pricing. But Pericles really turned the screws when the Board announced a sale. And, when Pericles came in as the high bidder, they went into high gear. Five of my best suppliers demanded that they be brought current or else they'd stop shipping. Guess what? I don't have eight million dollars to bring them current. So I found new vendors for those parts and subassemblies I could, and I'm pulling everything I can out of stock for the rest. Come September 30, the cupboard is going to be bare on a lot of inventory."

Lynn heard some anger in his voice, but also resignation. SoftRidge had fought from the position of underdog for years. Now, the fight was finally over. She asked again for the bills of materials, the master list of parts needed to build SoftRidge's key products.

Kepner took his feet off his desk and turned to his computer. He typed a series of commands and a laser printer behind him churned out a dozen or more pages.

Lynn took them and placed them in a file folder. "You don't plan to be around after the sale?" she asked.

Kepner snorted. "I think my life expectancy after the deal gets signed is about three minutes. Those guys hate us and the feeling is mutual. All they want to do is get us out of the way so they can raise prices. I just pity their customers."

"So what do you plan to do?"

Kepner threw a glance at a large map behind him. It was a trail and elevation map of the White Mountains. "Lady, on October 1, I plan to start hiking. I'll stop when the snow gets too deep, but not until then, and I can walk through some fairly good size drifts. Then, and only then, I may start looking for a job."

She studied Kepner more closely. He appeared to be in his late thirties though his stocky build could hide five years either way. He ought to be in his prime, family-rearing years. "No family?" she asked.

Kepner shook his head. "Not for the past few years. My wife couldn't put up with my hours here and I... well, I had things I couldn't put up with either. She's remarried to a guy who clocks out every afternoon at five sharp. It's better that way, I guess." His voice trailed off and Lynn had started feeling uncomfortable.

"I'd better get to my next meeting," she said.

Kepner picked up a stack of papers, put his feet back on his desk, and waved. "You know where to find me."

Bill Griffin, by contrast, was simply annoying. Short, fifty-ish and dumpy-looking, he glared at Lynn through thick glasses. His office was filled with boxes.

"Why do you want to know about royalties?" he repeated.

Just give me the stupid information, Lynn thought. "There's a schedule that lists every royalty payment SoftRidge makes to third parties. My job is to make certain that the list of payments is complete." She had answered the question twice already.

"But you already have a list," Griffin said.

"And I need to make certain it's complete. Look, you can turn over the royalties file, or I can go see Larry Driscoll and tell him you're stonewalling me. Either way is fine with me."

"But you're talking about a total of a hundred grand a year of payments," Griffin said. "It isn't worth your time. We've got to get this agreement in place and we've got two weeks…"

"Just give me the list." Lynn fumed. *Who are they to tell me how to do my job?*

"But I…"

"You'll get the request formally from Larry Driscoll in a few minutes," Lynn said and stood up. She didn't listen to the protestations that came from behind her. She walked the fifty feet to Driscoll's door, which was closed. She simultaneously knocked and opened the door.

Inside, Driscoll was in conversation with a man Lynn recognized from the meeting on Monday as Sandy Calo. Driscoll was behind his desk, Calo seated at a chair in front of it. Both looked up at the interruption.

"Mr. Driscoll, I'm sorry to interrupt you, but your controller is being a pain in the ass. He refuses to turn over the royalty files to me and keeps saying it's a waste of my time."

Driscoll nodded at Calo. "Sandy, see if you can get your boy to toe the line. If he doesn't, tell him we can get someone from Accountemps and save the salary until the close." Then to Lynn, he said, "I think you've met Sandy Calo, our chief financial officer."

Calo nodded and rose. "We'll pick this up later," he said to Driscoll. Then, to Lynn, he said, "We need to talk anyway, Ms. Kowalchuk. Let's kill two birds with one stone." Calo was tall, well over six feet, and with the slender build of a basketball player. He appeared to be in his late 40s and walked with authority. He wore a dark blue, pinstripe suit that was clearly custom fit. The suit draped on him effortlessly.

Lynn followed him to Griffin's office. The door was closed. Calo opened it. Griffin was on the phone. Calo walked over and put his finger on the handset, cutting off whatever call Griffin had been on.

"You'll have the file she needs in my office in one minute. If it isn't there in one minute, you're out of here in two. Got it, Bill?"

Griffin, his mouth open as though to continue the phone conversation, simply nodded slightly.

"Let's go to my office, Ms. Kowalchuk," Calo said.

"I haven't been avoiding you," Calo said when they were in his office. "I'm just up to my ears in things to do. Larry made clear that you were to get whatever cooperation you need. I hope that was demonstrable proof." Calo opened his hands in an 'I have nothing to hide' gesture. Lynn saw the manicured nails. Calo also had brilliantly white teeth when he smiled.

"Yeah, it was pretty impressive," Lynn said. "My list for you is still taking shape, but I can give you a partial one right now."

"Fire away."

They were interrupted by Griffin's knock at the door. Calo motioned him in. He took the file, riffed through its contents, and said, "Give it to Ms. Kowalchuk. And the next time she asks for something, just give her what she wants." There was an acid tone to his voice, as though talking to a child who had stolen a cookie.

Griffin mumbled something, took the folder and handed it to Lynn, and backed out of the office as though leaving royalty.

When Griffin was gone, Calo said, "I hired that guy because he squeezes every nickel possible out of the operation. He's smart with numbers. He's just dumb as dirt when things get into a two-minute offense like we're in now."

Lynn smiled. *He recognizes time is of the essence.* "I like the two-minute offense analogy. What I most need right now is orders by customer by month for the past eighteen months. The top 100 customers will do for now."

"The top ten customers are on a spreadsheet," Calo said. "The rest, I'll have to give you as raw files. Is that OK?"

"Can't you get Griffin to do it?"

"I'll give you odds Bill was on the phone with a headhunter, Ms. Kowalchuk. That's what we're all doing, most of the time."

"No one seems to expect that they're going to be kept on."

"And with good reason, Ms. Kowalchuk. Pericles just won a – please pardon my French – pissing duel that's been going on for ten years. You ever hear the phrase, 'it's just business, it's not personal'? Well, it doesn't apply to this acquisition. For Ross Maynard, it's intensely personal, and he won."

"Why has it been going on for ten years?" Lynn asked. "And Pericles has bought lots of businesses. Why is SoftRidge the one that gets Maynard hot and bothered?"

"Because of our late CEO," Calo said. "He used to ridicule Maynard and Pericles' products publicly. Said they were poor imitations of ours. I wasn't here then, so I don't know if he was right, but it was down and dirty for a very long time. Our two companies were roughly the same size back then, though Pericles was always more profitable. Anyway, what our CEO said got under Maynard's skin. Made him mad and made him swear to get even. Maynard started making acquisitions – smart acquisitions. And Maynard never missed a chance to shoot back at us. It wouldn't be an overstatement to say that Pericles became the billion-dollar colossus that it is because Ross Maynard had to prove that he was better than Pete Kincaid – that was our CEO."

"Well, Pete did some stupid things in response. It was personal for him, too. But slowly, we got ground under. When Pete had his heart attack, Maynard doubled up on the pressure. When Pete died, the Board caved and started looking for a buyer for the business."

Calo shuffled some papers on his desk. "But I'm sure you have plenty of things to do other than listening to the whining of a soon-to-be-acquired company. Give me the list of whatever you need and I'll have it for you by close of business today. You'll have the top 100 customer data in ten minutes. Either I or someone on my staff will find you." And with that, he picked up a phone and dialed an extension, barking out an order to someone elsewhere in the building. Lynn let herself out of his office.

Her final stop was Jeff Wright, vice president for human resources. Lynn was mildly surprised to find a man in the position. HR was typically the pink collar ghetto, the executive post that could be safely filled by a woman to demonstrate that the company did not discriminate in the hiring or promotion of women. Moreover, by putting a woman as the head of human resources, male-dominated managements automatically had a woman spokesman to tell the world that their executive ranks were gender-blind, when the *prima facie* evidence stated otherwise. And by staffing the HR department with women, companies could show that women were also well represented in their middle management ranks.

Except for SoftRidge. Jeff Wright wore a white shirt with a faded blue patch at the bottom of his shirt pocket where a pen had once leaked. Rather than throw away the shirt, Wright had elected to try to bleach out the stain, and then had deluded himself into believing that the stain was not noticeable. Instead, Lynn could not help but keep coming back to the stain as she spoke with him. Wright seemed oblivious to the effect. He was a bland-appearing man, pleasant features but an empty look behind blue eyes. He hair was blonde but rapidly thinning though he appeared to younger than forty.

"...Employment agreements, commission agreements, non-disclosure agreements, and any employee for whom you don't have signed agreements on file," Lynn was saying. She could see Wright copying down the list. He was at least three items behind her.

"Do you want me to repeat any of those?"

"No," Wright said, "I'm doing fine."

Lynn's eyes moved from the ink-stained shirt to Wright's tie. It featured several hundred black ants marching against a red background, and the effect was jarring on the eye. The bits of food on the tie, coupled with stains from previous meals, completed the effect.

"And I'll need all on-the-job injury reports going back two years."

Lynn saw Wright put down 'employment agreements'. She decided to wait for him to catch up.

"I take it most managers don't expect to be made job offers by Pericles," Lynn said when she saw he had written out 'injury reports'.

Wright looked up from his note paper. "We'd be fools to expect otherwise."

"But HR people are always in demand, aren't they?"

Wright shook his head. "They're in demand if you have a Masters in human resources management and a lengthy resume. I'm here by accident. I ran business development until last year. When we reorganized after Pete Kincaid died, the department got eliminated. The VP of Human Resources quit. I was offered the job on an interim basis. When the sale was announced, 'interim' became 'until the sale is completed'. That's not a lot to recommend me to a new employer, and Pericles is pretty well fixed for both business development and HR types."

"Most of the people I've spoken with seem to think Ross Maynard set out to undermine SoftRidge." Lynn threw out the statement, wondering if she'd get the same response.

"We did a perfectly adequate job of undermining ourselves," Wright said. "Eight years ago, we had a hundred million in the bank. Today, we can barely cover our bills. We frittered away the money. We bought back stock to prop up the price, we overpaid for acquisitions we didn't need."

"But you said you ran business development? Isn't that the group that buys things?"

Wright gave a wry smile. "CEOs and boards of directors buy things. And, in the case of SoftRidge, what Pete Kincaid wanted to buy, we bought. The independent board was not alive and well here."

"And you recommended against making those acquisitions?"

Wright nodded. "No head of business development has ever acknowledged liking an acquisition that subsequently went south. But in this case, I was adamant. We were letting money burn a hole in our pocket."

"Why did you stay?"

He shrugged. "Because I thought I was part of the solution. Especially when Pete had his heart attack. Not that it matters now."

* * * * *

What does this damned woman know? he thought to himself. *How close is she to discovering something?*

All afternoon he had listened as people dropped by with Lynn Kowalchuk stories. The woman was everywhere. She was friendly, yet she demanded mountains of information and then came back with still more requests. She probed into their post-acquisition plans. She wanted to know company history. She wanted to know things that were of no possible use unless she was attempting to piece together how a company's internal controls could break down, as they had done at SoftRidge.

His own encounter with her had been no different. She was much too thorough, her questions too wide-ranging. She would not be shaken off of her due diligence course. She had to go.

He had been waiting for the call from the middleman all day, keeping the phone on top of his desk when he was in his office, in his pants pocket when he was elsewhere. His greatest fear was that the phone would ring when Limp-haired Lynn was in his office. Now, frustrated and sensing that every hour brought fresh peril, he found the sheet of paper in his briefcase and called the middleman's number. It was answered on the second ring.

"I thought I said I'd call you before the end of the day, or don't you hear so good?" The middleman apparently had caller ID.

"It's almost the end of the day," he said.

"Well then I ought to call you right at sundown. But I got the information. Your lady can be sidelined just like we talked about last night. I got someone lined up. They're good, they're reliable, they're fast."

"When and how much?"

"Tonight. Fifteen grand."

"Fifteen thousand?"

"Be happy. I talked the guy down from twenty-five. Are we doing this or not?"

"How about ten?"

"This ain't 'Let's Make a Deal', pal. You tell me 'OK' and your problem is taken care of. You come down to Boston, you bring cash. The job gets done tonight."

"Twelve-five."

"You're pissing me off now. Right now, I don't know who you are and I don't care. You piss me off again and I'm going to make it my business to learn your home address. This is 'yes' or 'no' time. You understand?"

"I understand."

"So do we have a deal?"

He thought for a moment. He imagined trying to carry out such an assignment himself. He had the fifteen thousand in cash. He had budgeted twenty thousand.

"We have a deal. Where do we meet?"

"Same place. Same time. Nothing but fifties." The phone went dead in his hand.

At eight o'clock, he was in front of the Victoria's Secret display window. Fearing that he might be trailed, he had parked at a more distant garage – one even more expensive than the first – and walked a circuitous route to get to Quincy Market. The middleman arrived a minute later.

"How are you carrying the money?" the middleman asked.

"Two plain white envelopes," he said.

"All in fifties?"

"Just like you said."

"Where can my guy find this woman?"

"She's working at a company called SoftRidge. It's on Spit Brook Road. She'll be there for a couple of more hours."

"We're going to walk over to Cheers and stand at the bar with all the tourists. I'm going to walk in after you. You don't look at me, I don't look at you. When I say it's OK. You give me the envelope. You start walking, I'll follow."

He walked to the bar, ordered a beer, and bridled at the idea of paying six dollars for a draft beer that had cost the bar substantially less than a dollar. Five minutes went by. It was crowded and a Red Sox game was on the bar's large screen television. There was some cheering, though the Sox were quickly fading from contention. *Playing for pride*, he thought. *A game for losers.*

The Sox had two men on with Jacoby Ellsbury at the plate. Ellsbury popped a ball over the head of Tampa Bay's second baseman, scoring one and advancing the other runner to third. The cheering in the bar reached a peak. There was a tap at his shoulder.

"Now," the middleman said. He had appeared from nowhere. While Dustin Pedroia took a hesitant swing at the first pitch, he pulled the envelopes from his jacket pocket and handed them behind him to the man.

"Stay here until I call you. Order another beer, do something to make certain the bartender remembers you," the middleman said quietly. "That's important. If the police ever want to know where you were tonight, you need an impartial alibi. Do that, then go home. When I call you, it means it's going to be taken care of."

* * * * *

It was past 9 p.m., and the pizzas and salads from Papa Gino's hadn't sat well with either of them.

"We need a New York fix," Deb had said, poking at several uneaten slices. "I don't know how you ever ate this stuff when you went to school up here."

Lynn was distracted by the vendor list supplied to her by Frank Kepner. "Look at this," Lynn said. "More than fifty new vendors in the past six months, some of them for critical parts. When SoftRidge went up for sale, the bottom really fell out on them."

"You don't feel sorry for them, do you?"

Lynn shook her head. "No, everyone here agrees the company brought it on themselves. But that's an enormous drain on resources. Every supplier has to be qualified and then multiple qualified suppliers need to be found to bid on each item. The time required is incredible if it's done right, and if it isn't done right, it's a hit to quality that a company might never recover from. Vendors know they're supplying for the short term and there's no incentive to…"

Lynn looked more closely at Deb. Deb was on her computer, typing.

"You're not listening to a word I'm saying," Lynn said.

"Bagels," Deb said.

"I'm talking about the life and death of corporations and you're researching bagels."

"There's a place in Nashua that claims to make real, New York bagels."

"And they're open?"

"It's a café and bakery. They're open until ten."

"Let's go."

Lynn and Deb pulled together their files, shut down their computers, and walked to the parking lot. There, they got into a Ford Focus, the most economical car available at the Manchester airport.

In investment banking, as in all consulting professions, 'out of pocket' expenses are charged back to the client. Such expenses are supposed to be 'reasonable' though partners had been know to charter jets and charge the expense back to the client because it made more effective use of the partner's time. And a vice president, offered the opportunity to upgrade to a Lexus at a rental car counter 'for a few dollars extra', will never hesitate to drive away in the more luxurious vehicle. Lynn's innate sense of thrift would not allow her to choose a larger car.

Lynn entered the Everett Turnpike, otherwise known as Route 3, at Exit 1, intent upon driving the few miles to the exit that served downtown Nashua. She merged into the right-hand travel lane and accelerated in the light traffic.

"I'm sorry I didn't listen to your commentary on the problem of replacing vendors," Deb said, breaking the silence. "But that pizza was the last straw. It pushed me over the edge."

"And I'm sorry I started lecturing," Lynn said. "This assignment is starting to give me the creeps. Everyone in management waiting to be fired."

"It's just ten more days, Lynn. Put on the blinders and get the job done."

"And my feeling that someone's trying to run out the clock?"

"So don't put on the blinders. Did you learn anything?"

Lynn looked out the driver's side window and saw a large black SUV crowding into her lane.

"Idiot," she said and blew her horn.

The SUV pulled a few inches away but kept its speed and still rode over the white striped lane divider.

Lynn blew her horn again and moved to the far right side of the lane.

The SUV responded by crowding farther into her lane.

Lynn leaned on the horn. "I swear this guy must be drunk."

The SUV – Lynn now saw it was a Chevy Tahoe – nudged into the side of the small Ford. They heard a dull 'thunk' as the huge fenders of the SUV rubbed their car.

Lynn mashed her hand down on the car's horn and moved into the breakdown lane. "And I didn't take the insurance," she muttered to herself.

The SUV veered sharply right and Lynn felt her car being pushed off the road. There was no guard rail and the shoulder became a steep, grassy embankment. She slammed on the brake and the Ford fishtailed, the left tires finding asphalt and gravel but the right tires encountering only grass.

"Lynn!" Deb shouted and the SUV gave one more push to the Ford's front end.

The car spun around, but then tipped as its center of gravity shifted with the sloping side of the road. *Turn into the direction of the skid*, Lynn thought, but could not determine which way was correct with the car both tipping and skidding simultaneously.

The car hit the bottom of the embankment, tottering on two wheels. With its forward momentum suddenly terminated but its mass still accelerating, the Ford flipped, landing on its roof.

7.

New Hampshire State Trooper Lou Bergeron was heading southbound on Route 3 when he heard the call. *'Car overturned northbound at exit 3. Possible injuries.'*

"Got it," he said into his mike. "I'm making the turn now."

He turned on his flashing lights and siren went across the bumpy median. *What do you want to bet its alcohol?* he thought to himself. *A pair of 18-year-olds with a back seat full of beer cans.*

Three cars were stopped on the shoulder. He pulled in ahead of them and grabbed a flashlight.

The car – a gray econobox that could have been any of half a dozen different makes and models – rested on its roof at the bottom of an embankment. Two men were peering into the car.

"I'll need a wrecker and an ambulance," he said into his shoulder mike. "One vehicle, unknown number of passengers."

Lou Bergeron was in his third year as a state trooper. It hadn't been the career he had envisioned for himself, but then, little in his life had ever turned out as expected. He had grown up one of five children in Berlin, a poor, fading mill town fifty miles south of the Quebec border. He had played four years of hockey in high school, setting multiple school records in the process. But the college scouts did not come to his games or even those of the division finals that his school won. At nineteen, he faced either the prospect of a minimum wage job at one of the summer resorts or else the long wait to make it onto the remaining mill's payroll.

Bergeron had joined the Army instead. That was in 2002. Coalition forces had forced the Taliban into a few corners of Afghanistan, and the recruiter said the principal job from here on in was peacekeeping and nation-building. Moreover, if Bergeron committed for six years, he was guaranteed – in writing – college tuition. Free college tuition was the hook that got him to sign up.

Besides, it beat busing tables somewhere in the White Mountains.

'Nation-building' turned into firefights, first in Kandahar then, a year later, in Iraq. Bergeron spent three of his six years in the 'the Sandbox'. When his six years was up, the pressure to re-enlist was enormous, with a five-figure bonus, promotion, and stateside postings "all but guaranteed."

He decided six years was enough. It was time to earn a degree.

But at twenty-five, he found he was too old for college. He no longer fit in with the carefree teenagers who sat around him in classes. After a desultory semester at Plymouth State, he took the state police Trooper 1 Recruitment Test and aced it. Thanks to those six years in the Army, he scored first in each of the physical dexterity and endurance exams that followed.

It wasn't what he had envisioned, but it beat the alternative.

Bergeron politely edged by two men at the driver's side window of the overturned car. Luckily, he smelled no gasoline, though he had investigated other crashes where fuel had ignited seemingly out of nowhere.

He pushed aside several deflated airbags and shined his flashlight into the window. A young woman with brown hair hung by her seatbelt. She appeared dazed. On the passenger side, another woman, a blonde, was crying in pain. He tugged at the door handle. It refused to budge.

"We'll need cutters," Bergeron said into his shoulder mike. "I have two women, both alive but both trapped. Possible injuries."

The driver's window was open, a lucky break. He stuck his head inside. No evidence of alcohol in the cabin. The investigation wasn't going to be open and shut.

The driver opened her eyes and blinked. "Would you mind not shining that in my eyes?" she said.

Bergeron obediently turned the flashlight to the dashboard. There was no alcohol on her breath, either.

"I'm going to try to get you out of here as quickly as possible, ma'am."

The first woman turned to the passenger. "Deb?" she asked.

The passenger said softly, "I hurt."

The driver turned back toward Bergeron. "You get her out of here first. I'm not hurt. I'm fine for now."

Coolness under fire, Bergeron thought.

The lights of a second trooper's car appeared, followed about thirty seconds later by the distant wail of the EMTs. Bergeron watched the second trooper stumble down the hill. The large bulk told him it was Fred, whose usual duty was sitting at the state line a few miles south, waiting to scare northbound drivers into slowing down. The tactic usually worked for about a mile.

Bergeron noted the Avis sticker on the windshield. He had earlier seen the New Hampshire plate. A rental car, probably from Manchester. *Headed back for a return flight? Busy talking on their cell phones and not paying attention?*

Bergeron watched as Fred caught his breath from the short hike down the embankment. *Too many bear claws*, Bergeron thought. *God, don't let me look like that when I'm forty.*

"The driver is alert and appears uninjured," Bergeron told him. "The passenger indicates she's injured." He turned to the driver. "Ma'am, we can't get your friend out until we get equipment to cut open the car door. But I can get you out through the window. That strap is probably starting to get uncomfortable."

The woman looked at him and then back at the second woman. "I'd rather stay inside until you get Deb free."

The EMT van pulled into place. Three people got out. Two loped down the incline, the third began taking equipment from out of the back of the truck.

"The cavalry reinforcements just got here," Bergeron said, and smiled. But at that moment, he caught the first whiff of gasoline fumes.

"Ma'am, I've got to get you out of here now." To the other trooper, he said. "Passenger side, now!" To the two men coming down the incline, he yelled, "Gas!"

"Brace yourself," he said to the woman. "This may hurt." He pulled a special seatbelt cutting knife from his pocket and cut through the shoulder of the belt, then the lap assembly. The woman dropped about eight inches.

"Give me your hands," he said, and the woman extended one through the window. He began easing her out, the smell of gasoline was becoming more pronounced.

"Dispatch, get me a fire truck," he said into his shoulder mike. "We've got a leaker."

He pulled the woman free of the car, then leaned over and picked her up, bracing her shoulder and legs.

"I'm going to get you a safe distance from the car. My partner is doing the same for your friend…"

"My papers!" the woman said. "Oh, my God, I've got papers in the car, and my computer. There's a brown briefcase in the back seat…"

"I'll get it," Bergeron said, reassuringly, though the papers would wait until he had the other woman out of the car. He set her down, gently, in the grass. One of the EMTs was by his side and had an emergency bag already open. "She's yours for now," Bergeron said. "I'm going back for the other one."

The other EMT was working with metal cutters on the passenger side door. Fat Fred, while not standing by passively, did not appear to be helping.

"Let's see if two of us can force the door," Bergeron said. They positioned themselves and pulled. Nothing happened. "One more time," Bergeron said.

The second pull yielded a groaning sound. The car door opened. The gasoline smell was becoming pervasive.

The EMT positioned his arms under the woman while Bergeron cut the seat belt. This time, there was no drop. The EMT lifted her out and he and Bergeron began to carry the woman away from the car. "Everyone get away from the vehicle," Bergeron shouted as loud as he could.

"Fred!" he shouted, and the trooper ran to his side. "I promised to look for a briefcase. Can you take her for me?" The other trooper nodded and took the woman from Bergeron.

Bergeron looked through the window and spotted two briefcases. He reached in and grabbed them with one hand.

And then the gas ignited.

Bergeron threw himself backward, landing painfully on his back, his left hand still gripping the handles. He rolled away from the car, which quickly became engulfed. He got to his feet, wincing at the pain in his back and the heat of the fire searing his face. He looked around and saw that everyone appeared to have taken his warning seriously.

The fire reached the gas tank and the car exploded into one final orgy of flame. Bergeron circled around to the two women, who had been transferred onto backboards to be carried back up to the ambulance.

He found the driver. She was strapped to the backboard. He held the briefcases so that she could see them.

"You looking for these?"

The woman closed her eyes.

"I could kiss you," she said.

* * * * *

He could see the assemblage of fire trucks and police cars from half a mile away as he drove north on Route 3. A gawker's block brought traffic to a crawl and he took the opportunity to see that it was the smoldering remains of a small car, upside down. He wondered if it was Limp-haired Lynn's car. His contact had said that it would happen tonight.

Five police cars and two ambulances were on the shoulder, indicating to him that there had been injuries. *They weren't supposed to kill her*, he thought. *Just sideline her. Get her back to New York. But how do you control that sort of thing?*

He shrugged and drove the rest of the way home carefully.

8.

Thursday, September 20

Bergeron spread his notes out in front of him, attempting to reconcile Lynn Kowalchuk's statement and the physical evidence he had observed at the scene of the accident with any known 'usual circumstance' in his experience.

I left the offices of SoftRidge Corporation on Spit Brook Road at approximately 9:25 p.m., Kowalchuk's statement began. *I was accompanied by Deborah Fowler, who works with me at Clarenden Brothers in New York. We made the turn onto Route 3. As soon as I attempted to merge into traffic, I found that a dark colored Chevy Tahoe was crowding my lane. As I accelerated, it matched my speed. When I braked, the car did the same. I honked at the SUV, and it briefly moved away, then almost immediately moved again into my lane, hitting my fender. I started to brake, and the SUV moved next to me and forced me off the road. Because of the incline of the shoulder, I lost control of my car, which flipped over. I did not get a license plate number for the Tahoe, nor did I see the driver.*

To the best of my knowledge and experience as a driver, the Tahoe's driver appeared to be acting in a deliberate manner to force my car off of the road. I cannot rule out that the other driver was intoxicated, but the fact that the Tahoe accelerated and braked with me leads me to believe that the driver's intention was to run me off of the road.

It was strong stuff. The physical evidence would take time to evaluate. The driver's side was indeed dented, though the Ford had sustained much more serious damage in the process of overturning. As to finding black paint from another car, that would be nearly impossible without detailed investigation. The Ford had burned to its shell by the time the fire was brought under control.

But Nashua police had reported a black Chevy Tahoe stolen from the parking lot of the Pheasant Lane Mall a little before 9 p.m.

The Tahoe had been recovered from a supermarket parking lot

an hour ago. The SUV had sustained damage on its passenger side, including streaks of white paint that presumably could be matched to the Ford Focus. The left rear window had been smashed in, likely the original point of entry for the thief or thieves.

New theory: A couple of kids decide to steal a car for a joyride. They get some beer, get giddy, and decide to run a car off the road, just to show they can do it. Then they abandon the car.

The theory broke down too quickly. The Tahoe had been hotwired, bypassing the fairly sophisticated alarm system that would otherwise have disabled the SUV after a few blocks. Teenagers lacked that skill. There was no beer or other liquor in the car. For teenagers, stealing a car without drinking in it was pointless. The car had been wiped clean of prints and it had been left in a corner of the supermarket parking lot out of the field of view of surveillance cameras. Teenagers did not possess that kind of foresight in disposing of the cars they stole unless it was by dumb luck. And they never wiped away their prints.

By morning, mall security would have turned over a video showing the theft of the Tahoe. But he had seen such videos before. It would show whether it was one man or three. It would show whether they had used a small sledgehammer or a large rock to break out a window. Then, depending upon the thief's or thieves' sophistication, the video would show that after thirty seconds or two minutes, the car drove out of the parking lot. He would be able to get a rough height and weight estimate of the man or men involved, but there would be no facial features. It was a mall parking lot security camera, for crying out loud.

He tried a different theory:

Two guys steal an SUV from a parking lot. They're headed north with the intention of selling it to a chop shop or shipping it out of the country. But they have an argument as they're driving on Route 3. The driver isn't watching where he's going. He bumps into the Ford. 'Dumb broad,' he says, 'I'll get even with her for damaging this perfectly good car.' He runs the little subcompact off of the road, then ditches the car at the nearest supermarket lot.

It was slightly more credible, but professional car thieves didn't break out windows of cars they intended to sell, and they took pains to steal only recent-vintage cars without body damage because that's where the money was. According to the stolen car report, this was a four-year-old Tahoe with 65,000 miles on the odometer and a Blue Book value of about $13,000. To a chop shop, it was worth about $1,500. The same risk and energy would have yielded a much more valuable car. Tahoes just didn't bring much money.

He tried a third theory:

A guy has a contract to run two fairly low-level women investment bankers off of the road. He steals a battering ram of a car, follows them onto Route 3, and pushes them down into a ditch at the first opportunity. He gets rid of the car and is home by 10 p.m.

He poked at his theory. The one part that didn't make sense was that two women in their twenties were worthy targets for such an activity.

OK, so it's an angry boyfriend who one of them dumped for a handsomer guy. He hires someone to get even.

Bergeron looked at the clock: 3:30 a.m. The paperwork was done. He was three and a half hours into overtime for which he would never get paid. He sighed.

Time for me to go see that damned Tahoe for myself.

* * * * *

The pain medication was starting to wear off and Lynn fidgeted in the semi-darkness, looking for the button that would summon a nurse.

She had not wanted to lie down on the pallet. She said she could walk to the EMT's van. Then the car had burst into flames and – damn it – she had fainted. *I could have been in that car. Deb could still have been in that car.* It had been too much.

Then the cute trooper had shown her what he said was their briefcases. They could have been anything; they were just a dark rectangles silhouetted against the flames. And she had passed out. But she had said something.

I could kiss you. Oh my God. Where had her head been?

Then they were at a hospital – St. Joseph, the illuminated sign had said. The EMTs were working with Deb, who was in pain. *I'm fine,* Lynn had said. *Deb's the one who needs you.*

Deb had fractured her collarbone and had contusions. And every male medical practitioner in Southern New Hampshire had come by to take a gander at the beautiful blonde in Trauma One.

Lynn had wrenched her back and she had bruises – including one on her forehead – that would take weeks to go away. But she was alive. She was alive thanks to Trooper Lou Bergeron, who had smelled gas and dragged her out of the car.

And he had come to the hospital to take her statement, writing it all down in neat script and nodding as she spoke. He had not missed a word. When she had said, '*...acted in a deliberate manner to force my car off of the road...*' he had not given the involuntary smirk that she had braced herself for.

Instead, he had asked her why she thought someone might have wanted to run her off the road. Her initial inclination was to say that she was not prepared to answer that question and that she needed time to think about it. But this trooper had an intelligent look in his eye. And so she took a deep, painful breath and said, "Because I think something is rotten in the acquisition that I'm working on."

She tried to expand on her story, trying it out in her mind before saying the words aloud, telling herself what she believed to be the truth. *"I'm a third-year deal grunt for a major New York investment banking house. I think someone at the company where I'm doing final due diligence is trying to run out the clock to hide something. I have no idea what it is, but it's sufficiently shady that they were willing to run Deb and me off the road to slow us down. I know all of this because they wasted a day on a slide presentation and a boozy dinner, and they left the two of us waiting in the lobby for two hours."*

Right, Lynn. So, instead, she said nothing else to the trooper.

A nurse appeared. "I'll bet I know what you want," she said.

Ten minutes later, Lynn was in a deep sleep.

* * * * *

The word swept through SoftRidge like a late summer mountain wildfire. The two chicks from Clarenden Brothers – the incredibly good looking blonde and the other one – ran off Route 3. Their car flipped over and burned to a cinder. Troopers pulled them out just in time. Man, what luck.

He had sat in the meeting as Larry Driscoll delivered the news officially. "They're both OK. One had a broken collarbone and she may or may not be back. The other got banged up a bit, but I spoke with her this morning and she says she'll be in later today. Clarenden is sending up reinforcements to keep us on our timetable. They'll have someone on site later on today. In the meantime, I want you to pull together every schedule…"

He didn't listen to the rest. *'She'll be in later today…'* That could only mean Limp-haired Lynn. Debby Big Tits was the one with the broken collarbone. She wasn't even supposed to be in the car.

'She'll be in later today…'

He went into his office and closed the door. Shaking with a mixture of anger and fear, he pulled the disposal cell phone from his briefcase. He dialed the number.

"You better have a Plan B." He wanted to add, 'asshole' but feared angering a man to whom he had paid $15,000 for a job poorly done, and whose job was arranging personal injury to others for a fee. "The lady got a few bruises. She's fine and she definitely hasn't been sidelined."

"I'll get back to you," was the terse reply. And then the line was dead.

* * * * *

Bergeron had verified Lynn's story with Deborah – Deb – Fowler. She did not know if the SUV had followed them up the entrance ramp. The first time she became aware of the truck was when Lynn had complained that it was crowding into their lane. She verified that the truck had matched their speed and not responded to Lynn's use of the horn. She had been adamant in saying that the Tahoe had pushed them off the road, waiting until the side of the road banked most steeply so as to inflict the most damage.

"Did you discuss this with Miss Kowalchuk?" Bergeron asked.

"Sure, we got our stories straight while we were hanging upside down in the car."

Bergeron leaned forward. "This is a tough question to ask, but I have to cover all of the possibilities. Do either of you have a boyfriend who might have done this to get even with you?"

Deb had laughed. "Boyfriend? Do you think either of us have time for a *boyfriend* up here?" She had emphasized the word and Bergeron felt acutely embarrassed.

"How about a boyfriend back home who took it bad when you broke up with him?"

"Believe me, you can have a love life or you can be an investment banker," she said. "Whoever did this – and it was deliberate – wasn't some jilted lover."

Bergeron had spent an hour with the Nashua police at the impound lot, going over the Chevy Tahoe. The vehicle had all of the detritus of a suburban family in the back seat, plus the shattered window. Fast food wrappers, drink cups and unreturned DVDs from Red Box. But the front seat was pristine. It had been wiped with a disinfectant, as had the steering wheel, dashboard, and front windshield. There was no sweat, saliva, or clothing fragment from which to draw DNA. The person who had stolen this car had been a pro, and had been thorough.

The alarm had been bypassed using a tool well known to pros, and carefully not mentioned by automotive manufacturers. The ignition had been popped. The entire process had likely taken about sixty seconds.

The body damage was entirely consistent with the story told by the women. Bergeron traced the creases with his hand. "The SUV as battering ram," he had said to the Nashua policeman.

"Four thousand pounds of steel against some lightweight chassis," the policeman agreed. "That's not exactly a fair fight."

* * * * *

Lynn was replying to emails on her phone when she saw the trooper come into her room. Acutely embarrassed that she was still in a hospital nightgown, she pulled the covers up over herself and reached for the cup of ice next to her bed.

The trooper smiled. It was a very nice smile and a kind face. Curly brown hair, thick eyebrows, and hazel eyes. He looked to be in his late twenties, but there was a hardness in his jaw, as though he had lived an uncertain life. Her eyes darted to his left hand. No wedding ring, but it did not mean he wasn't living with someone or otherwise taken.

"I could kiss you", she had said. Her face reddened at the memory. *They must have had me on morphine.*

"Miss Kowalchuk, may I speak to you again?"

She kept the straw to her lips for a few extra seconds, the better to allow her face to return to a normal color.

"Sure."

He pulled up a chair, never taking his eyes away from her face. She saw that his eyes did not roam down the blankets and sheets, wondering how or if she was dressed. He had carried her from the car a moment before it burst into flames. It was the first time she had been carried by anyone since she was a child. *He would have felt those ten extra pounds. The girl who ought to weigh 130 weighs 140.*

"I don't know if you remember me from last night. I'm Trooper Lou Bergeron. I need to review your statement."

She snapped to attention.

"Everything I've learned since last night indicates that what you said is completely accurate. We found the car that sideswiped you, but not the person or persons who were in the car."

They were gratifying words. But she heard *"…however…"* coming up.

"The condition of the other car – which was stolen – indicates that whoever stole the car intended to use it for just such a purpose."

Here it comes.

"What I can't figure out is why did he or they choose the two of you?"

She sucked on the ice chips.

He leaned forward. Waiting.

A thought occurred to her. The accident had been shortly after nine o'clock last night. It was now nearly ten o'clock.

"You can't still be on duty?"

He smiled. Wonderful white teeth, but some of them could have been caps.

"Why did someone want to run two investment bankers from New York off the road?"

"What do you know about investment banking?"

"I saw *Wall Street*." He took a pad of paper out of his shirt pocket and clicked a ball point pen.

She nodded. "There's a company here in Nashua. It's called SoftRidge. It's being acquired by a company in Boston called Pericles. I'm not telling you anything that hasn't already been in the papers. SoftRidge put itself up for sale six months ago, and Pericles was the high bidder. The deal is supposed to close at the end of the month. On Monday morning, a team of people descended on SoftRidge to do what's called final due diligence and to get together everything that's needed for the contract. We've got a little less than two weeks."

"Most of what's done in this period is rote: make sure that when the contract says the buyer is acquiring a hundred widgets, that there are really a hundred widgets in stock. There are accountants doing that sort of thing. But there are also a lot of things that could be land mines. The buyer is assuming the lease for the building. What if there's a pending EPA action against the landlord? It's the buyer's responsibility to find out, and to adjust the price accordingly. Deb's and my job is to go over everything looking for those land mines."

"And you found one?"

Lynn shook her head and sipped on more ice. "No. Just a hunch that there is one to be found. To be included in the September quarter, the deal has to officially close on or before

September 30. We wasted all of Monday listening to some dumb company overview that we already knew. Then, Monday night, the company hosted a dinner for us. From what I hear, everyone got thoroughly wasted, which meant Tuesday was a bust for getting anything done. Then…"

"Who arranged for the dinner?" Bergeron asked.

Lynn thought for a moment. "I don't know."

"You weren't there?"

Lynn shook her head. "We – the bankers – skipped it. You don't want to be buddies with people when you're spending all day looking for deal killers."

"Deal killers?"

"Things that would make the acquisition come completely apart. Things that you couldn't cure with money."

Bergeron made a note. "Go on?"

"Well, then the company started enforcing this stupid rule that someone from the seller's management or banker had to be in on every meeting. Deb had to call the CEO of Pericles to get that taken care of."

"She called the CEO of Pericles? She works for him?"

Lynn's face reddened again. "She's met him once. But he took her call."

"I would imagine."

Lynn sipped her ice. *He doesn't have to rub it in.*

"Who did the CEO of Pericles call?"

"Larry Driscoll. He's the chairman of the board of SoftRidge. The company hasn't really had a CEO since the old one died last year. That's why the company was for sale."

Bergeron made more notes. "And did Larry Driscoll break the logjam?"

"Very quickly. He gave us the names of four executives and said that they would get us anything we needed and, if they didn't cooperate, to tell him immediately."

"So it isn't Larry Driscoll who's playing garbage time?"

Lynn shook her head. "Garbage time?"

"In hockey – or I guess in any sport. It's when you're ahead and you're trying to use up the clock. You pass the puck without taking a shot. You just try to keep it away from the other team."

"Larry seems like a straight shooter."

"What about the other managers? Are any of them trying to put you off?"

"The controller…"

"What's a controller?"

"The guy who does the grunt work on numbers. Bill Griffin. He works for Sandy Calo, the chief financial officer. Griffin kept asking me why I was wasting my time on little stuff and refused to give me files."

"Was he right? Were you wasting time?"

"It's the little stuff that hides the land mines. A company pays royalties to someone for something. It may be just a few thousand dollars a year, but what if the right to pay that royalty isn't transferable? What if someone could hold you for ransom over some little thing and demand millions? It's happened."

"Who are the other managers?"

"Frank Kepner – he's manufacturing. And Jeff Wright. He's human resources, except he used to run business development."

Bergeron wrote down the names.

"You've met with all of them?"

"At least once."

"Go out on a limb, Miss Kowalchuk…"

"Lynn. My name is Lynn." *Why did it take so much courage to say that?* she thought.

He smiled again. The smile seemed very genuine and very friendly.

"Let your imagination run free, Lynn. What could a company hide that would be worth running two attractive young women off the road?"

He said two attractive women.

"Money. One person in management has done something that they're afraid will get exposed if there's full due diligence. It could be a lot of things, but it comes down to money. These guys are getting shafted in the deal: there are no golden parachutes. No lump sum payments from options. And they all know it. So it isn't a collective thing. Someone did something that didn't get caught when Pericles did its own review."

"Is Pericles good at this due diligence?"

"They've done a dozen acquisitions on the past five years. But they don't do it for a living."

"Give me an example of something someone could miss that would mean money in someone's pocket?"

Lynn thought for a moment. "A secret employment contract. 'If I lose my job in a takeover, you have to pay me two years salary.'"

"And if you caught it before the deal was completed?"

"We'd deduct it from the purchase price. It would be a downward adjustment. That, or else we'd insist that SoftRidge's Board tear up the contract."

Bergeron tapped his pen against his lip. "These guys make — what? — a couple of hundred thousand a year?"

Lynn closed her eyes and recalled SEC filing forms. "The highest comped guy is the CFO at about $200,000. The others are around one-thirty to one-sixty."

"It isn't a secret employment contract," Bergeron said.

"And you know this because…"

"The person who ran you off the road was a pro. A pro might charge ten thousand bucks against the risk of being caught. The guy who *hired* the pro had to be playing for higher stakes than $150,000 to shell out that much money and take that kind of risk of being caught."

Lynn looked at him in surprise. "Is this something they teach state troopers?" Then, she immediately realized what she had said. "I didn't mean that you…"

Bergeron smiled. "I've spent a lifetime observing human nature, seeing what my fellow man would and wouldn't do for money. The last couple of years have been working to find people breaking the law. There's a risk-reward ratio at work."

"I don't need a lecture on risk-reward ratios," Lynn said, curtly.

"Maybe you do when it comes to killing people or having them killed. These are businessmen. Going to jail would be the end of their career – effectively, the end of their lives. No one will shell out ten percent of a year's salary against the possibility that they might sneak an extra hundred thousand out of the company. It isn't worth it. The stakes have to be a lot higher. In the millions."

Millions of dollars, she thought.

"So think big, Lynn. What could someone hide from the folks at Pericles that you might find in less than two weeks? What would net someone in the company a couple of million bucks?"

9.

Lou Bergeron slept until 2 p.m., then showered and dressed. By 3 p.m., he was at the Bedford barracks in full uniform, hat under his arm.

He knocked at the door of Captain Sam Hurley. "Beg your pardon, Captain."

Hurley motioned him in.

"Have you reviewed the file on the accident last night?" Bergeron asked.

Hurley glanced at a six-inch-thick pile of papers on the front right-hand corner of his desk. No. He hadn't looked at the report. "Why don't you tell me about it."

Bergeron stood awkwardly, having not been invited to sit. "A car was run off the road. Two women, one of them injured. The car burned."

Hurley nodded. "I heard about it this morning. Nice rescue effort. Are you putting in for a commendation?"

"No, sir!" Bergeron said briskly. "I did some additional investigating, sir. We found the car that sideswiped them. It was abandoned at a Market Basket. It had been stolen. It was a professional job. Wiped clean of prints."

"And you want me to do what, son?"

"I've got some ideas of how to pursue it, Captain. There are some people I'd like to question..."

"Stop," Hurley said.

"Yes, sir."

"You've been with us just shy of three years. You did a heroic rescue. You saved those women's lives. You'll get a commendation and a letter in your file. Don't go playing detective. Do your job."

"Can I refer it to one of the detectives, sir?"

Hurley drummed his fingers. He reached into the pile and found

Bergeron's report. He flipped through the pages.

"Take it to Johnson. See if it interests him. And be on the road at four."

* * * * *

Detective Claude Johnson listened to Bergeron's story and read the file. Johnson was sixty and gray-haired with a high widow's peak. His skin was pale, with loose folds of skin under his eyes. Bergeron noted the nicotine stains on his fingers and the impatient demeanor as Johnson flipped pages. Johnson wore a light gray suit that looked as though it may have been the only suit he owned.

"I suppose the hospital ran a tox screen?" Johnson asked.

"Yes, sir. No alcohol. No drugs."

"Then it's chicks on cell phones," he said. "Road rage. Xanax. New Yorkers who don't want to admit that they don't really know how to drive because they all take taxis. I'll pull their cell phone records. Fifty bucks says one or both of them were yakking with their boyfriends and they creamed the Tahoe, not the other way around. Oh, the Tahoe was stolen, I'll grant you that. And the guy who stole it ditched it because after they veered into him, the car wasn't worth squat."

"Then you don't want the case," Bergeron said, the disappointment showing in his voice.

"I didn't say that. I'm going to run the cell phone records," Johnson said. "And you're going to have learned a lesson that's going to cost you fifty bucks. Just 'cause the girl's cute doesn't mean she isn't lying through her teeth." He pulled out the accident scene photo. "If someone runs into her, it's a loss for Avis. If she runs into someone, it's a jackpot for Avis. They get the cost of the car plus processing fees plus 'loss of use' charges. Forty thousand bucks for a fleet car that cost them eighteen-five."

"And if they weren't on the phone?"

"Trust me, they were."

* * * * *

Lynn took a cab to SoftRidge and was greeted at the door by

Larry Driscoll. He put an arm around her and ushered her into the lobby.

"We all heard. We can't believe you're here," he said.

"Thank you, but I'm fine."

"That's a nasty looking bruise on your forehead," Driscoll said.

Lynn touched her forehead. It was quite tender.

"Miss Fowler has a broken collarbone?"

"Yes, and we both appreciated the flowers," Lynn said.

"The two other members of your team are in the conference room. They just got here half an hour ago," Driscoll said.

Lynn already knew they were here. She had spoken with them non-stop from the time their plane landed in Manchester until just a few minutes earlier. She chose not to share this information.

"I'll need some time with them," Lynn said.

* * * * *

He watched as Limp-haired Lynn walked through the hall with Driscoll. *All she has is a bruise. Other than that, it's like nothing happened. She isn't even limping. And I paid that asshole fifteen thousand dollars?*

He busied himself with work, fuming. And waiting for the call from the middleman.

Then there was a knock at his door and Lynn was standing there, with a fresh-out-of-B-school guy at her side. He looked like he was about twenty.

Startled, he stood up.

"We're all amazed you're in this afternoon. You must have been incredibly lucky."

Lynn smiled and indicated the young investment banker standing beside her. "This is Alan. He's going to be helping us until Deborah is back on her feet. Alan has a list of requests that will probably take a bit of your time. I'll leave the two of you together."

She smiled again and then was out the door, throwing a glance backwards as she left.

Alan pulled out a sheet of paper from a file folder. "I have about two dozen items I'm going to need…"

* * * * *

Lou Bergeron was four hours into his patrol. He had written up a DUI and warned a handful of speeders while patrolling his section of Route 3 between the Massachusetts border and Manchester. He was entitled to a 30-minute break at 8 p.m. and he drove the short distance to the Pheasant Lane Mall.

But instead of heading for the food court, he walked to the mall security office.

"I'd like to see the parking lot videotapes from last night," he told the elderly man sitting in front of the bank of screens.

"Nashua Police were here this afternoon, so I know just what you're looking for," the man said. The man rose and shuffled to a desk. He selected a video cassette and pushed it into a monitor.

"You're lucky this was on the north side of the mall," the man said. The Pheasant Lane Mall sat directly on the New Hampshire – Massachusetts border. The body of the mall was in New Hampshire, which imposed no sales tax. Much of the mall's parking was in Massachusetts. Had the Tahoe been parked in one of the southern lots, the grand theft auto case would have been, however technically so, a Massachusetts crime.

"Here's your man. He's walking the aisles like he's lost his car." The video showed only a dark, indistinct shape. Based on the height of the vehicles he passed, he guessed the man to be about 5'10". In the video, the Chevy Tahoe pulled into an empty space near the man, and the man crouched behind a car. A lone woman got out of the SUV and walked briskly toward a mall entrance. The man waited for about a minute, then walked deliberately toward the car. He waited just a moment, then pulled a short-handled sledge hammer from his jacket and broke out the left rear window. He athletically jumped through the window of the car. Sixty seconds later, the lights went on and the car backed out of the space.

"Is the time stamp accurate?" Bergeron asked.

"No question. The theft took place at 8:24 p.m. The woman reported it at 8:45."

Which meant that the thief had an hour to kill, Bergeron thought.

"No chance of an image enhancement on one of these frames?"

"This was state of the art in 1995," the man said with only a hint of an apology. "What you see is what you get."

Bergeron got a sandwich and sat in his car, thinking as he ate. *This is a guy who hurts people for a living. He had been told that the women would be occupied until at least 8:30 and possibly much later. He had to stake out the parking lot at SoftRidge and wait for them to leave the building.*

The man would need something to eat or drink. There is nothing on Spit Brook Road, which is lined with apartments and office buildings. Whatever he found would have been on Daniel Webster Highway.

He started the cruiser and exited north out of the parking lot as the man would have done. Chain restaurants lined either side of the road. He ruled out the sit-down restaurants as taking too long. Which left the Big Three: a McDonalds, a Burger King and a Dunkin' Donuts.

He pulled into the Dunkin' Donuts.

"I need to see the manager," Bergeron said.

"I'm the night manager," said a boy in a baseball cap, who was probably not yet eighteen.

"I need to look at your security camera tapes for last night." Bergeron was careful to phrase it as a request. He didn't want this guy wondering if he needed to call someone for approval.

The boy nodded. He heard an official request from a state policeman. He authoritatively said, "Kathy, take over for me," and led Bergeron into the manager's office.

"It's a 24-hour loop," the boy said.

Bergeron looked at his watch. 8:25. He might already be too late. "Let's play the start of the loop. Go back the full 24 hours. As far as you can."

The kid nervously pushed buttons. Four screens appeared. One showed the dining area, a second was the parking lot. The third focused on the cash register – an apparent effort to make certain the help didn't steal from the till. The fourth showed the drive-thru.

Three minutes into the tape – 8:28 p.m. – a black Chevy Tahoe pulled into the drive-thru lane. The left rear window was missing. A man placed an order for a large coffee and chocolate muffin.

"Freeze it there," Bergeron said.

The man was Caucasian, Somewhere in his late 30s or even early 40s. He had thinning, black hair worn long, and a Fu Manchu mustache that draped down the side of his mouth. He had a muscular build and a thin face. When he reached for the coffee, there were tattoos on the knuckles of his fingers – likely prison tattoos.

"You ever see this man before?" Bergeron asked, pointing to the screen.

The boy shook his head. "Not that I recall."

"I'll need the tape."

"Did he do something?"

"Well, he stole that SUV for starters."

* * * * *

Lynn sorted through spreadsheets and lists. Across from her in the conference room, two Clarenden Brothers associates – deal grunts, by any other name – did the same. She looked at them with a sense of amazement. They were her, three years earlier. A few months out of B-school and immersed in the reality of why they were being paid $125,000 per year. Clarenden expected seventy to eighty hour weeks out of them and to drop everything in their lives on an hour's notice.

And, in return for that $125,000 salary, they would pore over every number and flag anything that did not tie back to a line of the balance sheet or the income statement. In six months, they'd think they knew everything there was to know and they'd still make mistakes. Right now, they were still in the mode of asking questions about anything that wasn't readily apparent. They continually interrupted her.

"Lynn, the European sales VP's salary is shown in UK pounds in this schedule, but in dollars in this schedule. Which currency do you want to use?"

"Lynn, this schedule is different from the one in the data room. Which one should I go with?"

"Lynn, the actual marketing expense for the June quarter was $110,000 over budget, but they're showing the September quarter as flat to June. Should I flag it?"

"Lynn, they've got a part here that's over 180 days' supply that they're showing will be used this quarter. Do you want me to flag it or look for a reconciling order?"

And, through it all, Lynn looked – and listened – for the hidden multi-million-dollar error. *Think big, Lynn. What could someone hide from the folks at Pericles that would net someone in the company a couple of million bucks?*

So far, she had found minor inconsistencies. A significant number of the laptop computers listed on the inventory were not in stock – they probably had been secreted out of the building by departing employees. Office supplies had disappeared en masse – doubtlessly taken by employees expecting to be laid off and needing to create home offices.

The big missing dollars, however, eluded her. *What could account for hidden funds?* Lynn's list, drawn up earlier in the day, included:

- *Phantom employees*
- *Phantom inventory*
- *Understated accounts receivable*
- *Overstated accounts payable*
- *An entire phantom department or business*

Lynn was working on employees, matching SoftRidge's 538 employees to job descriptions and length of service. She flagged several headquarters employees that seemed like obvious duplications and would ask for personnel folders in the morning. But the aggregate salaries of the employees involved amounted to less than half a million dollars. There was also a mysterious service group in the Philippines that defied logic: twenty people at one site. But their salaries averaged $15,000 and the group had been in existence for half a dozen years. The group reported to Frank Kepner. She would confront him in the morning.

At 10:30 p.m., she saw the two associates starting to nod off. From long experience, she knew that coffee was no longer a sufficient stimulant.

"Let's knock it off and start fresh in the morning," she said.

They looked at her with gratitude.

* * * * *

His phone rang at 9:45 p.m.

"You'd better have a solution," he said.

"My guy did what he was supposed to do," the middleman said. It was a statement, not an explanation. "The car went off the road. The damn thing burned to a cinder. The fact that your lady friend walked away from it was pure dumb luck. The other doll has broken bones, I hear."

"So what are you telling me?"

"I'm telling you that he thinks the job's done. He earned his money. But he feels like that's probably not a satisfactory answer. And so he says that for another five grand – and that's talking him down from ten – he'll finish the job, but he'll do it his way."

He thought back to the humiliating session with the fresh-out-of-school junior woodchuck that Limp-haired Lynn had pushed into his office. Two dozen individual data requests, including material that could point to his retirement fund. In talking with other managers, all had received similar requests from cocky kids who thought nothing of asking for mountains of data, then coming back an hour later to ask why it hadn't yet been assembled.

And he had seen suspicion in her eyes. She suspected that the accident hadn't been a matter of being on the wrong ramp at the wrong time. She suspected that he – or one of the other managers – had pushed her off the road, or arranged for someone else to do it.

"Do it," he said.

"Do what?" the middleman replied. "Don't give me no dangling participle answers. I said he'll finish the job, but he'll do it his way.

Are you agreeable?"

He held his breath. "Yes."

"Do you have the money?"

"Yes."

"Then get your ass down here now. We don't do this on a handshake and I don't take IOUs."

"Quincy Market is closed by now."

"That's what you country people think. Cheers is open until 1 a.m. You walk in, you don't order a beer this time. I'll be there in an hour."

The line went dead.

An hour later, he was at the crowded tourist bar where he waited by the entrance. Five minutes later, the middleman sauntered in. This time, he saw the man's features more clearly – a pockmarked face as though from acne. A darker complexion than he would have imagined, and a nose bent as though once broken badly in a fight. As soon as the middleman saw him, he pulled his cap low over his face. As quickly as they had been visible, the features disappeared.

"Just turn toward the bar, give me the envelope, and go back to the boonies."

"When does the job get done?"

"It gets done when you give me the money."

"Tonight would be real nice." He handed the middleman the envelope, offering his hand behind him. His watch said 10:48.

* * * * *

Immediately after leaving the Dunkin' Donuts, Bergeron had radioed in asking that, if Claude Johnson made an appearance at the barracks, that he be notified. At 11 p.m., the call came.

Bergeron made a U-turn and headed north for Bedford. If it meant a speeder got away with going 80 in a 65 zone tonight, so be it.

Johnson was at his desk, going over paperwork. Bergeron knocked.

"I'm still waiting for the cell phone records," Johnson said.

"You don't have to pay me yet."

Bergeron handed him the video cassette. "I think you'll want to look at this."

There was an old VCR in the duty room. Bergeron cued up the tape and gave a background explanation. "The SUV was stolen at 8:24. The incident was at 9:20. I surmised that the perp staked out the parking lot waiting for the two to leave the building…"

"You're 'surmising' a lot, Trooper Bergeron," Johnson said, emphasizing the 'trooper'. "We still haven't established who hit whom."

"It's less than a mile from the mall to the accident site, sir. Why was the stolen vehicle only a mile from where it had been stolen an hour earlier?"

Johnson said nothing. Bergeron pushed the play button.

"This is the Dunkin' Donuts a few blocks from the mall."

They watched as the man ordered his large coffee and chocolate muffin. Bergeron froze the image at the clearest point to see the man's features.

"Huh, Slick Willie," Johnson said, leaning into the television set for a closer look.

"You know him?"

"William Catalano," Johnson said, still peering at the image on the screen. "The guy's been sent up to Concord twice. I didn't know he had made parole. You name it, he does it. Breaks legs, steals to order. He's got the IQ of a Big Mac and he is one mean son of a bitch. I've never collared him personally, but it looks like that's about to change."

"I figured he would need coffee and something to eat while he waited for them…"

"Yeah, yeah, yeah. I get it. That's good work. You pulled those two ladies out of burning car last night?"

"The car wasn't burning yet. I was getting their briefcases when it exploded."

"You were rescuing their purses?"

"Well, the one woman asked…"

"Slick Willie and you got something in common."

Johnson turned to his computer and typed a search string.

"Released last month," Johnson read from his computer. "Served eighteen months on a two-year sentence. Supposedly, he's living with his sister in Hudson."

Hudson was a small town across the Merrimack River from Nashua.

Johnson looked at his watch. "Oh, hell, those guys are supposed to be on call 24/7." He dialed a number from the computer screen.

"Hey, Ray, it's Claude… Yeah, I know what time it is… Screw you, too… You got the jacket on Slick Willie. I hear he's out. Is he really with his sister? …No, I didn't ask if he's doing his sister, just if he's staying there… Yeah… Well, we're on our way over to see him and you may want to be there. He did a GTA on a Chevy Tahoe last night that subsequently got used for a battering ram… Ten minutes… OK, fifteen."

Johnson put down the phone. "Let's roll, Trooper Bergeron. You just hit the big time."

At 11:45 p.m., they pulled onto Central Avenue and parked several houses down from the home of William Catalano's sister. A silver Taurus was across the street. "State issue," Johnson said. "That's Ray."

Johnson got out of the police car and tapped on the Taurus' windshield. "Wake up Ray."

Ray Malone was Johnson's contemporary in age and appearance. *Civil service lifers*, Bergeron thought. *God, don't let me be like them.*

Together, they walked to the house, a sagging structure that was probably once housing for mill workers. Bergeron, who had grown up in just such a house, walked around the side of the house, looking for the possible escape routes. Light from a television screen flickered in the living room.

Ray rang the doorbell, then knocked on the door. It opened after a minute. A sallow woman who could have been thirty or fifty, with stringy hair pulled back from her face, answered. The polyester house dress she wore had grease stains on it.

"We need to speak to Willie," Ray said.

"He's not here," the woman said. She seemed to accept as natural that policemen would be at her door at this late hour.

"Is he staying here?" Johnson asked.

The woman nodded. "But he isn't here right now."

"When did he go out?"

"About an hour ago."

"What was he driving?"

The woman stared vacantly. She shrugged.

"Does he have a car?"

"He uses mine, he uses friends'." Knowing what Slick Willie was driving would have meant leaving her living room, an unlikely event.

"Did he get a phone call before he went out?"

She considered the question. "He got a couple of calls this evening."

"Any of them from people you know?"

"He picks up the phone. He lets me know if it's for me."

"Mind if we look to make certain he isn't here?"

"I ain't lying to you." She stepped back from the doorway, as close to an invitation to enter as they would likely get.

Bergeron had a creeping sensation that caused the hair on the back of his neck to stand on end. "Claude, can you get a ride back to the barracks with Ray?"

"What's wrong?"

"I just had a thought that Willie might be trying to finish his job."

"That's a hell of a leap of faith, kid."

"Do you mind? I know where she's staying."

"I only mind if you're planning to go without me." Johnson turned to Ray. "Call me if you find anything interesting here."

Seven minutes later – almost exactly at midnight – they were at the Crowne Plaza.

The desk clerk said Lynn Kowalchuk was in room 514.

They took the elevator. When the door opened on the fifth floor, they came face to face with a man attired in a dark red waiter's jacket, walking down the corridor, carrying a bouquet of flowers. The man had long, thinning, black hair, a mustache that draped down the side of his mouth, and tattoos on his knuckles. The man was Slick Willie Catalano.

10.

Bergeron launched himself at Catalano, an instinctive move that nearly got him killed when Catalano, his reflexes sharpened by jail fights, tossed aside the bouquet and flashed a knife. Bergeron threw Catalano hard into the wall opposite the elevator. An end table crashed to the floor, one leg crumpling as it did.

Catalano wiggled away, simultaneously slashing at Bergeron with the knife. Six years of Army self-defense training flooded Bergeron's mind and muscles. He waited until the knife went by his chest, then kicked hard at Catalano's groin. The kick missed, catching Catalano on the thigh. Catalano rolled away, jumped up, and raced toward the stairwell.

Bergeron recovered and started running after him. He suddenly felt something trip him, looked down and saw Johnson's leg. "Stay down!" Johnson said, angrily. Bergeron landed chest first and – more Army training – stayed down.

Johnson stood in the center of the hallway, pulled a gun from his shoulder holster, and took careful aim in a two-handed stance.

"William Catalano! Police! Stop! Now!"

Catalano kept running. He was perhaps six feet from the stairwell door.

Johnson fired once. The sound of the firing gun inside the hotel hallway was deafening. Catalano screamed and went down as his hand touched the door.

Bergeron got up and raced in the opposite direction, toward room 514.

The door was locked. He hammered on the door, yelling, "Lynn – Lynn Kowalchuk – it's the police!" There was no answer. He braced himself and kicked the metal door with all his strength. The door would not yield.

"Get the manager!" Bergeron screamed at Johnson. Johnson,

though, was at the far end of the hallway, leaning over the man he had shot.

He heard the door unlock from the inside.

* * * * *

Lynn had gotten back to her room at 11 p.m. She checked emails and responded to questions from New York. She called the hospital and learned that Deb was asleep and resting comfortably.

I ache everywhere, she thought. *What I need is the world's longest shower.*

At ten minutes of midnight, she got into her nightgown and pulled back the covers of the bed, setting her alarm for 7 a.m. She planned to go to the New York bagel shop, completing the shopping episode that had been interrupted by the accident. She would have breakfast with Deb and tell her everything she had learned so far. She was drifting into sleep when she heard a crashing sound like someone fighting, followed, a few seconds later, by an unintelligible shout and a loud noise like a car's backfire, except that it seemed to come from the direction of the corridor rather than the parking lot.

Seconds later, there was pounding on her door and then it shuddered with the effort of someone trying to kick it in. Groggy, she snapped on the bedside light and reached for the telephone to call the front desk when she heard her name being called and a muffled shout of 'get the manager!'

The voice sounded familiar.

Lynn, now awake, jumped up from the bed, turned on the room lights, ran to the door and looked through its wide-angle peephole.

It's that state trooper, she thought.

She grabbed her raincoat from the closet and unlocked the door.

Lou Bergeron stood there, his mouth open, sweating profusely, the front of his uniform slashed horizontally. He saw her, his eyes closed with visible relief, and he smiled.

"Thank God you're OK," he said.

Lynn stepped out into the corridor. At the other end, next to the stairwell, a man in a gray suit leaned over another man in a red jacket. There was the smell of gunpowder in the air. The table in front of the elevator had been knocked over, a leg broken. Incongruously, a bouquet of flowers was in front of the elevator.

She looked back at Bergeron and put together what had happened.

"You saved my life again, didn't you?"

She did the only thing she could think to do. She threw her arms around him and hugged his chest as tightly as she could.

* * * * *

For the next half hour, the fifth-floor corridor was a blur of paramedics and policemen. Johnson had shot Slick Willie Catalano in the leg, a non-life-threatening injury that resulted in a large pool of blood but left a potentially valuable witness in a position to testify.

Catalano was revived by the paramedics. As soon as he realized he hadn't been mortally wounded, Catalano began screaming that he had done nothing, and that neither Bergeron – even though he was in his state trooper's uniform – nor Johnson had identified themselves as policemen, and that Johnson had not warned him before firing his gun. He threatened a multi-million-dollar lawsuit and demanded that he be provided a court-appointed lawyer to pursue his charge of police brutality.

Lynn changed into slacks and a blouse, the rush of adrenaline pushing aside the near state of sleep of a few minutes earlier.

While the crime scene unit worked the hallway, Johnson and Bergeron sat in Lynn's room. Lynn put on a pot of coffee using the small drip coffeemaker in her room. The hotel's night manager was occupied explaining to Nashua police how Catalano, unchallenged, had walked into the restaurant's linen supply room and taken a waiter's jacket, then picked up a vase of roses from the restaurant's waiting area.

"As near as we can tell, Catalano was going to knock on your door and say that flowers had been left earlier for you at the front desk," Bergeron said. "Catalano would wait out of sight until you opened the door. What he had in mind once you opened the door is anyone's guess, although that knife offers a reasonably good clue.

He isn't talking – at least not yet. It may take some time before it dawns on him that he's on the hook for attempted murder."

"The question is who hired him," Johnson said. "By morning, we'll know who placed calls to the house where he's staying. It was almost certainly a contractor." Johnson saw a look of non-comprehension on Lynn's face. "The contractor is the go-between. He's the cut-out man who protects all sides – in exchange for a fee. He wouldn't have met with Catalano in person, and he may never have met Catalano at all. The contractor would know Catalano from someone he did time with in prison. So, we'll also go through a list of Catalano's known associations to get a sense of who else might be involved."

"How did someone at SoftRidge get the contractor's name?" Lynn asked.

Johnson leaned forward, his hands clasped in front of him. "We've got to take your word for it that the person who instigated this is associated with the company where you're doing that investment banking deal. But you've got to help us take that leap of faith. So, here are my questions back to you: are you working on anything else that would make you a target, or have you just completed any deals that would have made someone angry enough to want to come after you? And, is there anyone in your life – past or present – who has that kind of anger? I want you to really think about those questions before you answer, because otherwise, we might be putting all of our resources against something that turns out to be a dead end while the real bad guy sets up his next attempt."

Lynn thought carefully. The last two deals on which she had worked had been completely routine. Her efforts had been effectively anonymous because there were no major disclosures prior to closing. She had been one of a group of six people and, as far as she knew, she had not stood out in any way in the eyes of the clients.

As to other, current deals that might make her a target, this was the only deal to which she was assigned. She had an IM on a likely deal she would join once this work was completed, but so did half a dozen other associates. And, as to her personal life…

"I can say without reservation that I haven't crossed anyone in a long time," she said to the two of them, keeping her voice even and unemotional. Then, looking directly at Johnson, she said, "There's no one in my personal life. There's no way someone could be coming after me except because of my work with SoftRidge."

She saw a look pass between Johnson and Bergeron.

"Then tomorrow morning, we start talking to the fine folks at SoftRidge," Johnson said. He stood up and extended his hand. "Lou seems to be your guardian angel, Miss Kowalchuk. He not only figured out who had tried to run you off the road, he had the feeling the guy was about to try again. And, by the way, he's going to drive you to and from that office for the next couple of days."

Johnson waited to see if there was any reaction from either of them. Both merely nodded agreement. "Also, I'd like for you to switch hotels tomorrow morning. While it's unlikely anyone will try anything, your whereabouts ought to be unclear." He patted Bergeron on the shoulder. "I'll talk to Sam Hurley in the morning. You've earned the right to help out on this investigation. I'll see you in the morning."

And then it was only the two of them.

Lynn looked at Bergeron's shirt. "You didn't know he had slashed your shirt?"

Bergeron looked down and shook his head. "Not until you pointed it out. I thought Catalano missed me completely. Of course, I didn't know he had a knife until it was almost too late."

"No one has ever saved my life once before. Let alone twice."

Bergeron blushed. "Let's hope there isn't a third time."

"I need to find a way to thank you," she said. "Can I at least buy you dinner on your day off?"

Bergeron did not hesitate. "Let me buy the dinner, you buy the dessert. And I'm off on Saturday."

My God, he thought. *I could never have asked her out, but she asked me.* He looked into her face. *She has beautiful eyes.*

11.

Friday, September 21

He was fixing breakfast at 7 a.m.; the radio in his kitchen tuned to a Boston all-news station. He almost didn't hear the item, included in the news recap:

New Hampshire state police last night shot and wounded a man who they say was planning to attack a New York woman staying at a hotel in Nashua. The man, William Catalano, 36, is hospitalized with non-life-threatening wounds and is expected to be arraigned later today…

He turned the radio dial, seeking a local station that carried news. Twenty minutes later, he heard essentially the same news snippet, with this added information:

Police allege Catalano also ran the woman and a companion off the Everett Turnpike, resulting in a fiery crash Tuesday evening. Police did not speculate why the man was attempting to injure the woman, who is from New York City and in Nashua on business.

He fumbled with his briefcase, retrieving the disposable phone. He dialed the middleman's number, his anger growing by the second.

"I guess you heard," the middleman said, almost nonchalantly.

"So what are you going to do about it?"

"The guy's not a screw-up," the middleman said. "The police either figured out something or else they made one incredibly lucky guess and were in the right place at the right time. But this guy isn't going to sing. He got paid to do a job, and he got caught. That's part of the risk and it's built into the price. He'll do the time for the highway job. And that's if they can convict him, because he's real good at covering his tracks. As for the hotel, they've got nothing because he didn't do anything. And he can't tell the police anything because he doesn't know anything. He doesn't know who you are. He doesn't really know who I am. It's perfect because the trail begins and ends with him."

"What do we do?"

"*We* don't do anything. They'll be watching your girlfriend from now on. I wouldn't send in anyone for a week or more."

"It'll be all over in a week," he protested. "Then I want my money back. I paid you to do a job."

There was a silence on the line for nearly thirty seconds.

"You can get back half. That's fair."

He knew better than to push for more. He had been threatened once by this man.

"When and where do we meet?"

"Tonight at eight. Same location."

He ended the call. He calmly went back to the task of preparing his breakfast.

I have a little over twelve hours, he thought as drank his coffee. *I need to devise a foolproof plan. Part one is to silence the middleman as a witness who could ever identify me. That part I need to carry out tonight. Part two is to silence my old friend Joey Gavrilles. Sorry, Joey, but they can trace me through you. And, third, I'm going to finish the job on Limp-haired Lynn. The middleman is right that I can't do it immediately. But I will do it. And I know now that I should have done it myself in the first place.*

* * * * *

At 8:00, Lynn was at Deb's bedside; a bag of bagels, a tub of cream cheese, and something called a 'Big Tote' of strong coffee in her hand.

"I've got two newbies who are utterly clueless about what to do," Lynn said. "They have to ask questions about everything. It's driving me nuts. It's like I'm teaching kindergarten. Tell me they're going to let you out of here soon before I completely lose it."

Deb chewed on a pumpernickel bagel. "Not Zabar's, but not bad. More of an East Side bagel." She took a sip of coffee. "Andy wants me back in New York as soon as I can travel, and the doctor said that can be today. My collar bone is set, flying isn't going to be worse on it than driving. I could be home tonight in my own bed."

Lynn lowered her voice. "C'mon Deb, if you have any say in the matter, *please* stick around. I need someone else on this with more than a month's worth of experience in this stuff. Besides, don't you want to be there when they slap the handcuffs on whoever from SoftRidge hired the guy who ran us off the road?"

"Given what happened to you last night, I'm trying to figure out why you're not on the morning flight out of here," Deb said, sipping her coffee.

"I thought it over last night and this morning," Lynn said. "About what happened to us and what's happened so far at SoftRidge. Something huge is getting hidden at that company. Something Pericles missed. Something that is going to mean a couple of million dollars to one person there – the person who had this guy, Catalano, hired. For whatever reason, that person decided it was the investment bankers who were most likely to discover it – not the accountants, not the lawyers. It means it's a 'big picture' thing, not something that's easy to spot."

Deb looked at Lynn skeptically.

"I mean it," Lynn said. "The thing out on the highway was just intended to put us both in the hospital, or scare us back to New York. When I showed up at SoftRidge the next day, the guy – whoever he is – probably flipped. Now, he's going to get nailed. You should take a lot of satisfaction in that."

"Then tell it to Andy."

"Tell Andy what?" Lynn asked. "That some drunk ran us off the road? That a guy who may have been the same guy that ran us off the road was caught in my hotel? Deb, we know what's going on, but there's not a shred of proof yet. Unless you're living it, it's all speculation. Some paranoid fantasy. If I bag out of here, Andy – and everybody above Andy – will conclude that I see monsters under my bed, probably caused by PMS or drugs. Which means I can wave 'bye' to my career in investment banking. No, I've got a trooper escort to and from the office, that's all I need."

"The same guy..."

"Yeah, Lou Bergeron. The cute one."

Deb smiled. "That's sweet…"

"He figured out who Catalano was, and where he would be last night."

"Is this trooper guy following you around for any special reason?"

Lynn turned red. "I invited him to dinner – to say thanks."

"Jeez, it's about time you got a personal life. When he takes you home tonight, ask him to check out your room to see if it's safe. Then jump his bones."

"Deb, he's right out in his car!"

"And he's going to hear us?"

"It wouldn't surprise me."

Deb reached out and touched the bruise on Lynn's forehead. "Before you go out with this guy, I get to do your makeup."

* * * * *

Lou Bergeron and Claude Johnson sat in the office of Sandy Calo. Bergeron observed the trappings of a confident, high-level corporate executive. Calo dressed and acted the part. His suit was well-tailored, his hair neatly trimmed. Calo looked to be between 45 and 50, but his face was tanned and unlined. The office was large, with four windows and a broad desk that allowed for neat groupings of papers and files. Behind Calo, a credenza and file cabinet wrapped around the wall, providing a ten-foot-long work surface. Neat stacks of papers were in piles next to one another, with yellow Post-it notes on the wall – '2.1(c)', '3.3'. A pair of potted palms flanked the doorway. A small conference table and three chairs allowed for private meetings.

"What are those?" Bergeron asked, pointing to the row of papers.

"The exhibits for the contract," Calo said. "Or at least the beginning of the exhibits. The numbers refer to the contract sections. Section 2, paragraph 1, subparagraph c. 'Seller shall deliver at closing an assignment of all real property leases except for those specified in Section 8.4 (d).' When I get a lease assignment completed, it goes in this pile. When all the lease assignments are completed, they go to the lawyers to get collated into the contract."

"What do the bankers from Clarenden Brothers have to do with things like lease assignments?" Johnson asked.

Calo shrugged his shoulders. "As much or as little as they want. They don't work for us, they work for Pericles. They're watching out for their client's interests. It's our lawyers and investment bankers who are doing all the work of gathering this material and making certain it's right."

"You think Clarenden being here is superfluous?" Johnson asked.

"They have a right to be here," Calo said emphatically. "They have a right to look at everything as it is being assembled. What I'm saying is that, from the CFO's perspective, Clarenden is an extra set of eyes that can slow the process. If I'm pulling together lease assignments and, suddenly, someone from Clarenden takes it into their head to review those leases, I'm stymied. I have to wait for them to satisfy themselves that whatever they're looking for isn't there. The alternative is that I work around them. I'm saying it can get frustrating."

"You've met Miss Kowalchuk from Clarenden?"

"Certainly. I've responded to any number of her requests."

"You're aware that someone ran her car off of Route 3 Wednesday evening, injuring one of her co-workers?"

"I think we all are thankful neither she nor Ms. Fowler was seriously injured. I wasn't aware that it was a case of someone running her car off of the road."

"Last night, we intercepted the same person outside Miss Kowalchuk's room. Fortunately, we arrived before he could enter her room," Johnson said.

Calo blinked several times, seeming to absorb what Johnson was saying. "Do you mean, like a hit man?"

Johnson waved his hands dismissively. "We don't know for certain. I'm just saying that someone set out to do injury to Miss

Kowalchuk, and they found a fairly nasty individual to carry out that assignment."

"Would you provide us with a list of your various telephone and cell phone numbers, Mr. Calo?" Bergeron asked. "Those would include ones from your home as well as from the office."

"By all means," Calo said.

Johnson pointed to the wedding band on Calo's left hand. "I see you're married, Mr. Calo. Can your wife account for your whereabouts Wednesday and Thursday nights – what time you got home, whether you went out, that sort of thing?"

"Judy – my wife – is in Connecticut this week. Her sister is going through a rough patch – she has son who has been diagnosed with leukemia – and Judy is there to more or less run the household for a few weeks. Also, with all of this…" Calo gestured to the pile of materials along the credenza. "I haven't been home much these past few weeks."

Johnson made a note on his pad. Bergeron noted mentally that Calo did not have an alibi for the two evenings.

"I don't expect you to have an answer to this question, Mr. Calo, but can you think of any reason why anyone at SoftRidge would want to see harm come to either Miss Kowalchuk or Miss Fowler?"

Calo looked incredulously at Johnson for a moment, then shook his head. "The idea that someone here would want to cause bodily harm to those two women is pretty far-fetched. They're just investment bankers. They're trying to get a deal done, just like us."

* * * * *

Jeff Wright's office was not nearly as grand as Sandy Calo's, Bergeron noted. It was not as large and the furniture in the office was old, showing the wear and tear of long use by multiple owners. Also, Wright's office had no windows. The edge of the cuffs on Wright's white dress shirt were frayed, his New England Patriots tie showed a grease stain under his chin.

Either this is a guy who doesn't give a damn about his personal appearance, or else he's perpetually broke, Bergeron thought.

"That's partly functional," Wright said after Bergeron pointed out the lack of windows. "This is human resources. There's a lot of sensitive data in this office. A lot of files that need to be kept under lock and key. A window is an extra point of entry and a potential security weak link. You'll find that most HR people accept that the sensitivity of their work means certain tradeoffs, and the view is the first thing to go."

"I understand you headed corporate development until last year," Bergeron said.

"Until the department was eliminated," Wright said. "Back then, I had a couple of windows." He smiled, but then coughed for several seconds. "Excuse me," he added.

"Cold?" Bergeron asked.

"Ex-smoker," Wright said. "Three years since I had a cigarette, but I still get these coughing fits."

"Corporate development," Johnson said. "What's that?"

"Buying and selling product lines," Wright said. "And raising money."

"Why was the department eliminated?"

"It takes money to buy stuff," Wright said. "And there came a point where we weren't going to raise any more money."

"After running corporate development, is heading up human resources a comedown?" Johnson asked.

Wright swiveled his chair to face Johnson and glared at him. "I thought you had some questions about the traffic accident the investment bankers were in?"

"I didn't mean to ask such a personal question, Mr. Wright," Johnson said, returning Wright's stare. "Miss Kowalchuk says that most of the company's management doesn't expect to be retained by Pericles. Do you agree with that?"

Wright swiveled his chair again and slightly raised its seat height. "We're going to find out pretty soon. Agreeing or disagreeing with it is fairly academic at his point."

"Would derailing the acquisition mean managers would keep

their jobs?"

Wright laughed. "If this deal doesn't close on September 30, we'll have a lot more serious things to worry about than a few management jobs. We won't have enough money to meet our payroll."

"It's possible that one of SoftRidge's managers hired someone to injure Miss Kowalchuk and Miss Fowler. Can you think of any reason why someone would want to do that?"

Wright's brow furrowed and he shook his head. "Lynn made a nuisance out of herself the past few days, but she's just doing her job. Deb asked a lot of questions that first day, but pretty much kept her head down afterwards. Making a nuisance of yourself is no reason to get hurt by someone. Stopping two investment bankers isn't going to slow down the process. It might even speed it up."

"How old are you, Mr. Wright?"

"Thirty-nine."

"Are you married?"

"No."

"Living with anyone?"

"Not right now. I had a girlfriend who lived with me, but we broke up a couple of months ago."

"Can anyone account for your whereabouts outside of the office Wednesday and Thursday evenings?"

Wright looked up toward the ceiling and thumped the eraser of a pencil on his desk. "My dog, but that's probably not good enough for you. I'm in a rented house. I had been living in my girlfriend's condo, and I had to move somewhere. People in the neighborhood don't really know me and I certainly don't know them. Someone in the street may notice when I come and go. Mind you, I've been here a lot of time since final due diligence began."

"And you can provide us with a list of your telephone numbers – personal and business cell phones and the like?"

"No problem."

* * * * *

Bill Griffin's tiny office made it difficult for Bergeron and Johnson to be seated without their knees crushed up against Griffin's desk. File boxes of papers were everywhere, stacked against walls. Some of the stacks were five feet high. Griffin was the oldest of the executives they had met; probably fifty, give or take a year.

"You don't believe in filing cabinets, Mr. Griffin?" Johnson asked.

"This is all of the material that was in the Data Room," Griffin said. "These are the hard copies. I'm the repository."

"What's a data room?" Bergeron asked.

"When a company puts itself – or a division of itself – up for sale, the bankers create what's called a Data Room," Griffin said. The Data Room has all of the information – the data – a buyer needs to make a decision about whether to come in for due diligence. It used to be a physical room – a conference room usually – with all of these boxes arrayed on tables. Now, it's online. Companies can decide what they want to release to competitors versus financial buyers. And investment bankers can keep track of who spends how much time in the Data Room, even what documents they look at and for how long."

"But it all starts with hard copies," Griffin explained. "We scan the hard copies and put them up into the Data Room. Now that we're into the contract, we need that material to create the schedules. Keeping it here makes it a lot easier. It's a little crowded, but nobody asked me if it was OK to use my office."

"Miss Kowalchuk had trouble getting certain materials from you on that first day," Bergeron said.

"Miss Kowalchuk is a first-class pain in the ass," Griffin replied quickly. "I'm sorry about her car and I'm sorry that her partner got banged up, but she's in here every ten minutes asking for stuff that just doesn't make any difference. Now she's got these kids fresh out of college running around asking for even more stuff. We're trying to finish a contract by a deadline. She's acting like we've got all the time in the world. We don't, and she knows it."

"You sound angry about it," Johnson said.

"We're all angry about it," Griffin said sharply. "Some of us are just more honest than others. Pericles did their due diligence. They were here for four frigging weeks looking over every scrap of paper they could lay their hands on. They went away satisfied. We did a deal. We agreed on a number. Now, these Clarenden people are coming in, trying to justify their fee, by starting all over. Hell, yes, I'm angry." Griffin's face was red.

"Can you tell us where you were Wednesday and Thursday evenings?"

"Why?" The response was brusque.

"Because we need to know where you were Wednesday and Thursday evenings for our investigation."

"You think I had something to do with that accident Wednesday night? Well, I didn't." Griffin's voice was growing more testy with each response.

"Please don't make us have to do all of this formally, Mr. Griffin," Johnson said. "Right now, this is a friendly discussion in your office. It's the same discussion we're having with each of the other senior managers. You're under no special scrutiny."

Griffin was silent. He looked behind Johnson and Bergeron at the door, making certain it was closed tightly. "My wife thinks I was here at the office Wednesday evening. I was somewhere else."

"And where was that?"

"I was at my girlfriend's."

"We'll need a name and address."

* * * * *

The orderliness of Frank Kepner's office was in stark contrast to that of Griffin. The manufacturing VP, whom Bergeron judged to be a few years either side of forty, had one neat stack of paper on the left side of his metal desk. The rest was bare. Charts on two of his gray walls showed productivity and unit cost trends. The graphs showed steady improvement in whatever they were tracking. Behind Kepner's desk was a large-scale topological map of the White

Mountains. Kepner himself looked like an athlete who was still in training, with biceps bulging under a Van Halen concert tee shirt.

Bergeron visually traced the upper edge of the map, finding Berlin, where he had grown up.

"Lynn and Deborah – and those two new guys – are here because Pericles wants them here," Kepner said. "I don't bear them any ill will. Hell, I'd be doing exactly the same thing if I were the one doing the buying."

"One of your other managers says you're all really angry about their requests and the time it takes to comply with them."

Kepner laughed. "Yeah, I'm sure Bill thinks he speaks for all of us. He's got enough anger for half a dozen people."

"Why is that?" Johnson asked.

"Because he's got a very expensive lifestyle that's going to get tossed in the crapper as soon as this deal is done."

"What do you mean, 'expensive'?"

Kepner folded his hands with his fingers pointing upwards. "He's got the big house out in Hollis, two sons in private colleges, a boat over in Portsmouth. He didn't figure out that SoftRidge was slowly going down the drain. He thought the gravy train would all go on forever, and that he could count on stock options to bail him out. Guess what? Like all of us, he's got lots of options. And they're all worthless, just like ours."

"There was a dinner Monday night in Nashua," Bergeron said. "Do you remember who organized that?"

Kepner put his hands behind his head and turned his neck back and forth. "I got the command performance invitation from Larry – Larry Driscoll. I imagine he's the guy who put the thing together."

"And dinners like that – with lots of wine and an open bar, paid for by the company – are rare?"

Kepner laughed again. "Since Pete Kincaid died, you can count them on one finger of one hand. This has not exactly been party central around here for the last year."

"Who paid the bill?"

"I saw the waitress give the check to Sandy Calo. I also saw him open that little leather folder. I thought he was going to have a stroke right on the spot."

"Are you married, Mr. Kepner?"

"Not for the past five years."

"Can anyone account for your whereabouts Wednesday and Thursday evening?"

"From when to when?"

"From eight to eleven, say."

Kepner massaged the back of his neck with his big hands. "I watched the ball game Wednesday night – the one that officially guaranteed that our beloved Red Sox will have a losing season. I was here until fairly late last night – probably until close to 10 p.m. I brought out a fair number of files to the Clarenden people, so they could vouch for me."

"We'll also need a list of all of your telephone numbers – cell phones, home phones and the like," Johnson said.

"You mistake me for a wealthy man. I have a home phone and the company issues me a genuine, old-fashioned circa 2004 Blackberry for when I travel. You're welcome to those numbers."

"Do you think it's possible that someone inside SoftRidge could hide a couple of million dollars that would escape the attention of Pericles' due diligence?" Bergeron asked.

Kepner laughed one more time. "They might have escaped Pericles' first round of due diligence. That was done by their internal people. The clowns we hired to sell the company – Highsmith – are next to worthless now that the letter of intent is signed. They're not looking for anything except to get out of here as fast as humanly possible. But escape Lynn and her crew? I walked in this morning and she and her guys gang-tackled me. Made me go over every dime of spending for the Philippines repair facility. I had to pull up email correspondence, repair bills, and travel reports. I offered a Skype session and I think that may have convinced her those people are real, but she may send one of her people over there to take photos."

"But could someone do that? Hide money that would come back to that person after the acquisition?" Bergeron asked.

Kepner considered the question before answering. "It would be enormously difficult. We have very tight controls on what we spend. We once had an accounting clerk who figured out that she was in a position to cut hand checks to herself. We caught her on the second check – and that was for about two hundred bucks. We spend a huge amount on internal audit just to prevent things like that. So, could it be done? I guess so. I just don't know how you could get around the audit side of the equation... unless you ran audit."

* * * * *

I've got to get this back under control, he thought after the two policemen left his office. *This isn't how it was supposed to be. The idea was to get the damned deal closed without scrutiny. Lynn Kowalchuk looked like she was going to be a problem. Fine, so I did something to get her out of the picture. Not kill her. Not maim her. Just get her away from here and replace her with someone less bright.*

Except that the cretin hired by the middleman didn't do the job right. And I panicked when Kowalchuk showed up yesterday. That was my fault. I got caught up in wanting to get it over with. Except that the guy, Catalano, blew it. Shows up at her hotel with a knife.

So now they've figured out it's someone inside SoftRidge. Because that woman has no personal life and so no angry boyfriends to go look at. The cops talked to just half a dozen people. Are we the first ones, or is there a wider cast of suspects?

The middleman said Catalano couldn't identify him. I don't believe it. Catalano has to get paid. Catalano wouldn't do business without knowing who was hiring him. And I don't believe that the middleman doesn't know who I am. This business about thinking that Kowalchuk is my 'girlfriend' is just a smokescreen. He's put it all together.

And, the middleman knows that if the police catch me, I'll roll on him. I've met him. I could pick him out of a lineup.

Which means I'm in danger, too. No wonder the middleman agreed to give me back half of the money. He wants to meet me one more time.

Probably to kill me.

So, I am the hunted.

But starting now, so is he. And I have the element of surprise.

12.

Lynn looked through her list, drawn up the previous day:

- *Phantom employees*
- *Phantom inventory*
- *Understated accounts receivable*
- *Overstated accounts payable*
- *An entire phantom department or business*

She crossed through 'phantom employees' and 'phantom businesses'.

That would have been too easy, she thought to herself.

Frank Kepner had taken the request with great amusement. "You want me to prove that those twenty people in the Philippines really exist?" he had said, laughing. "You think I've invented an entire group?"

"I'm just trying to complete the due diligence," she had said, expecting anger or defensiveness from him, but not laughter.

"Well, let's go see what we've got by way of documentation," he had said. And, for an hour, they had gone through files. He had pulled out office blueprints, emails, expense reports, and correspondence with customers. After fifteen minutes it was obvious that her suspicions were misplaced, but he continued bringing out material. "Let's be absolutely certain," he had kept saying. "You never know what kind of stuff we're hiding around here. Damn, I may even have invented a country."

Finally, she had said, "Enough!" She handed him back the material and offered an apology.

* * * * *

Through the afternoon, Claude Johnson checked the incoming and outgoing phone records. Carla Catalano's numerous calls to her doctors and her children's school were crossed off, leaving half a dozen that he circled, including one that came in at 11 p.m. the previous evening. The call came from an 857 area code, one of the cell phone overlay area codes for Boston. There had been two calls to Catalano from the same number on Wednesday.

The phone that called Catalano, in turn, was a Tracfone – essentially, an untraceable cell phone. Tracfone's records showed that it had been purchased at a convenience store in South Boston and activated three months earlier. Speaking minutes had been replenished using pre-paid cards acquired for cash. The subscriber's name was given as John Smith. The address given tied to a point roughly fifty yards offshore from the L Street Beach in South Boston.

God damn burner cell phones, Johnson thought to himself. *But at least I know how they communicated. That's the first step.*

The records on the South Boston cell phone were only slightly more illuminating. Apart from the three calls to Catalano's sister, most of the calls were made to yet other untraceable phones. There were multiple calls in recent days to a cell phone with a 603 area code – New Hampshire. *That* phone had been purchased three weeks earlier for cash at a WalMart in Nashua. The name given to Tracfone was George Smith with a street address that corresponded to no location in New Hampshire.

"Real wise guys," Johnson murmured.

The New Hampshire cell phone had been used only a handful of times. There were five calls to the South Boston number starting Tuesday afternoon. And one, shortly after the cell phone was activated, to a bar in downtown Nashua.

"This is why they pay me the big bucks," he said, circling the Nashua bar telephone number with a red marking pen.

Johnson put the records from the three phones alongside one another and created a timeline in his notebook:

Friday 8:55 p.m. – SoftRidge exec calls his local bad guy contact at the bar where he hangs out

Tuesday 4:20 p.m. – SoftRidge exec calls a fixer somewhere in Boston – arranging a meeting?

Tuesday 8:00 p.m. – SoftRidge exec calls the fixer – I'm here, where are you?

Tuesday 8:01 p.m. - Fixer calls SoftRidge Exec – why was this call made?

Tuesday 9:22 p.m. – Fixer calls Catalano. Interested in a job?

Wednesday 4:14 p.m. – SoftRidge exec calls fixer – to set another meeting?

Wednesday 8:11 p.m. – Fixer calls Catalano to say it's a go.

Wednesday 8:30 p.m. – Fixer calls SoftRidge exec. All set!

Wednesday 8:30-9:30 – Catalano steals car and runs Kowalchuk off the road

Thursday 10:43 a.m. – SoftRidge Exec calls fixer. Probably panicked that Kowalchuk showed up at offices

Thursday 9:25 p.m. – Fixer calls SoftRidge exec. Probably wants more money. Meeting?

Thursday 11:02 p.m. – Fixer calls Catalano

Thursday 11:30 p.m. – Catalano goes to hotel to finish off Kowalchuk

Today 7:48 a.m. – SoftRidge exec calls fixer. Heard or saw news on Catalano? Does he want another meeting?

The phone calls told a story. Johnson needed to make certain he was interpreting the story correctly. Finding the local contact was the best way to put names to that story. The bar was his best opportunity to put all of the pieces together.

* * * * *

The Galen, a shabby, twenty-foot-wide storefront on Spring Street in the center of town, was a remnant of a fast-disappearing Nashua. A bar with neither a theme nor wines by the glass, and without Cosmopolitans on the menu. In fact, there was no menu. Only a long counter that smelled of years of spilled alcohol and cigarette smoke. The lawyers, stockbrokers, and civil servants flocked to the brew pubs for lunch, leaving places like the Galen to serve the serious drinker.

Johnson walked in to the darkened room and the four people in the bar all looked up. Conversations did not stop because there were no conversations ongoing. The Galen was a place to get drunk, not to talk.

The bartender looked up from the pages of the *Telegraph* and studied him. The stranger was in a suit, therefore this was an official visit. He put down the newspaper and waited, expectantly.

Johnson showed him a badge, something he rarely needed to do any more.

"You're the owner?"

The bartender nodded.

"I'm looking for one of your regulars," Johnson said.

The bartender threw a glance at the handful of patrons in the bar. "They're all regulars."

"Someone who gets phone calls here."

The bartender nodded, getting a glimmer of where the conversation was headed. "I don't keep track of phone calls," he said cautiously. It was a statement, offered neither defensively nor with intent of being of use to a member of law enforcement.

"Then tell me who gets phone calls here and I'll be a happy guy."

The bartender shifted uneasily. His eyes went to the front door. "There must be two dozen guys who get calls here over the course of a week. Most of them are just first names."

Johnson was starting to feel frustrated. This was his one proper lead out of dozens of calls to untraceable numbers, and a bartender was not cooperating. The bartender looked at him impassively. He intended to say nothing more.

So, instead, Johnson decided to up the ante. He took out his cell phone and began pressing numbers. "The alternative to your not helping me is for me to request, from my cell phone right now, that my fellow agents at the Liquor Control Commission do a thorough audit of your inventory and records to make certain that you're not bringing in out-of-state liquor. Failure to have proper tax stamps for your inventory would, by statute, result in a two hundred dollar fine per bottle and mandatory hearing to determine if you should retain your liquor license. Do you want me to complete this call?"

The odds were that at least a third of the bottles in the bar would lack a tax stamp.

Johnson's finger was poised over the keypad, ready to tap the final number.

The bartender licked his lip. Buying time. Hoping for a meteorite to come crashing through the ceiling and put an end to his dilemma.

"I got two guys who get calls here regularly. Juan Gonzales and Joey Gavrilles."

"Little Joey G?" Johnson asked.

The bartender shrugged. "I hear him called that sometimes."

"And when does Mr. Gonzales make an appearance?"

"Mostly Thursday, Friday and Saturday nights."

"You'll do me the favor of pointing him out if he comes in tonight?"

The bartender nodded.

"And Little Joey G?"

"He'll be in tonight, probably after ten."

Joey Gavrilles, aka Little Joey G., Johnson thought. *A useful man to know. Receiver of stolen goods and a man who will steal a car to order on four hours' notice. A guy who had been in and out of prisons in Massachusetts and New Hampshire often enough to have acquired a wide circle of nasty friends.*

How would an executive of a company have come to know Little Joey G? And, why did they first get in touch a week ago? Johnson thought of scenarios: *Our perp buys a cheap ring for his wife or girlfriend. They went to school together. They were in the drunk tank together....*

Claude Johnson looked at his watch: 4:30. He had been on this case, with only a few hours break, since the call last evening from the Bergeron kid at 11 p.m. He needed a few hours sleep. Go home, get some rest, get back to the bar and wait for his two most likely perps to walk in the door.

* * * * *

At 6:30 p.m., he loaded his car and began the drive to Boston. At 7:30, he was parked and ready. His disguise was, in his mind, perfect. A Red Sox cap pulled low over his eyes, a dark blue windbreaker with the collar turned up, jeans, sneakers, and a shopping bag from Crate & Barrel. He looked like every tourist in Boston. A pair of tinted glasses completed the look. He was indistinguishable from the crowd around him.

He made two passes by Cheers and Victoria's Secret to see if the middleman was waiting for him. He wasn't but, on both passes, a beefy, bearded man with an ear ring – a man who looked decidedly out of place at Quincy Market, was standing about thirty feet from the entrance to the clothing store, watching the Victoria's Secret entrance. The man bore a vacant expression as he waited, as though waiting to be activated by someone or something.

At 7:50, he called the middleman's cell phone.

"Traffic was backed up in the tunnel," he said. "I just got off the highway and I'm running a couple of minutes late. Do you want to meet at Victoria's Secret or Cheers?"

"'The same place' means the window in front of Victoria's Secret," the middleman said caustically. "It's this ritual I have, and I'm the one handing over cash this time. Humor me."

He ended the call and watched the bearded man. Almost immediately, the man reached into a jacket pocket and extracted a ringing cell phone. The man listened and then spoke a few words. He nodded at what he was hearing, then put the phone back in his pocket. He walked briskly toward one of the South Market arcade entrances.

The bearded man and the middleman are acting together, he thought.

Two policemen were talking by one of the kiosks that lined the center of the market. He walked hurriedly up to them. "Officers, I'm pretty sure I just saw a pickpocket at work."

That got their attention.

He pointed to the arcade entrance the bearded man had gone into. "I saw him dip his hand into a woman's purse less than a minute ago – she's walking toward that building over there…"

They asked for a description of the man. He provided a detailed one.

"Stay here," one of the policemen said, as both began walking toward the arcade entrance.

He waited a few seconds, then stripped off his jacket and cap and walked the short distance to Victoria's Secret. The Crate & Barrel bag went into a waste bin. The tinted glasses went into his pocket. As he walked, he called the middleman's cell phone.

"Can you believe it? I found an on-street space," he said. "I'm here."

The middleman said, sarcastically, "Congratulations. This must be your lucky day. Maybe you want to buy a Powerball ticket on the way home."

"Let's get this over with," he said. "I'm at Victoria's Secret."

"I'm almost there," the middleman said and hung up.

A minute later, they were standing alongside one another, the middleman again with his cap pulled low and his windbreaker collar turned up. The middleman extracted an envelope from his jacket pocket.

"Ten grand," the middleman said. "Don't embarrass me and count it here. You want to do something in a couple of weeks, you give me a call."

And with that, the middleman walked away.

Way too easy, he thought. *The plan is that I'm supposed to be being watched. The bearded guy will intercept me on the way to my car. The middleman gets the money back, and a New Hampshire man dies in an apparent robbery. Except that, if the Boston PD are doing their job right, they're questioning the guy right now and, while they didn't find some lady's wallet on him, they found a knife or a gun. And because he's out of place in this sanitized tourist trap, they're going to question him for a long time.*

Right about now, the middleman is going to call the bearded guy and say, 'he's all yours.' Except the bearded guy isn't going to answer. And the middleman is going to get nervous, because he doesn't want to be out ten thousand bucks. So, I've got to move fast.

He walked quickly back to the waste receptacle and retrieved the Crate & Barrel bag and, from it, the windbreaker, cap and a pair of surgical gloves. He put back on the tinted glasses. He also brought out the screwdriver. A big screwdriver with a yellow handle, the Phillips head sharpened to a fine point.

The middleman was nearly to the arcade underpass that led to the Rose Kennedy Greenway. In theory, the Greenway was intended to extend the tourist 'experience' of Boston. In reality, it was a bleak, barren expanse of uninviting grass and concrete paths and walls that, at least at night, kept visitors on the 'safe' side of Atlantic Avenue. Right now, the middleman was in a crowd. As soon as he reached the service road, he would be in a mostly deserted area, such was the sharp nighttime distinction in Boston between the well-lit safe tourist zone and the dark streets that the out-of-towners avoided.

Where was the middleman headed? He could cross Atlantic Avenue and head for the North End, or he could be walking to his car. If the middleman was looking for a cab, he might have only seconds to act.

The middleman paused at the curb, waiting for traffic to clear. He stepped into the street. He raised an arm.

Damn, he thought. *Now or never.*

There were a few people around. They looked mostly to be tourists. They were not lingering, nor were they making videos or taking pictures. They seemed intent upon getting back to their hotels because this forlorn area was as uninviting as they imagined any big city could be.

The middleman waved his arm impatiently. Cabs cruised this area and, from his vantage, he could see one, the light atop the vehicle indicating it was not engaged. Between the middleman and the cab were only two large trucks, both moving briskly though the thinning traffic.

He saw the trucks and knew it was his opportunity. It wasn't his plan, but it could work. He got a running start. He shoved the middleman with both hands, pushing him well into the traffic lane. The first truck blew its horn, even at the moment of impact. The driver slammed his brakes with a horrific squeal. The truck behind him, following too closely, could not stop and rammed the first truck, pushing it forward.

He looked back only briefly, to see that the middleman's body was under the truck's second set of wheels, motionless, with who knows how much weight on top of him. Several horns blew as traffic suddenly stopped.

He ran back under the arcade, stripping off the gloves though retaining the windbreaker, glasses and cap pulled low over his head against the likelihood of security cameras. He heard the first scream as someone understood that a man was dead under the wheels of the large truck. He slowed his pace to a fast walk through the Quincy Market plaza, where he was startled to see the bearded man, handcuffed, being led by four policemen, including the two whom he had approached. He slowed his pace further so as not to attract the policemen's attention, crossing to the far side of the esplanade.

From the corner of his eye, he saw two of the policemen leave the bearded man and begin running back toward the arcade. He continued walking, now quickly and deliberately, taking off the windbreaker and hat as he walked. When he perceived he was a safe distance in front of the two policemen and their charge, he put the items of clothing into separate waste receptacles. When he reached the Congress Street end of Quincy Market, he threw the sharpened screwdriver into a water drain.

He made it to his car, half a mile from Quincy Market. Remarkably, he was not sweating. He wasn't even breathing hard. Instead, his pulse felt normal. He had just killed a man, and it had no physiological impact on him.

Remarkable, he thought to himself, feeling his pulse again. *I can't understand why I agreed to pay someone to do this.*

* * * * *

It was 9 p.m. The smoking gun was staring Lynn right in the face.

"I can't believe how stupid I am," she said to herself. Across the table, her two assistants both looked up in unison.

"It was right here all the time," she said. "I can't believe no one saw it."

They looked at one another, then back at her, perplexed.

"We just saved Pericles a couple of million bucks," she said. "I just discovered who was going to get rich on the sale of the company."

13.

Lynn spent two hours verifying her information was correct. The two associates, comprehending that this was a potential career-making move, eagerly fetched all materials required to document her analysis.

At 11 p.m., Lynn phoned Andy Greenglass to discuss what she had found. Andy, in turn, phoned a managing partner and briefed him. Though it was now nearly 11:30 p.m., they agreed for the need to bring in Pericles' CEO, Ross Maynard.

"Maynard needs to make the decision whether to squeeze their gonads or call the deal off, and he needs to decide before word gets out," Andy said in support of the decision to call Maynard.

Ross Maynard was beside himself with glee.

"Those bastards are going to suffer," he said after Lynn explained the deception.

"It's only one person," Lynn cautioned. "I'm fairly certain he did it on his own. Anyway, he's the only one who benefits. If it was all of management, you'd have spread the stock around."

"But there could be an agreement to distribute the proceeds afterwards," Maynard said.

"It's risk/reward," Lynn said, realizing that she was quoting Lou Bergeron. "Somebody isn't going to risk his career – or going to jail – for a couple of hundred thousand dollars. You've got to be talking millions to make that risk worthwhile."

There was silence. And a "Hmmm…" on the other end of the line.

"So why do you think my bright brains here didn't catch it in due diligence?" Maynard wanted to know. "And how did it get past the fancy-pants bankers from Highsmith when they put together the Information Memorandum?"

"Because the share count was still bouncing around," Lynn

explained. "You have a weighted number of shares that fluctuates with the share price and the final purchase price. Your guys were focused on the deal breakers – the customer list, the technology. They didn't care about the share count. That's the divisor. Everyone knew SoftRidge had 'about twenty-one million shares' outstanding, and that the purchase price was two hundred million, give or take."

"What Bill Griffin did was simply to add 300,000 phantom shares into the final count. He created them and then instructed the transfer agent to issue the shares – or, more accurately, the electrons that represent the shares. Instead of 21.1 million, it was 21.4. It still rounded down to twenty-one."

"And the bastard would have gotten away with it."

"It was all set up," Lynn said. "Pericles would have cut checks to shareholders right after closing – more electrons. All he had to do was clean out the dummy accounts when they settled, three days later. Electrons in, electrons out."

"And because he was entrusted with the relationship with the transfer agent, he just added the shares," Maynard said.

"Exactly. He was the fox guarding the hen house."

"I'll be damned," Maynard said. "Those bastards are going to suffer big time."

"Are you still going to go through with the deal?" Andy asked.

There was a moment's silence on the line.

"Yeah." Maynard said. "But I've got a couple of demands in mind for their board. They're going to love it. They're going to scream. But after this, they're going to say 'yes' because they have no choice. God, I'm going to enjoy watching them crawl."

Then, Maynard appeared to shift gears. "So this is probably the same son of a bitch who hired someone to run you and Miss Fowler off the road the other night?"

"We think so," Lynn said. "Or, at least I think so. I haven't called the state police yet. We wanted to talk with you first."

"Is Miss Fowler doing OK?"

Lynn bit her tongue. "She was fine this morning. She was trying to decide whether to go back to New York or finish up the due diligence here. I'm hoping she stays."

"Well, give her my best. I suppose there will be criminal charges against this Griffin bastard. For hiring someone, I mean. Not just for – what? Attempted theft? Misappropriation of funds?"

"We'll let the police in New Hampshire sort that out," Andy said. "The key thing is to get the contract finished."

The conversation drifted into tactics. Maynard was to demand a board meeting for Saturday afternoon. He would lay out his demands for agreeing to go through with the acquisition. The price would drop from $9.50 per share to $8.50, otherwise, SoftRidge's Board would be considered in material breach of the binding letter of intent they had signed, and each director would be on the hook for fraudulent misrepresentation.

"You should be thinking about the kind of bonus Miss Kowalchuk is going to get," Maynard said at the end of the conversation. "I think it ought to be a really big number."

"Lynn is one of our rising stars," Andy said. "We'll take care of her."

* * * * *

It was a long time since he had been in this neighborhood. An even longer time since he had been at this house. The building itself was unremarkable: two stories, probably three bedrooms. Just a white, frame home built in the 1920s, similar in style to the houses up and down Linden Street. The porch needed repairs and the whole house could use a coat of paint.

He remembered standing on this porch on a summer night, decades earlier, ringing the doorbell. Katie's father had answered the door, in his undershirt, a can of beer in his hand. Mr. Gavrilles had squinted at him. "Do I know you?" he had asked. Then he looked at the clothes. "You don't look like one of Joey's buddies. What's your name?"

He had shown up in a sports jacket and slacks. Appropriate

dress, he had thought, for a first date. He told Mr. Gavrilles his name.

"From down the street?" Mr. Gavrilles had said. "Eddie's kid? So you've come sniffing around my Katie?"

He didn't know how to answer. 'Sniffing around Katie' sounded sordid, like something a dog would do. He was getting ready to turn around and leave – call the whole thing off – when Joey had come up behind his father.

"Relax, Dad, he's OK," Joey had said, clamping his hand on his father's shoulder. "You said Katie ought to be going out with nice guys. Well, this is one of the nice guys. He gets straight A's. He's going to UNH in September."

Mr. Gavrilles had squinted again. "Ain't you a little old for her?"

"Hey, Dad, she's seventeen. Let her decide for herself."

And they had gone out. He and Katie. All that summer. Once or twice a week. Movies, parties, even a couple of trips over to Hampton Beach. Katie was great. Always laughing at his jokes, always being a sport. And then they had stopped.

I remember why, he thought. *I remember why very well. Because she made a fool of me. Because she used me, the 'good boy' when she needed something. What a lesson she taught me. What a sap I was.*

That was what went through his mind as he stood on this porch. That first night, so long ago, that he came to pick up Katie on that first date. The bitterness of how that ended welled up with a freshness that surprised him.

He rang the doorbell and heard the sound of footsteps.

* * * * *

It was nearly midnight. Lynn sat at the conference table, fingering the card with Lou Bergeron's name and phone numbers on it.

I should call him, she thought. *He's supposed to drive me back to the hotel, regardless of what time it is.*

I should wait until morning, she thought. *He's been getting by on two or three hours' sleep for the last several nights. He'll need to be fresh tomorrow to arrest Griffin. To put the case to rest. But then I might not see him…*

She called the barracks number. Trooper Bergeron had asked to be paged when she called.

He's probably home, asleep, she thought.

Less than a minute later, her cell phone rang.

"I've been right outside the building for two hours," Bergeron said. "Were you planning to work all night?" He sounded bright and energetic, the opposite of what she expected.

"There's a lot to tell you," Lynn said. "We found the fraud."

At midnight, there was no place to go to talk. And so they sat in his patrol car.

"Bill Griffin, the controller, 'invented' 300,000 shares of SoftRidge stock and created dummy shareholders in multiple accounts," Lynn explained. "I only caught it because the share count kept coming out higher than what I had on the trial balance sheet."

"What's a trial balance sheet?" Bergeron asked.

She shook her head. "You don't want to know. But it was there, all the time. And everyone would have just assumed that the share count was a little higher than predicted. We were all focused on assets, liabilities and shareholders' equity, not on the number of shares. It was ingenious."

"Griffin says he was with his girlfriend Wednesday and Thursday evenings – that's as opposed to being home with his wife," Bergeron said. "Claude and I were going to interview her tomorrow. Then, this afternoon, Claude got a line on two guys – one of which was likely Griffin's original contact to find the guy who hired Catalano. A 'fixer' down in Boston called Catalano at his sister's house just before he went to the Crowne Plaza. The fixer got a couple of calls from one of those disposable phones from here, probably setting up meetings. But before all that happened, that same disposable phone called a bar that two guys use as a clearing house. Once we catch up with those guys, we can tie them into Griffin."

It was a lot to absorb and Lynn realized she was tired to the point of exhaustion. But she was drawn to Lou Bergeron's excited voice and the animation in his hands. *He is so good looking,* she thought. *And it's going to be over too soon.*

And out of that realization came a decision. That morning, Deb had said, *"when he takes you home tonight, ask him to check out your room. Then jump his bones."*

"Can you take me back to my hotel?" she asked. "I'm cold, I need something to drink. I've got a coffeemaker in my room. And I'd appreciate it if you checked out my room, just in case."

Bergeron paused and grinned. "That's a great idea."

* * * * *

At 11:45 p.m., Claude Johnson sat on a bar stool at the Galen, waiting for Joey Gavrilles. Juan Gonzales had been a dead end. Gonzales' interests were confined to the small Latino community in southern New Hampshire. After twenty minutes of questioning, Johnson was convinced that Gonzales knew no one at SoftRidge and had set up no Anglo with a fixer in Boston. Gonzales was a go-to guy for loan sharking, fencing, and a half-dozen other vices, but he had not set in motion the events that led to the hiring of Willie Catalano. He was an interesting guy to keep in mind for future, Latino-centered crime, but he was of no interest in this case.

Which left Joey Gavrilles as the logical candidate, assuming the bartender had not held back information, which was always a distinct possibility when dealing with the flotsam and jetsam of New Hampshire society.

But Joey had not made an appearance this evening. He looked at his watch and then at the bartender.

"I don't know what to tell you. He's usually here by now," was all the bartender could offer by way of an explanation.

Johnson took out his phone and called the Bedford state police barracks. "I need a home address for a guy who's in the system: Joey or Joseph Gavrilles. He's somewhere in Nashua... Yeah, I'll wait... Linden Street? Yeah, I know where that is..."

And then a look of anger tinged with shock came over Johnson's face. He closed the phone and looked at the bartender.

"I hope you didn't let little Joey run a tab," Johnson said.

The bartender shook his head. "Why?"

"Because Little Joey's house is on fire, and they just pulled him out of it."

* * * * *

Lynn watched as the coffee dripped through its filter and into the pot. She was acutely conscious that this smaller room at the Radisson provided only a pair of chairs to accompany the bed. Bergeron stood close to her, close enough that she could smell a mix of aftershave and sweat. The scent of a man who worked for a living instead of sitting in an office making phone calls and tapping keys on a computer.

It's now or never, kid, she thought.

The coffee maker stopped dripping. She took two cups from the counter.

"I'm not very good at this," she said.

"Not very good at what?"

"Anything," she said, shaking her head. "Making coffee. Small talk. Being around people. And I'm probably going to get it wrong."

She put the cups back down and faced him. He was at least six inches taller than she was. She took the two steps toward him and, standing on her toes, kissed him on the lips.

She felt him return the kiss, at first tentatively, then with enthusiasm. He wrapped his arms around her and she began to feel that, yes, this was the right thing and the right time.

Then, without warning, she felt his body stiffen. His arms released their grip and he stepped back.

He was shaking his head. "No, I can't do this…"

"I'm sorry," she whispered, staring at the floor.

He took her face in his hands. "I can't do this *tonight*… I'm supposed to be guarding you… The kiss was…" He was too flustered to complete the sentence.

And then his phone rang.

They both stared at the phone clipped to his belt.

On the fourth ring he said, "I'd better answer this."

He pressed the phone to his ear. All he said was, "Yeah" several times. And then the conversation was over.

"I need to leave, Lynn," he said, gently, looking her in the eyes. "There's been a fire. The home of a guy who may have helped set this whole thing up. I need to be there."

Lynn poured a cup a coffee and pressed the cup to her lips, ensuring that there was no choice to make in how he would depart.

"Then you need to go," she said. "I'm in my room now. I'll keep the doors locked. I'll be fine." She tried not to betray emotion.

Bergeron looked torn, uncertain of the right step.

"Me, neither," he finally said.

She looked up. "What?"

"Me, neither," he said again. "I'm lousy at small talk and being around people. But I'm going to try to get better, starting tomorrow."

He smiled. "I'll see you in the morning." He reached out and touched her cheek with his hand. And then he was gone.

* * * * *

The smell of gasoline was overwhelming. Whoever had set the fire had made no effort to conceal that this was arson. The gas had been poured all over the first floor and on the porch. As a result, the house went up like a tiki torch with three neighbors phoning 911 within seconds of one another.

And because the house was less than a mile from a fire station and there were no competing calls, response had been swift. Two companies had controlled the fire within minutes, leaving the police and fire investigators with a clear trail of evidence.

"Have you ever gone through an arson scene?" Johnson asked Bergeron, shining his flashlight on the charred, soaked furnishings in the living room of the house.

"Not as a cop," Bergeron said. "I got plenty of experience in the Army, though. I was attached to an MP unit my last two years in the service and we had to write up anything with a loss of life. Burned-out buildings were fairly common in Afghanistan and Iraq."

"Well, look at this," Johnson said, sweeping his light around the floor.

"An accelerant, probably gasoline," Bergeron said. "Poured from a gas can, to judge from the width of the spray. Whoever did it didn't do the corners, just splashed it as they walked. They were probably in a hurry. And, except for the porch, everything's on the interior. I'd say our arsonist was an amateur."

Johnson did not respond except with a grunt. He walked to the sitting room and shined his flashlight on a reddish stain on the floor.

Bergeron got down on one knee and put a finger in the stain, both evident and still sticky despite the barrage of water that had put out the fire before the evidence was destroyed.

"Blood." Bergeron shined his light around the area and pointed to spots on an upholstered chair. "Blood spray. I'd guess your Mr. Gavrilles bought it in here."

Johnson nodded. "Pretty good for a rookie. Let's have a look at the body."

The body of Little Joey G lay on a stretcher on the sidewalk. He, too, had been doused with gasoline and his clothes were mostly burned off. But here was no mistaking an indentation in his skull.

"Too sharp for a baseball bat," Bergeron said, examining the wound.

"Think tire iron," Johnson said. "Or construction re-bar. But I'd put my money on the tire iron. It's the weapon of choice for people who don't think ahead."

"The attack was inside," Bergeron said. "Gavrilles invited his killer in."

Johnson squinted. "They taught you a lot in the Army. Yeah. Gavrilles knew his attacker and invited him in – or the attacker forced his way in by waving that tire iron around in the air. But it's the porch thing that gets me." He splayed the flashlight beam back and forth across the front porch. "The attacker risked being seen by neighbors or anyone driving down the street to douse the porch with the gasoline. Inside, he had all night. Out here, he was visible. He didn't like this porch. That was personal."

"Something bad happened on the porch?" Bergeron asked. He thought about porches he had been on and things that had happened there. Porches were for children and old people. Old people sat on them. Kids played on them. In between, you just went up the stairs, knocked on the door, and went inside. "How long did Gavrilles live here?"

Johnson didn't hesitate before answering. "His whole life, except when he was doing time."

Bergeron nodded. "Then, if you want my uneducated guess, I'd say your perp was someone who knew Gavrilles growing up. Someone who knew this porch as a child and had something bad happen on it."

Johnson grinned. "That's just guesswork. Amazingly enough, though, I thought exactly the same thing."

"Are Gavrilles' parents still around?"

Johnson shook his head again. "Mother died twenty years ago. Father died in 1998. One sister. She lives over in Portsmouth."

"I suppose you'll be taking a drive over to Portsmouth tomorrow," Bergeron said.

"No," Johnson replied. "I suppose you'll be taking that drive."

* * * * *

He sat alone in his kitchen. It was after 2 a.m. He popped the top on a can of beer, joining the three other cans on the table. He took a long drink, feeling the good taste of a cold beer, and thinking how good it felt on a hot night.

He had felt such heat, just for a moment. The gasoline had erupted as soon as he touched the match to a surface. It wasn't like lighter fluid, slowly creeping across the face of charcoal briquettes. It was an explosion. The entire room was suddenly in flames and he barely had time to retreat through the house to make his escape. He had thought he would need to light the porch separately. Instead, the flames raced him to the door and he had needed to jump the stairs to escape unharmed. He had raced to his car, half a block away, in under a minute and already he could see the fire from the house. The building would undoubtedly be reduced to ashes is a matter of minutes and, with it, the body of Joey Gavrilles. The body might even he burned beyond recognition.

He drank another slug of the beer. Two witnesses, eliminated. Two men dead in one evening. One of the men he had never met until this week and then only for a few minutes. The other, a guy who had once been someone he thought of as a friend.

Well, never a close friend. Joey had always been mixed up with a bad crowd. He and his friends had shoplifted from the K-Mart and grocery store almost from the time they had been old enough to ride bicycles, which were probably also stolen. He had never been part of that crowd. He and Joey would play Monopoly on the porch at his house, contentedly buying and selling houses on Baltic Avenue or the other cheap spaces. Then, at some point in the afternoon, Joey's cohorts would show up on their stolen Schwinns or exotic, multi-geared bikes. They'd taunt Joey. Telling him he was wasting time there on the porch. There were girls to corner at the swimming pool. Candy to be pocketed at the A&P. Cherry bombs to be set off in the exhaust pipes of teachers' cars. And Joey would look at him with his crooked smile and say, 'We'll pick this up later.' 'Later' might be the next day or it might take a week. Slowly, too slowly, he learned a bitter truth: that the time Joey spent with him was the time being marked until his real friends arrived.

And, in the end, Joey Gavrilles had been no friend at all. For among the papers in his kitchen were a detailed listing of favors done, entered into a spiral-bound notebook. The most recent entry bore his name and the notation:

Put in touch with G. Sullivan 9/16 to arrange accident. $1000.

The other names on the ledger were unfamiliar, the tasks a mind-numbing array of stolen cars, houses broken into and stolen property fenced. But it was all there: names, dates, and amounts. He burned the notebook in the kitchen sink before pouring gasoline around the first floor of the house.

But he now, at least, had a name of the middleman whom he had killed. G. Sullivan. Gordon? Greg? Would the murder even make the newspaper in the morning?

He finished off the beer with a long pull and decided four were enough for one evening. Two dead men and four beers.

Farewell, Joey, and farewell G. Sullivan, he thought. *You have given me the courage and the experience to take on my last task: getting rid of that bitch before she causes me any more trouble.*

14.

Saturday, September 22

Larry Driscoll's pale, sleep-deprived face matched the cracked voice each of them had heard on the phone that morning. The calls had gone out at 7 a.m. Be at the office at 8 a.m. sharp, no exceptions, no excuses. Driscoll looked worn – beaten. Something horrible had happened.

Around the conference room sat six of the seven members of the executive staff of SoftRidge. There was one outsider: the company's general counsel, an attorney from a firm in Manchester. When they saw his face they, too, became worried.

As evidence of the somber, no-nonsense tone of the meeting, each man saw there was no coffee; no tray of pastries. Those who had brought coffee sipped from their paper cups. Those who had no coffee fidgeted with their hands or made meaningless notes on pads of paper.

"I had a call last night from Ross Maynard," Driscoll said, reading from a page of handwritten notes. "He has reset the terms of the deal. There's a board of directors meeting this afternoon to make it all official, but I want you to know what's happened."

Everyone looked around the room at one another. No one spoke. *'Reset the terms of the deal'* could mean nothing good. It was only a matter of how bad things were about to get.

"You may notice that Bill Griffin isn't here. Bill was terminated with cause at four o'clock this morning, but that's the least of his problems. He was arrested an hour ago. Over the past six months, Bill concocted an elaborate scheme to skim several million dollars off the deal. Essentially, he invented a private placement of 300,000 shares, got those shares registered, and put them into dummy accounts. When the sale of SoftRidge closed, he would wait for those shares to be paid from the proceeds, and he would clean out the accounts."

"What he actually did was considerably more complicated. It got by Sandy. It got by me, it even got by our accountants, outside counsel, and investment bankers." Driscoll motioned at the attorney seated by him. "It certainly got by Pericles when they did their due diligence."

"But it didn't get by the bankers that are here with us now. One of the bankers from Clarenden – Lynn Kowalchuk, whom I imagine all of you have met – spotted it last night and called Ross Maynard. Because we – meaning 'we' as a corporation – overstated the number of shares, which artificially inflated the price of the company, we – meaning the officers and directors of the company – are in material breach of the agreement. Never mind that no one except Bill knew what had been done and that we've certainly bent over backwards to make the deal go smoothly."

Driscoll looked around the table. He saw faces that showed fear. *These are frightened men and what I am about to say will scare them even more.* He continued. "Pericles has the right to sue us for misrepresentation. Ross Maynard also has the power to force us into Chapter 7 bankruptcy. What Ross has done is to re-set the price from $9.50 per share to $8.50. That's a $20 million hit to the deal price in addition to not paying the phantom shares. He has also sent me a list of other changes. Given the circumstances, the Board has no choice in the matter. It's his deal or the company will be dead on Monday morning. And, because those other changes affect all of you, you need to hear them."

There was a collective intake of breath from around the table.

"First, all managers agree to take two weeks' severance pay and voluntarily waive any previously agreed-upon package."

No one at the table made a sound.

"Second, all managers agree to make no claim for unused vacation, sick pay, or other benefits not previously used."

"This is just dancing on our grave." The acidic comment came from Sandy Calo. It was addressed to no one in particular.

Driscoll made no comment in reply. "Third, he expects all managers to voluntarily accept a pay cut between today and the date of the deal closing to the federal minimum wage of $7.25 per hour."

"And if we don't?" The angry question came from Jeff Wright.

The response came from the attorney, who had not spoken until that point. The attorney spoke in an even and unemotional tone. "The failure of any manager to agree to these changes, or the decision of any manager to leave the company prior to the completion of the acquisition as a result of these changes, or the failure of any manager to fully cooperate with the various final due diligence efforts will result in Pericles exercising its right to sue SoftRidge's officers and directors for breach of contact. Ross has spelled out that those suits will be filed against both the company and all managers as individuals."

"Is that it?" Frank Kepner asked the question. "Or is there more?"

Driscoll bit his lip. "That's what he told me last night. Oh, for whatever it's worth, he also made the deal contingent on our investment banker, Highsmith, cutting their fee in half. That's their punishment for not catching it during their own due diligence. Other than that, I think I got everything."

"And is there any negotiation in this?" It was Calo, again.

Driscoll shook his head. "Bill did this. He got greedy. He had apparently been planning it since the board meeting back in March." Driscoll looked at each of the managers in turn. "I've been over this with our attorneys six ways from Sunday. Ross Maynard holds every card in the deck. We all signed off on the numbers. We are collectively and individually liable. The only way we can keep from getting sued – and I mean sued by every strike suit attorney in the country – is to follow through on the deal exactly as Ross is offering it. So is there any negotiation room? Absolutely none. Consider yourselves screwed, courtesy of Bill Griffin."

"What about directors and officers insurance?" It was Calo, yet again.

The attorney answered. "This is company malfeasance. There isn't a prayer in the world that a D&O claim would be paid under these circumstances."

Driscoll looked around the table for reaction. He saw only faces drained of color. "The only good news is that Bill is going to jail. In addition to securities fraud, which is both a state and a federal matter, he's got those two attempts on the bankers' lives: hiring someone to run their car off the road Wednesday night, and sending the same attacker back to the hotel on Thursday night. However painful this is going to be for us, Bill has it infinitely worse."

"Is that it?" The question came from Kepner. He sounded impatient, rather than angry or distraught.

"Yes, Frank, that's it," Driscoll said. "There's not much point in continuing this meeting. I understand the lawyers and the bankers are both here today, so it's likely that most of you will be needed, too. Get it done. Get it behind you. There's life after this. Ross is being Ross. He's having his moment of victory. It will undoubtedly make the next deal harder for him to do, but I don't think he cares. This is the deal he has been savoring for the better part of a decade."

Driscoll stood, said a few murmured goodbyes, and left the room with the Manchester attorney at his side.

Some managers also rose, others stayed at their chairs, seemingly stunned by the ten-minute meeting. They said little to one another.

They had been told that not only was the war over, but that they had lost and that they were expected to fall on their swords.

* * * * *

"Let's take it from the top, again," Johnson said.

They were in a small conference room; the only one at the state police barracks in Bedford set up for interrogations. Three people were in the room – Johnson, Bill Griffin, and Griffin's attorney. Griffin's attorney was neither a securities lawyer nor a criminal lawyer. As far as Johnson could tell, his specialty appeared to be matrimonial disputes. Perhaps Griffin had been consulting with the guy about leaving his wife. That Griffin and the attorney were overmatched was not his problem. Getting to the truth was the immediate requirement.

"My client has already responded fully to each of your questions," the attorney said.

"Then bear with me for being very stupid," Johnson said. Turning to Griffin, he said, "Do you own a so-called disposable cell phone, Mr. Griffin?"

Griffin nodded. "I *owned* one. My wife found it and smashed it with a hammer."

"And that cell phone number was what?"

"I have no idea. I never had reason to call that phone."

"Why did you have that phone?"

"I used it to call a woman – Elaine Summers."

"Did you ever use that phone to call Joey Gavrilles?"

"No."

"Do you know Joey Gavrilles?"

"I never heard of him until this morning," came the exasperated reply.

"When did your wife destroy the disposable phone?"

"A week ago."

"Why did she destroy it?"

"Because she found it and she figured I was up to something."

"And did you purchase another disposable phone?"

"No."

"How have you contacted Miss Summers since then?"

"I've used the office phone."

"How long have you lived in New Hampshire?"

"Six years in November."

"Did you ever live in New Hampshire before?"

"No, I lived in Pennsylvania and New Jersey."

"Did you go to school in New Hampshire?"

"I went to Rutgers."

Johnson excused himself and went out to the barracks bullpen, where Bergeron was examining and circling phone records.

"How's it going?" Johnson asked.

"I've got a creepy sensation that this isn't our guy," Bergeron said. He held out a page of print. "Here's the girlfriend's phone records for the past four weeks. Until last week she made and received regular calls to the number highlighted in yellow. That number is a disposable cell phone, but it isn't the same one our perp used. Then, the calls stop. For the past week, she's called SoftRidge half a dozen times. Before that, no calls to the company in the prior month. And there's nothing on his home phone to tie him in to any of this."

"Unless he had two phones," Johnson said. "One for the girlfriend, one for the scam. Any luck tracking down Miss Summers?"

Bergeron shook his head. "Gone to Foxwoods for the weekend. I've left two messages on her home phone and two on her cell phone. You want to go the route of an APB?"

"Not yet," Johnson said. "I've got the same problem. If Griffin knew Gavrilles, they had to have met in the past few years. The whole thing with the house suggests a much deeper connection. Also, Griffin is at least ten years older than Gavrilles and he's no athlete. If this guy came after Gavrilles with a tire iron, Gavrilles would have sidestepped it and had Griffin on the floor in about ten seconds. Griffin would be the guy in the morgue, not Little Joey G."

The two men said nothing for several seconds.

"Let's call the reservation police or whatever they are and see if they can locate Elaine Summers. And you better get yourself over to Portsmouth."

Johnson went back into the conference room.

"Mr. Griffin, we need to go over a few more details."

The lawyer slammed his hands on the table. "This is irresponsible!"

"Your client should have thought about that before he embezzled a couple of million dollars from his company."

"*Allegedly* embezzled," the attorney said, "and we are here on condition that your questions are restricted to your investigation into the incidents involving Mr. Gavrilles and the investment bankers."

Uh huh, Johnson thought. *Wait until the feds get here. You'll look back on this conversation as the good old days.*

"We've been unable to contact Miss Summers either at home or on her cell phone. We're going to ask local authorities to find her. I'll need as exact a location as you can provide for me – her time of arrival, that sort of thing."

"I told you. She was going to Foxwoods," Griffin said. "She said she was going to leave early this morning. She didn't say what time. It's about a three-hour drive. She drives a red Honda Accord. I don't know the license plate number. Her girlfriend's name is Linda. I have no idea of the last name…"

15.

He sat in his office, contemplating his next move. For the first time all week, he felt the gnawing sense that things were no longer on track.

That was close, he thought. *Far too close for comfort.*

Griffin, the idiot, had taken the bullet meant for him. If Limp-haired Lynn had been focused on manufacturing vendors instead of share counts, that meeting might have been all about him, and he would be the one everyone was now cursing as they made their way back to their offices.

Everything looked perfect before. Everything still looked perfect. It would continue to look perfect because he had carefully set up fourteen accounts over six months, all of them properly papered, all of them competitive bid. None of them among the top twenty-five largest vendors. They'd be paid out by Pericles and then sent letters saying their products and services were no longer needed. They'd be paid regardless of whether Ross Maynard was paying $9.50 a share or $2.50. Shareholders got shafted, not vendors.

Unless the bitch screwed it up.

His fourteen phantom vendors were owed an aggregate $4.2 million, among hundreds of genuine vendors that were owed $56.7 million. Unless someone went looking for and found a reason to withhold payment, Pericles would write checks to those vendors when the deal was completed. Pericles would then close all but a few of those accounts. All he had needed to do was run out the clock without anyone with the right intellectual curiosity asking questions about the accounts payable ledger.

The first of the $4.2 million owed by SoftRidge to the dummy corporations he had set up would hit the magic thirty day window for payment on the projected closing date of the transaction. The last of the payments were due twelve days later. In past acquisitions,

Pericles had issued payments to vendors three days after closing. On October 3, he should be a very wealthy man.

It was important that his dummy vendors not be paid by SoftRidge prior to the sale, and so it was crucial that the closing date of the sale not get extended beyond September 30. The company's own accounts payable staff typically culled out any unfamiliar check for a large amount and ran it through internal audit, calling the vendor to match purchase order numbers and payment amounts.

On the day the acquisition was completed, those safeguards would disappear, at least for a brief period. In the days just after Pericles acquired SoftRidge, accountants unfamiliar with the names of vendors would be disbursing more than $60 million of checks and automated payments as the acquired company's debts were cleared. Pericles' staff would also process a substantial volume of severance checks and other payments associated with the acquisition. In this blizzard of ledger-clearing, his theft would go unnoticed.

His assessment of everyone else involved in the due diligence process had proven correct. They were dull people watching a clock and ticking items off of a checklist.

Except for the bitch. She had to be stopped.

An end had to be put to her meddling. Not just because she was dangerous, but because... because she was young and plain-looking and carried those extra pounds. Women were supposed to be attractive and wear dresses than showed leg and cleavage. They were supposed to wear makeup and care about their hair. They were supposed to giggle when you said something nice to them and flirt with you.

Lynn Kowalchuk did none of these things. She hunched over the conference room table and studied numbers through those big black glasses. She drank coffee by the gallon and wore the same damn sexless blue shirts and brown slacks, day after day. She barely noticed him when he tried to be nice.

He had killed two men in the past twenty-four hours and had gotten away with it, cleanly and without leaving a trail of evidence.

Killing one useless woman should be easy. Getting rid of the bitch should be a public service.

* * * * *

Lynn sat nervously in a chair at the back of the room. She had attended dozens of board meetings in her three years with Clarenden Brothers. She had given presentations at several such meetings. But there had never been a time when a board meeting had been called specifically because of her.

The largest conference room at the Crowne Plaza was near to capacity. The seven members of the SoftRidge Board were at the long table, as were three attorneys from SoftRidge's outside law firm. Four investment bankers representing SoftRidge were present, including the three who had done little during the last week except crack jokes and watch videos online. The fourth Highsmith & Co. banker was a large, rotund man who made careful notes of everything said during the meeting. His age indicated he was a senior partner.   All now wore serious expressions, as did three representatives from SoftRidge's public accounting firm. Those two organizations – the seller's accountants and bankers – had the most to lose in this meeting because they had the deepest pockets.

In total there were seventeen people at the table, each one legally culpable for fraudulent representation. Everyone at the table had reviewed and signed off on the Information Memorandum or SoftRidge's SEC filings. None of them had ever focused on something as mundane as share counts.

The investment bankers would claim that they were only working with the information provided to them by the company and its accountants. The accountants, too, would claim they were duped by management. The attorneys would plead that they were not experts in accounting and should not be responsible. And the first question raised by a plaintiff's attorney in deposition would be, "How much did SoftRidge pay you in audit/banking/legal fees last year, and did you sign off on their most recent filings?"

The accountants and law firm would – and probably already had

– resigned the account, but it was far too late to avoid financial and legal culpability. And so they were here, listening to the tone of the meeting to assess how much damage would be caused to their finances. That their reputations would suffer was secondary.

Not at the table but seated in chairs arrayed behind those at the table were those who had come to gloat. Two of Pericles' lawyers were there to observe as were two accountants. Andrew Greenglass had flown up with his boss, Mitch Rundle. Both had headed directly for Lynn when they entered the room, both were effusive in their praise. Deb, released from the hospital, was seated by Lynn.

On her other side were the two associates who had worked through the night to get ready for this meeting. They both looked owl-eyed and haggard. They both believed that Lynn's coup was also their own, and that they had distanced themselves from the pack of first-year associates with whom they vied for attention and plum assignments.

At noon, the conference room doors opened one final time. Ross Maynard, followed by Pericles' CFO, and vice president of corporate development entered. Maynard was a short man, flanked by his two, much taller executives. He had the tanned face of someone who, at sixty, spent his summers at a beach house in a pleasant climate. He moved with the ease of someone who never doubted his superiority and had the wealth and success to back it up. Maynard scanned the room. Lynn saw the CFO touch Maynard on the arm and point at her. Maynard walked over to Lynn.

"You did a great job, young lady," he said, shaking her hand. "If you get tired of that New York rat race, there's a place for you at Pericles."

"Either of us could have been lucky," Lynn said, indicating Deb. "I just happened to be working in that area last night."

Maynard then smiled at Deb. "You get yourself better, Miss Fowler. We've got a celebration on October 1, and I'm counting on you to be there."

Deb smiled back. Maynard walked to the head of the

conference table. As soon as his back was turned, Deb whispered to Lynn, "Pervert."

"We are here to amend our offer for SoftRidge Corporation," Maynard said. There was no preamble, no 'hello' or 'thanks for coming out on such short notice.'

"As I believe all of you know by now, we found a significant misstatement in the number of shares outstanding. That misstatement constitutes a material breach of the letter of intent signed between our two companies. We are, therefore, exercising our right to amend our offer, the alternative being to outright withdraw the offer and allow SoftRidge to seek another buyer."

Maynard looked up and down the table and seemed satisfied with the reception of his blunt news. "I am distributing the amended terms and conditions so that everyone can study them." Maynard motioned, and his two staffers passed a stack of documents down either side of the table. "Our amended offer will remain open until two o'clock this afternoon. If it is not accepted by that time, Pericles unilaterally withdraws its offer to acquire SoftRidge, and we will seek restitution for our out-of-pocket costs associated with the transaction. We will also pursue other legal remedies that we are told are open to us." Maynard paused and gave a slight smile before saying the last sentence.

He's saying all of this with a straight face, Lynn thought. *He knows the company has no alternative. The other buyers lost interest as soon as Pericles got their people inside. Pericles knows everything they need to know to put this company out of business. So, at this point, Ross Maynard doesn't care if he goes through with the deal or not.*

Maynard continued talking. And the more he talked, Lynn came to the decision that she did not like this man. In fact, 'not liking' was too mild. She detested Ross Maynard. He was a bully in an expensive suit.

"I've asked Clarenden Brothers to walk you through the facts of the misstatement so that there is no question in anyone's mind," Maynard said.

Deb nudged her. "Time to shine," she whispered.

Lynn rose and went to the table beside Ross Maynard. A digital projector hummed into life, and a PowerPoint presentation filled the screen at the other end of the room. For the next fifteen minutes, Lynn took her audience through the fraud. She started off with some hesitation, then grew more confident as she saw comprehension on people's faces. It had all been there if anyone knew where to look; she had just been curious enough to dig below the dull surface of the number of shares outstanding, how those shares came to be in existence, and when.

"Do you think there might be anything else?" Maynard asked her.

"We're about two-thirds finished with the review," she said. "We haven't found anything else."

"So you believe we can still close on September 30?" A set-up question, designed to tell those assembled, *'this is all the blood I'm going to draw'.*

"If nothing else comes up," Lynn said.

"Do you have all the resources you need to finish the job?" Another set-up question.

"We have everything we need."

Maynard smiled and nodded. Her part was done. Lynn returned to her seat.

"We'll leave you to deliberate," Maynard said, his eyes moving around the table. "Larry Driscoll can reach me on my cell phone when you're finished. I'll be in the Nashua area."

With that, Maynard left the room. Those not at the conference table hurriedly gathered their briefcases and did the same. The entire session had taken under half an hour, with half of that devoted to Lynn's presentation.

"I'd like to buy the Clarenden people lunch," Maynard said when they were outside of the conference room.

Lynn looked at Andy, who gave her a look that said, *'Don't even think of begging off'.* For Clarenden Brothers, this was the opportunity to turn their one-shot due-diligence and fairness opinion assignment into an of-record investment banking relationship with a company that continually was on the lookout for acquisitions. Every asset needed to be deployed, and Lynn was the cornerstone of Clarenden's arsenal.

* * * * *

"I can't tell you how pleased I was to get that call last night," Maynard said as the group ate. "For the past couple of months, people have been saying to me, 'Ross, you're being too generous. The company has nothing you need. They're dying. Let them die on their own.' And I've had to defend my decision with the worst possible reason – 'what would happen if someone else bought them?' I don't like making defensive acquisitions. They never work out."

"The management team at SoftRidge is convinced you don't like them, and that it's personal," Lynn said, softly.

"I don't even know them," Maynard said, shrugging his shoulders, then picking up a forkful of salmon. "How can I like them or not like them? The company founder and I had a – some animosity. But these people? They're obviously not very good businessmen. Look at the hole they dug for themselves. So do I want them around for a minute longer than I'm required to keep them? Of course not. But I have nothing against them personally."

"What about their technology?" Lynn asked.

Maynard made little circling motions with his finger. "We do the same thing, and we build it for a lot less money. Their gross margins stink. We'll substitute our products for theirs. In a year, everyone will say, 'SoftRidge who?' You mark my words."

Exactly what the people at SoftRidge fear, she thought. "The managers at SoftRidge think Pericles used unfair tactics to put them out of business."

"Lynn, I don't think this is the time…" Andy Greenglass started to say.

"No, those are valid questions," Maynard interjected, his mouth still filled with food. "At Pericles, we use every tactic at our disposal to win. Is it unfair to point out to their customers that the company was out of money? No. Customers need to have a full range of information to make an informed buying decision. Was it unfair to tell those customers that if SoftRidge went under, they'd have no service or spares? I don't think so. SoftRidge put itself into a corner. Pete Kincaid should have sold the company five years ago. Instead, he burned through a hundred million of shareholders' cash and had nothing to show for it. Anyone who invested in the company was a sucker. They're getting exactly what they deserve."

I really don't like this man, Lynn thought. *And I've just helped him win what sounds like the most satisfying battle of his career.*

A cell phone chirped the first few notes from the Cole Porter song, 'You're The Top'. Maynard smiled and held up a finger, requesting silence. He flipped open the phone. He listened for a few seconds, then said, 'Thanks for the call,' and closed the phone.

"We have a deal," he said, grinning broadly. "On my terms." He clapped Lynn on the shoulder. "And all because of you, Miss Kowalchuk. All because of your diligence."

* * * * *

Lou Bergeron knocked at the door of the small house in Portsmouth. The smell of salt water was in the air. From the look of the house and the neighborhood, Katherine Gavrilles – married name Laconda – had traded her life in Nashua for a nearly identical one fifty miles away. It was an old neighborhood of frame houses, neatly kept up with small lawns and rows of trimmed hedges by the sidewalk. A neighborhood of men who worked at the Navy Yard across the river in Kittery, perhaps. Katie Gavrilles had not enjoyed the upward mobility that American society was supposed to provide.

A boy of perhaps twelve or thirteen came to the door. Bergeron had come in full dress, his trooper's hat held under his arm. The boy took in the uniform, Bergeron close-cropped hair and regulation shoes buffed to a high shine.

"Is your mother at home? I'm Trooper Bergeron."

The boy said nothing, but stared a moment at the gun holstered at Bergeron's side.

"Mom!" the boy yelled. "There's a cop here."

Katie Laconda came to the door. She was an attractive looking woman in her late thirties, perhaps a little wide at the hips. Her hair was dark brown and worn stylishly short, her eyebrows neatly echoed a pair of tortoiseshell glasses. A toddler, maybe three years old, held onto her dress. Her dress was a fashionable print, all of which belied the rather ordinary house. Perhaps Katie Gavrilles Laconda had in fact enjoyed some of that upward mobility after all, but was content to live in less ostentatious surroundings.

Seeing her, he stood more erect.

"You're here about my brother?" she asked.

"Yes, ma'am," he said. He introduced himself and asked if could come in for a few minutes. She opened the door fully and walked into a living room.

"I've been on the phone with the funeral home a good part of the morning," she said, moving toys from chairs and a sofa. "They tell me we really can't make any arrangements until after my brother's body is released." She looked up at him. "I'm told there's going to be an autopsy."

She offered him a Coke and he accepted. She walked out of the room and turned toward the kitchen, and he followed her walk. *Sensual*, he thought. *The way she moves. Is it conscious or unconscious?*

The same boy who had answered the door now came into the living room, still staring sullenly. "Are you going to arrest the guy who killed my Uncle Joey?" the boy asked.

"Yes," Bergeron answered. The correct answer ought to have been *'We'll make every effort'* but Lou sensed that the response he gave was the only one acceptable. "I'm here to talk to your mother about people who may have wanted to hurt your uncle. Do you know of…"

His question was interrupted by Katie's return. "Go back and help Louise and Darlene," she said to the boy. "This is between me and the policeman."

The boy looked at his mother and at Bergeron. He bit his lip, clearly wanting to stay and listen, and perhaps to speak. But he obeyed, turning slowly and walking to the back of the house where the voices of several women could be heard. Katie handed Bergeron the Coke and sat in a chair opposite him. "The neighbors have started bringing food," she said. "We don't know if the funeral is going to be in five days or two weeks, but they're bringing food like the wake is tomorrow."

"The medical examiner works on his own schedule, Mrs. Laconda. When I get back, I'll do whatever I can to get your brother's autopsy moved up."

Katie Laconda murmured a 'thank you'.

"Your children were close to their uncle?" Bergeron asked.

She nodded. "He was a fill-in father when he could." She saw the confused look on Bergeron's face. "I remarried a few years ago. I was divorced for about eight years. Joey did everything he could to help out." She shrugged, her explanation completed.

"We know your brother had a lot of brushes with the law," Bergeron said. "Our sense is that he crossed someone with whom he recently did business. Did he ever talk with you about those kinds of things?"

There was a crash from the direction of the kitchen. Katie Laconda quickly rose and excused herself.

While she was gone, Bergeron took in the living room for the first time. The furniture was, at most, a year or two old. A large, LCD-screen television anchored one side of the room, a pair of Wii consoles beside it. The drapes looked expensive and the windows in the room bore the thin silver strips of a top-end alarm system. His initial impression of a lack of upward mobility was completely wrong. The Lacondas were apparently doing just fine.

Katie returned and shook her head. "They want to be helpful, but there's really nothing they can do right now." More composed, she sat back down, smoothing the dress across her lap. "You had asked me a question."

"Did your brother ever share things about his life with you?"

She nodded. "There was a time when he did. Then I started to get worried that he might be making it sound a little too glamorous to the kids and so I asked him to talk about anything else – fishing, cars, whatever. Things little boys would like, but that wouldn't get them started... down that path. So, for the past few years, he's respected my wishes."

She shifted in her chair and moved forward. "But I need to know what happened. And I don't need to be spared the gory details. My brother was a thief. My brother spent ten years in prison for things he did and probably should have spent another ten for things he did but didn't get caught." There was a seriousness in her voice, a pleading for help.

Bergeron nodded. "Your brother met someone at his house. He let that individual inside, which indicates he knew the person. That individual clubbed him with something. The medical examiner will be able to tell us what the weapon was. Your brother died from that blow. Then that someone doused the downstairs and porch with gasoline and struck a match. Whoever did it wasn't a professional arsonist. The fire department got there pretty quickly and contained the blaze."

Katie nodded. "I understand he was burned pretty badly."

"Yes. But he was already dead."

He saw her eyes moistening with tears. "He chose his life. He knew the risks. But he always took care of me and the children. He never had a family of his own. I used to get checks – I still get them. 'This is for Danny's birthday' – that sort of thing."

"But he hasn't said anything to you this year about anyone he was working with?"

Katie shook her head. "No. Not for a couple of years."

"The detective I'm working with has a theory that it might have been someone Joey knew from his past. I have some names and photos. I want you to tell me if you recognize anyone of them."

Bergeron pulled the eight photos from an envelope. He had downloaded them from the SoftRidge web site, which helpfully provided photos of the management team. He arrayed eight photos in front of Katie.

"It may be possible that none of these men had anything to do with your brother's death, but each one is potentially linked to a crime your brother helped facilitate." He pointed to the photos and provided names. Paul Fuller, Alan Morton, Charles Li, Frank Kepner, Bill Griffin, Jeff Wright, Larry Driscoll, and Sandy Calo.

He studied her reaction as she looked at the photos. One by one, he put names to the faces, pointing to the photographs as he said the name. If Joey Gavrilles' connection to the person went back twenty years or more, it would be likely that Katie might not be able to immediately spot a man who had aged two decades, and not necessarily gracefully. He was more interested in how she reacted to the names.

Some were clearly long shots: he knew Charlie Li, the engineering manager, had grown up in California. Larry Driscoll, the board chairman, was at least a decade too old to have a connection to Gavrilles. Bill Griffin, he now knew, had not lived in New Hampshire until a few years earlier. Still, he recited the names slowly, waiting.

And saw no discernible reaction. Or saw a reaction within a narrow range to each name. She was either a good actress or she did not remember these people.

"Joey was older than me," she said after he had matched the last name to the final photograph. "He didn't bring his friends home. Our dad was very strict. And it was a long time ago." She looked from the photos up to him. "How are these people connected to Joey?"

"One of them may have hired your brother." He offered no other detail.

"But they're linked to one another somehow, though. Isn't that right? These are all – what – businessmen?" She had that pleading sound in her voice again.

Bergeron paused and considered whether he ought to answer the question. He gathered up the photos and returned them to the envelope.

"You've been honest with me up to now," she said, looking at his face. "Please, don't start hiding things now."

He paused again, then decided to answer as best as he could, but not telling her everything he knew. "Someone working at a company over in Nashua may have contacted your brother. Your brother called another person down in Boston who hired a local guy to hurt someone – a young woman. Because we caught the man who carried out the attack, we were able to trace phone records back to your brother. But that's as far back as we can go. It could also be that someone else Joey was working with killed him. As you said, your brother was no saint. He probably made a lot of enemies along the way."

"Why does your partner think it was someone from Joey's past?" she asked.

"Whoever set the fire took the time to put a lot of gasoline on the porch as well. It put the person at risk of being seen. The detective I'm working with seemed to think that's significant. Kind of like settling old scores from when they were kids."

"Let me see the photos again."

Bergeron displayed them again.

"Which one is Paul Fuller?"

Bergeron pointed to the photo.

"I know my brother used to hang out with a guy named Paul. The last name might have been something like Fuller. They had some kind of a falling out."

She's lying now, he thought. *Is she trying to be helpful and reaching, or is she covering up the person she recognized? And why would she lie?*

"That's very helpful," Bergeron said. "I'll follow that up when I get back."

As he was leaving, he turned and asked, "Mrs. Laconda, are you certain none of the other names or faces seemed familiar?"

Katie looked sad and shook her head. "They were just faces of men. Did Joey know a Frank or a Bill or a Charlie? Yeah, probably. But my brother's friends mostly went to jail. They weren't the type to go to work for some company."

Bergeron pulled out a business card from his wallet. He wrote his cell phone number on the card and gave it to her. "Something may come to mind," he said. "Or you may just need someone to talk to about this. You can call me any time on my cell phone. And I promise I'll try to get your brother's body released as quickly as possible."

As he navigated through the narrow Portsmouth streets, Bergeron thought to himself, over and over, *I blew it. I had my chance to get a lead in this thing, and I blew it. She recognized someone from those photos, I'm sure of it.*

State police are drilled with their duties and responsibilities while on the clock. High on that list is that the police radio is the only acceptable listening. While troopers' cars have AM/FM radios, they're not to be used at any time during duty hours.

But he had an hour's drive back to the Bedford barracks where he would own up to Claude Johnson that he had failed to read the changes in body language that would have provided progress in the investigation. And so he tuned to the all-news station in Boston, turning the police radio low. All he wanted was a distraction to the ugliness that was coming. And because he was lost in thought, he almost didn't hear the news item.

The report came as a follow-up to something that had apparently first been reported sometime the previous evening.

"Boston police are reviewing Quincy Market security tapes in their search for leads in the apparent murder of a South Boston mobster Friday evening. Police aren't saying if they have suspects in the death of Gerald Sullivan, 52. Sullivan, who has long been suspected to be linked to protection rackets and murders-for-hire, was pushed under a truck on the Greenway's surface road around 8 p.m. last evening. Witnesses said a man dressed in a windbreaker, sunglasses, and a

baseball cap, appeared to 'come out of nowhere' to push Sullivan into traffic as he was attempting to hail a cab. The man then disappeared back into Quincy Market. Police are asking anyone with information about the accident to come forward."

Bergeron turned on his siren and sped up, even as he consulted a highway map. If he reached I-93 in ten minutes, he could be in Boston in less than 45 minutes. He turned off the news station and radioed back to the dispatcher his change in plans.

* * * * *

In the back room of a bar in South Boston, Aidan Parker sat in a circle with four other men. They sat hunched over on simple wooden chairs, leaning on their elbows, smoking. Parker was of medium height but weighed 180 pounds, much of it muscle which he kept toned with the aid of a punching bag that occupied a corner of the room. His reflexes were kept fast by a twice-weekly sparring match at a Southie gym. Parker had never boxed professionally but he was known to have twice beaten men to death with his fists and, for this, he was both feared and revered.

To Parker's right was Tony D'Alessio, the only non-Irishman of the four and, indeed, the only non-Irishman of Parker's thirty-man gang or, as Parker called it, the Darts Club. D'Alessio was significantly larger than any of the other men and he was the only one with a beard and an ear ring, the latter affectation something the others thought too feminine. The conversation had been going on for twenty minutes already.

"Gerry called you and said his guy was late," Parker said, looking at D'Alessio. It was a statement. It was also a question.

"That's what I told you," D'Alessio said. "He called me on my phone. 'I just got off the horn with the Nashua guy. He's tied up in traffic. Go be inconspicuous for ten or fifteen minutes.' That's exactly what he said."

Parker knew D'Alessio was not the brightest man in the room. Moreover, though D'Alessio had lived his entire life in South Boston, as someone of Italian extraction he could never be entirely trusted by this group of men, none of whom was more than one generation removed from Ireland. But Parker also knew D'Alessio had looked up to Gerry Sullivan as a father figure and was part of this organization because of Sullivan's sponsorship. D'Alessio would not lie to him in this meeting.

"He never mentioned the Nashua man's name?"

D'Alessio shook his head.

"So you go to the men's room?" Parker said. These questions had been asked before, but it was necessary to fix in Parker's mind a sequence of events. He must know all he could about this man who had murdered, in cold blood, one of his most trusted lieutenants.

"I wasn't going to take a crap or anything. I just wanted to stay out of sight, like he told me."

"And what was the plan?"

"He'd call me when he heard from the guy. I come out. I'm going to watch the transaction to make sure the Nashua guy doesn't do any funny business. I follow the guy back to his car from a safe distance. I mess with the guy some. I get the money back. I keep a thousand bucks. I give the rest back to Gerry."

"But the cops showed up," Parker said.

D'Alessio nodded, content to repeat the story as long as asked. "Like I said. I'm in the can for about two minutes. I'm wearing a watch. Suddenly, I got two uniforms all over me. They tell me to assume the position. They find my knife and ask me why I'm carrying a switchblade. I ain't going to tell them anything. Then one cop says to the other, 'I don't see a wallet' and I ask 'what wallet?' The other cop says, 'a tourist saw you dip a lady's purse. This will go a whole lot easier if you turn over the wallet, plus any others you got stashed.'"

"I coulda taken these guys. They've got batons, not guns. Plus they're both kids. But I didn't want that kind of trouble. So I tell them I ain't got any wallets and they can check, and can I please go because I'm late for an appointment. But they've run my name and they know I got a record. So they tell me I'm under arrest for carrying a concealed weapon and I'm violating my parole. One of them calls for backup, and we all sit in the can for about five minutes while some more uniforms got pulled out of the nearest bar. By the time I get outside, Gerry ain't there anymore. Then I hear a screech of brakes and horns and people shouting. The two cops with batons say they'll go check it out. They've cuffed me and we start walking in the other direction. About ten seconds later, this guy goes walking by us, quick-like. Windbreaker, Red Sox baseball cap, sunglasses. The cops are talking on their radios asking what happened out on the other street and I hear some guy got hit by a truck."

"They're not paying attention to this guy walking in the other direction, but I am. And I got a good look at him. Thin, but he's got some muscle underneath. Five-eleven. Dark brown hair, sideburns down to here. Around forty. Clean shaven. I could spot him again in an instant, even with the sunglasses and cap."

"What makes you think he pushed Gerry under the truck?" Another man in the circle asked this question and learned farther forward.

"Because this guy is walking away when everyone else is screaming. Because this guy is wearing sunglasses at eight o'clock at night. I watch this guy walk all the way to Congress Street where he drops something down a gutter. I also watch him take off the windbreaker and cap and stuff them in trash cans. Finally, it's just me and one cop, and he's frustrated because every other cop in the city is in on this accident, except that the cop on the walkie-talkie is saying that it definitely ain't an accident because witnesses say some guy pushed another guy, and the description of the guy under the truck is Gerry. And the description of the guy who did it is the guy who walked right by me. But the cop is too stupid to put two and two together."

Parker said, "And you didn't tell the cops, 'Hey, why don't you go after the guy in the windbreaker?'"

"I figure that's a collar we'd like to make," D'Alessio said. That's a job I'd do for free. Plus he's got at least a thousand bucks that Gerry said was mine. Plus I had to post bail and pay a lawyer. I figure this guy is into me for three, four grand."

"What did Gerry tell you about the guy?" It was the second man in the circle again.

D'Alessio repeated a description he had provided earlier. "He's a guy from Nashua. Gerry set up an accident for him to get some woman out of the way. The deal got busted. The guy complained, and Gerry figured it was easier to say he'd give back half and then take the money back with a threat that he'd better keep his mouth shut."

"And the way you figure it, the guy made you in front of the bar, called the cops and made up the story about lifting the lady's wallet," Parker asked.

"Exactly. He was never stuck in traffic. He had already been there for a while, watching. But I didn't know what he looked like. I was waiting for the meeting to eye him."

The four men looked at one another. It was Parker's call as to what they would do. He thought about it for just fifteen seconds. Within this group, decisiveness and quick response counted toward maintaining the Dart Club's respect.

"Here's what we're going to do, Tony," Parker said. "We got sources inside the department. We'll see just what the cops see just as soon as they get it. You know what this guy looks like. If they get a name, you go find the guy. Right now, you go up to Nashua. Find someplace and lay low until we call you. We'll get in touch the minute we hear something. When you hear from us, you move fast."

* * * * *

Lynn looked up from a stack of personnel files. It was just after 2 p.m. She pushed her glasses up into her hair and rubbed her eyes. She was tired.

I don't want to be here, she thought. *I don't want any part of this anymore. Not after listening to Ross Maynard.*

Across from her, Deb looked up, trying to read her thoughts. "You could take the afternoon off," Deb said. "The munchkins and

I can take it from here. You could go shopping. Buy some clothes for your big date. And I still get to do your makeup."

Lynn rolled her head, hearing the creaks and snaps of muscles and bone that had been in the same position for far too long. She said nothing.

"Take the afternoon off. God knows you've earned it."

What she wanted was two or three hours sleep. What she wanted was to have this be over. But everything was wrong. She tried to envision Bill Griffin setting up a scam to create phony shares in the company, and she had no difficulty envisioning him doing just that. But then she tried to conjure up a scene of Griffin hiring someone – even two or three steps removed – to run her and Deb off of the road. She couldn't make that image work. She now knew Griffin had been carrying on an affair and planned to abandon his family using the funds from the scam to start his new life. But the rest of it didn't make sense. He wouldn't hire someone to hurt people.

If she was right, it meant that someone else had gone to Joey Gavrilles. Somebody else was behind Willie Catalano. Which also meant that someone else was hiding a multi-million-dollar payday in the books of SoftRidge.

"Oh, no," Lynn said.

Deb looked up again. "Oh, no, what?"

"It isn't over," Lynn said, the weariness leaving her body with a rush of adrenalin. "We're looking for something else. Let's give it another hour or two."

16.

Lou Bergeron listened as a Boston Police Department detective told him all the reasons why the assistance of the New Hampshire Highway Patrol was neither useful nor wanted in their investigation. The detective was a guy maybe one or two years older than himself, attired in a cheap, ill-fitting suit that had been worn too many times since its last cleaning. His tie was the kind that remained on the shelves, unpurchased even after deep, post-Christmas price reductions were taken. But he was clearly a detective, entitled to wear a suit and tie while Bergeron wore the lowly uniform of the New Hampshire State Police. The distinction set the tone for the conversation.

"You cross state lines and the feds demand to take over," the detective said in a lecturing voice that was probably reserved for talking to hayseed state troopers. "It's that simple. We've got a man with links to organized crime who got shoved under a truck. As long as we treat it as a local matter, we can make the case that it isn't their jurisdiction, organized crime link or not. Throw in something – anything – from a different state, and they're at the table, demanding to take over. And you've never seen red tape till you've seen federal red tape."

They were in the squad room of District A-1, which served downtown. The detective refused to take Bergeron back into the investigation's working area. He crossed his arms, a defensive move to enforce his 'no trespass' stance.

"All I need to know is whether Sullivan was carrying a cell phone and, if so, whether the number matches the one in my hand," Bergeron argued.

The detective gave his head a 'no, no, no' shake. "And I'm telling you that as soon as I answer that question, it becomes part of the investigation log and I'm going to have OCCB over this thing like white on rice." The detective stared at Bergeron, clearly wanting this uniformed yokel to get out of his city and go back where he belonged and set up speed traps for unsuspecting leaf-peekers.

Bergeron felt his anger getting the better of him. He closed his eyes and breathed deeply and evenly.

"You still alive there, kid?"

Bergeron hated nothing as much as being called 'kid' by someone under thirty. He did not respond. He just kept his face neutral and his breathing regular.

"If you have something you want to share as a private citizen..."

"Not unless you want to share that phone number," Bergeron said.

"I can't do that, kid," the detective said, his arms firmly crossed. The conversation, as far as he was concerned, was over.

"But you've got the phone – you could just look."

"You got a hearing problem?"

"Then I guess I'm on my own," Bergeron said.

The detective left the squad room. Bergeron waited until he was out of sight. Then he took out his own cell phone and dialed the number Gavrilles had called a week earlier.

From a room in the direction toward which the detective had walked, Bergeron heard a cell phone ringing. He hung up before someone could answer the phone or Caller ID could establish a link. Bergeron quickly walked out of the squad room. As he left, he could hear someone screaming into a now-dead phone, 'Hello, damn it!'

* * * * *

He began to relax, the morning's meeting of SoftRidge management receding into memory. Joey Gavrilles was dead and would tell no tales. The fire had occurred too late to make the Nashua or Manchester newspapers. And when it did, it would most likely only say that a local felon had been killed and his house burned to the ground. The motive would likely be ascribed to gang-on-gang activity. Criminals ran that risk every day.

'G. Sullivan', now identified as 'Gerry', was dead and, according to the news radio station in Boston, the police could say only that they were reviewing security tapes. He knew well that such tapes, especially at night, showed only vague shapes. A recognizable face was out of the question.

If the police focused on him, which was unlikely, they could say only that there was a man of average height who was walking away from the carnage on Atlantic Avenue. The man appeared to be a tourist. There were no telltale facial features to be seen in the dim light, no distinctive articles of clothing.

He was annoyed that the bearded man with the earring was being led away by the police just as he was making his escape. But the bearded man had never seen him, and his face was well hidden under the baseball cap and sunglasses. Chances were good that the bearded man had been found to be carrying a gun. Because he was also likely an ex-con, he had probably been arrested. Because of his size, reinforcements had been called in. The bearded man was almost certainly in jail and would remain there, wondering at his bad luck.

And Bill Griffin was in a jail cell somewhere. Upon reflection, he realized this was the luckiest break of all. Griffin's stupidity – and the more he thought about it, the more ludicrous the scam sounded – had given him a free ride to the finish line. Griffin would take the fall for the lower share price offer and for the indignities heaped on management by Ross Maynard. Griffin was a dream come true. There would be securities investigators all over him.

In the hours after the morning meeting, he had heard many explanations for Griffin's scam from other managers. The one that tied to his limited knowledge of Griffin's private life was that Griffin had been having an affair with a personal trainer at his country club. Griffin was deeply in lust with a 29-year-old bimbo. Griffin had planned to take the money, fly away with his honey to Mexico, and live like a king in Baja California. His wife would find the bank account empty, his sons would find themselves bounced from their fancy private colleges, the cars repossessed. It was a fat, middle-aged man's fantasy, and it had all come crashing down.

And with Gavrilles dead and the guy the middleman had hired – what was his name? Catalano? – not knowing who had initiated the job for which he was now in jail, Griffin would take the fall for the attempts on the Polish Princess's life as well. It was, in a word, perfect.

Well, perfect for him. Like the other company executives, he was in the office for the day, helping to close the transaction at his new wage of $7.25 per hour – and with a gun pointed at his head that, if he slacked off on his job, Pericles would exercise its option to walk away. His fellow managers pasted artificial smiles on their faces as they ferried data out to the lawyers and accountants, then went back to their offices and stared blankly at the walls, wondering if they would ever be employed or employable again. Bill Griffin and Ross Maynard had scuttled their careers.

He mimicked their funk and commiserated with them as they came by to share the reaction at their homes when the news was told to their wives and children. He said it was a terrible fate they had all been dealt, and that it was unfair. He shook his head with sympathy as they spoke of their fears of losing their homes and of robbing from their children's college funds to buy groceries in the coming months.

And all the time he listened to these heartbreaking stories, he kept his mind on the important numbers: *$4.2 million, tax-free, yields $273,000 of annual income.* That was his payday, and it was ten days away.

Which left the question, should he leave well enough alone? Should he forget about Lynn Kowalchuk? He had seen her just a few minutes earlier. She looked tired, worn out. A weak, plain-looking girl in need of a nap.

But this was the woman who had stumbled over Bill Griffin's scheme. She had found it when the bright guys from Pericles, who had pored over every aspect of their business, had missed the inflated share count, just as they had missed his accounts payable gold mine.

She could, in theory, get lucky twice. Thus far, only the dreary accountants had asked for details on vendors. They had 'ticked and tied' the numbers and pronounced themselves satisfied that the amount of money SoftRidge said it owed to vendors was, in fact, the same amount that was actually owed. They had probed no deeper. They didn't care.

But the bitch did. She needed to be dealt with, once and for all. She needed to have a fatal accident. She needed to have that accident very soon. And this time, it had to look like an accident. A tragic accident that cut short a promising young life.

Auto accidents were out. Two car crashes in a week would never be believed by the police. A fire, while convenient for him, was also off the table. He did not know how many arson investigations there were in Nashua each year, but two fires in one week would bring extra scrutiny, and his goal was a simple chorus of, *'she was so young, how awful...'*

He made a mental list of possibilities. Then, he began jotting notes. Most ideas were crossed off immediately. But he kept coming back to one. He circled it, then circled it again. His foot tapped out a rhythm.

This could work, his foot tapped. *This will work.*

* * * * *

In Portsmouth, Katie Laconda sat alone in her living room. In her hands she held a snapshot of herself with her brother she had found that morning in a photo album. Though undated, the picture looked to be a little over twenty years old. In it, she and Joey were smiling for the camera, though Joey had his usual, mischievous smirk. Joey sat behind her on the steps of the front porch of their house in Nashua, his arms around her. The big brother, watching out for his little sister. She was in a sleeveless blouse and her hair was worn the same length as when she was seventeen. Perhaps it was taken that summer. The summer everything changed.

That summer.

He had always been around, Joey's 'good' pal, as if befriending one boy from the neighborhood who made the honor roll offset hanging around with the half dozen delinquents who cut classes regularly, broke into vacant houses, and shoplifted anything that would fit in their ski jackets.

When he had asked her out that summer, she didn't know what to say. He had always been shy around her. It had been obvious for years that he liked her but she assumed he was too insecure to do anything about it. Besides, he was college-bound, and so would gravitate to and hang around with the smart students.

Not that she couldn't have been one of them. School came easy. She intuitively grasped the math and science in the textbooks and yearned for more. But her father was unyielding when she wanted to sign up for the after-school clubs and enrichment classes. 'You help your mother,' he had said. 'That's your job after school.'

Slowly, the initiative had been drained out of her. By the time she entered high school, she no longer asked about taking chemistry or advanced math. She hurried through her schoolwork and did the minimum necessary to pass courses. And inexorably, as she began to fill out her sweaters and jeans, she caught the attention of Joey's buddies. They flattered her and brought her presents – invariably stolen goods. She dated those that were cute and excluded those that made it clear their only interest was in getting into those jeans.

By the spring of her junior year, she was seeing Carl on a regular basis. Sweet Carl with his cool car and cooler clothes. Just what every teenage girl dreamed of, she mused. Slick Carl, who plied her with Tequila until, one night, he got inside of her. *Today, they would call it date rape*, she thought. *Back then, it was just boys being boys. And I was a fool.*

Because she was a fool, she had kept seeing Carl. Why? Because he was cool and being with him conferred status. And, to be honest, she liked the thrill of illicit sex in his Camaro.

And then *he* asked her out. And it was like a breath of fresh air. They went out a couple of times a week and actually talked during dates. They discussed politics and novels and places far beyond New Hampshire. The urge to learn was rekindled inside her and she vowed that, in the fall, she would sign up for the college prep courses and get herself into UNH one way or another, with or without her parents' approval.

Then, the first week in August, she missed her period. She had always been as regular as clockwork. In just two days, she knew something was wrong. She cursed that she had continued to go out with Carl and she had continued sleeping with him.

For two weeks, she agonized over what to do. From what her parents had said about other girls in the neighborhood who had become pregnant, she knew her mother and father would be of no help. 'No better than a whore and she shamed her family' her father had said of Connie, her close friend who had gotten pregnant in her sophomore year. She couldn't say anything to Joey. And if she said anything to Carl, he'd just brag and tell everyone that he had proven his virility.

And so she turned to *him*. They had been making plans to continue to see one another. He had already invited her up for a football game in October. Just a week before he was leaving for college, she asked for his help in ending the pregnancy.

His reaction had been one of sympathy and a promise to help her. And he did. The next day, he drove her to Planned Parenthood down in Cambridge and sat with her through the interviews and the counseling. He even paid for part of the cost of the abortion at the Women's Health Clinic though it meant he ate into his expense money for college.

He had stayed with her every minute except during the procedure, and then only because he had been told to sit in the waiting room. Afterward, he had held her hand as she listened to the checklist of things she must do over the following days. When the nurse talked about support, he had spoken and acted as though the fetus that had been inside her was his. By the time they got back to Nashua, she was ready to give her heart to him.

But sometime during that long, tortured day, he had changed. When they arrived at her house he was cool, his embrace was unenthusiastic. He called the next day, but only to say that his mother had a lengthy list of errands for him to run and that he wouldn't be able to see her that evening.

He did not call again.

Her mother, who counted her use of tampons with a near religious fervor, already suspected what had happened. Confronted, she confessed, and then all hell broke loose. She quickly gave up Carl's name and Joey immediately took off, found Carl – who had no idea Katie had been pregnant – and beat the crap out of him, breaking an arm and a leg and dislodging several teeth. Joey also took a sledgehammer to Carl's beloved Camaro, reducing it to un-repairable scrap.

It took only a few days for word to get around of what had happened both to her and to Carl. As a result, no boy had asked her out in her senior year.

But neither was she allowed to take the college prep courses or an SAT exam. She graduated, got a full time job at K-Mart, and watched her dreams fade to nothingness.

But she was smart, and she got promoted. She moved out and got her own apartment. When she married it was on her own terms and, while Roger had ultimately been a jerk, he was the man she had chosen.

When Roger left her, Joey was there. He stepped in as a surrogate father for nearly six years. Whether it was out of a sense of responsibility or the goading of her parents, she did not know and did not ask. But he was there for her, driving two children to school and doctors' appointments while she worked ten and twelve hour days. She could not have imagined how she would have made it without Joey's help.

It was Joey who had introduced her to Johnny Laconda. She knew almost from the start he was the right man for her. He didn't object to becoming an instant father to two children not his own.

His business was illegal – no friend of Joey's could have been completely legit – but he was a good man. That he exported stolen cars for a living was not a deterrent to her falling in love with Johnny.

When the state trooper showed her the photo array, she had instantly recognized the one boy who could have changed her life. She didn't need the confirmation of hearing his name. It had taken all her concentration not to change her expression or the tone of her voice when he asked if she recognized any of the names or people.

Joey had come for dinner a few weeks earlier and had mentioned that he had run into an old flame of hers. She had been too embarrassed to ask in front of her husband who it was. But Joey had passed it off without further elaboration and she had not cared enough to press the matter.

Now, she was caught between honoring her brother's memory by helping the state police catch Joey's killer and respecting her husband's professional opinion that the police were never to be helped or trusted.

Weighing on the side of silence was the fact that twenty-one years earlier, she had turned to him in a time of need and he had helped with neither hesitation nor judgment. Without that help, her parents would undoubtedly have forced her to carry Carl's baby to full term. She would have dropped out of school, becoming both unemployable and unmarriageable.

There was a further question of how exactly he was connected to Joey's death. The state trooper had said he had hired her brother, not that he had killed Joey. Joey's principal means of support was that he sold access. Joey bragged that he could make calls to a network of friends and associates to get things done. If you wanted a car torched for the insurance, Joey wouldn't set it, but he knew who would, and he would put you in touch with that person for few hundred dollars. If you needed to have someone beaten up, Joey knew the muscle all over New England. He was the perfect cut-off man who prided himself on keeping other people's secrets.

So he had gone to Joey looking for someone to do something illegal for him and doing that thing led to Joey's death. What was the illegal thing that he needed to have done?

More than two decades had passed and those long-ago conversations were clouded in a haze. He had talked of all the things he wanted to do, the places he wanted to go. There was a recurring theme in those discussions: what stood between him and his dreams was money. His family was mired in debt, his father a mailman who believed that fifty dollars a week in lottery tickets was his path to riches. He had raged that his father would bring home a fistful of tickets every payday and sit in front of the television, awaiting the drawing of the week's numbers. That he never recouped even one week's bets did not faze him. Every week, there were the same lucky numbers to be played.

On their dates, he had confided to her his inability to reason with his mother to get his father to stop or at least cut back on his betting. Instead of the good private school he yearned to attend, he could afford only a state college and even going to UNH would require borrowing money for room and board. In the meantime, there were weeks when his scant savings were used to put groceries on the family's dinner table because of his father's betting habit.

So, in all likelihood, it had to do with money. It was his blind spot. It was the thing that would cause him to cross the line.

In Katie's purse was the state trooper's card with his cell phone number. She wouldn't throw away the card, but neither was she going to call the number. Instead, she stared at the photograph and saw another time and another life.

* * * * *

Willie Catalano lay on the bed in his locked and barred hospital room, fuming. His leg still hurt like hell. The mid-afternoon sun was only a slightly lighter spot on the mottled, translucent glass. He didn't know that being in a locked room was going to be part of the deal. He wanted fresh air and sunshine. Yes, this room had slightly more space than a jail cell and the luxury of a private bath, which he didn't have at his sister's house, but he was still locked up. And he didn't even have a television.

The dumb-ass public defender assigned to him had just left and had been three hours late for his appointment. The guy was worthless, probably with a six-month-old mail-order law degree from some cow college. The PD had immediately started talking about a plea deal, with the goal of serving two years in Concord knocked down to fourteen months with good behavior. As though that was going to be acceptable.

Willie had a far different goal: it was to walk out of this hospital a free man. And preferably to walk out with a clean slate – all priors expunged from his record.

He had hinted as much to the detective who came to see him this morning. The same old bastard who had shot him in the leg back in the hotel. The guy he was going to sue because he was probably going to walk with a limp for the rest of his life. The public defender had said that suing governmental bodies was outside of his expertise and that Catalano would have to find a contingency lawyer to take on a suit against the state and that his chances were poor.

The old fart detective – Johnson – had sat down with him, offered him a cigarette, and said there was a deal to be made. The detective had on this rumpled gray suit and smelled of cheap aftershave and cheaper cigars. Willie's initial opinion was that the guy was a loser from the get-go.

"Willie," the detective had said, lighting up a Camel in defiance of all hospital rules, "you know a lot more about this that you're letting on. And you're a lot smarter than anyone gives you credit for."

A pretty good opening, Willie had thought. Maybe the guy wasn't such a loser after all.

"Willie, you could come out of this smelling like a rose," the detective had said. "You could be a goddam hero. Keys to the city. A new car. A new life."

"By not suing you?" Willie had said.

The detective had laughed. "Hell, Willie, you can sue me all you want. I'll even help you. I ain't got much, but what I got I'd rather give to you than to my ex-wife any day of the week. So, when this is over and if you still want to sue me, you go right ahead."

Willie's opinion of the detective was rising by the minute.

The detective had leaned closer. "What I need are some names, Willie. I know how you work because I've asked around. You don't take on jobs blindly. You watch, you pay attention. You got hired by a guy down in Boston. I want that name. The guy in Boston was contacted by Little Joey Gavrilles. We already know that. Somebody who knew Little Joey reached out to him and said he needed a job done. The somebody is at the company where those two women you ran off the road were working. I'm betting you know who that guy was, too. And you know why I bet you know? Because you're smart. Too smart to take a fall and end up back in Concord. Especially when you didn't even get paid."

The detective had sat back and clasped his hands behind his neck. "And if you tell me those two names, I'm betting we can work you a sweet deal. No jail. Not even a suspended sentence. No parole violation. Not even for the car. You walk away a free man."

"But I got to testify, right?" Willie had said, not believing that there wouldn't be a hitch.

"Not if I get my way," the detective had said, pursing his lips. "If I get my way, we get the two guys with lots of other evidence. In fact, if I get my way, they'll be falling all over one another to rat on one another."

"When do I get out of here?" Willie had said. The offer was tempting.

"Take a few days, I'd guess," the detective had said. "Once you give me those names, I can keep you here in the hospital instead of getting you shipped to the jail. That leg of yours is only good for about twenty-four hours here and, ordinarily, you'd be on your way to a cell on Panther Drive. Stay here and there's better food, more space and maybe some outside time. A lot nicer than your sister's house. Her and that pack of brats."

Willie had thought about it for a few moments. He didn't look forward to going back to his sister's ratty house with her mob of fat children always waking him up and eating all the good food. The hospital was better than that shack. Then the reality kicked in.

"I tell you the name of the guy in Boston, I'm as good as dead," he had said.

The detective smiled as he spoke. "As far as I'm concerned, the name won't have come from you. You'll have spat in my face and called me names. Besides, what I'm really interested in is the company suit. You don't owe him anything."

Willie had sat back, confused. It sounded too good to be true.

"You come back in a few days," Willie had said.

The detective had shaken his head. "I'll give you this life of luxury until tomorrow morning, then I tell them to transfer you to the city jail," the detective had said. "But keep in mind that I'm working on those names real hard. If I get them from someone else in an hour, this afternoon or tonight, there's no deal." And with that, the detective had gotten up, given him a salute, and walked down the corridor to the outside world.

Now, eight hours later, Willie wondered if he had done the right thing, not giving up the other name. Because he had both names. He knew Gerry Sullivan because he had done a dozen jobs for Gerry over the past year. Gerry was his best source of work and he paid promptly. Gerry had never stiffed him, never said he had the wrong figure. Gerry had even sent his sister money when he was in Concord. He'd never give up Gerry's name. He and Gerry were tight.

But the other guy, the suit from that company. If that was his ticket out of here, why not? After he had run the two broads in the dinky Ford off the road, he had gone back to the company the next morning and watched as people entered and left the building. Most people just walked in or out. This guy was suspicious of everything. This guy looked over his shitty car like he expected to find a pipe bomb. Catalano knew he was dirty just by looking at him. And so he had followed him home. He had written down the license plate number and the address.

The guy might be his ticket out of this hospital. He might also be a gold mine. Guys like that could pay. They'd pay him to keep quiet, and when they paid once, they'd pay again. There was one guy who had paid him for two years until he got so depressed he ate his gun. Served him right, though. Willie had knocked off the guy's father. You shouldn't never do anything like that to your old man. Or at least you shouldn't pay someone else to do it for you.

But he had to get out of this barred and locked room to get to the guy at SoftRidge and present him with a pay-me-or-I-go-to-the-cops proposition. And he couldn't get out of what amounted to a jail cell with a private bath because his dumb-ass public defender had accepted a remand without even asking for a bail figure. So now he was stuck.

He had the detective's number. If he couldn't figure out a better angle on this thing, he'd make the call.

17.

Bergeron had shown the photos of the four most likely suspects – he had eliminated Driscoll, Li, Fuller and Morton either because of their age or their having fully documented alibis for the two evenings – to restaurant, bar, and shop owners in Quincy Market. Everywhere he showed the photos, he got shrugs of non-recognition. At several restaurants and bars, he was told that shifts changed at 6 p.m. If he wanted useful information about someone who might have been there at 8 p.m. or 11 p.m., he needed to come back when they were on duty.

Bergeron had no intention of hanging around. He had a date.

At 4:30 p.m., he headed north out of the city and reported in.

"Claude Johnson's looking for you," the dispatcher said.

Damn, he thought. "Better patch me through."

"I blew the assignment, but I may have recovered a little bit, sir," he told Johnson.

"You've been in this business for about three days," Johnson said. "You're expected to make mistakes, as long as they're not fatal. And the next time you call me 'sir' I'm going to punch out your lights. Until we wrap this thing up, you're my partner. Got it?"

"Got it."

"Got it what?"

Bergeron smiled. "Got it, Claude."

"OK," Johnson said. "How did you blow it and what's this magical recovery of yours?"

"Joey's sister recognized someone," Bergeron said. "But I went through the names too quickly and she was pretty good about hiding it. She threw me what I'm pretty sure was a phony clue – she said she thought her brother used to run with Paul Fuller. But Fuller is six years younger than Joey Gavrilles, so that doesn't seem likely."

"On the other hand, a guy got shoved under a truck in Boston last night. Gerald Sullivan. He's a local mobster whose specialties include setting up things like murders for hire. He bought it just outside of Quincy Market a little after 8 p.m. A forty-ish white guy, medium height and on the slim side, pushed him out in front of a truck on the Greenway access road."

"I stopped in to see the Boston PD, and they treated me like I've got some kind of communicable disease. They're afraid that…"

"…By bringing in another state's law enforcement, they're going to lose jurisdiction to the feds," Johnson said, completing the sentence. "I've heard that one once or twice before. Plus, they hate sharing information with anyone, any time. They'd rather not solve the case than accept help from the outside. They're assholes, and we're beneath contempt because we're not big city police detectives like them. We smell of cow manure. Get used to it. What makes you think he's our fixer?"

"I called Sullivan's cell phone and it rang in the homicide office."

"Good for you, Lou," Johnson said, laughing. "You just earned yourself a bunch of enemies for life. God, that's clever. I wouldn't plan on double parking in Boston anytime soon, though. They hate to be beaten at their own game, and especially by some yokels from the Granite State."

"I showed four of the photos around Quincy Market," Bergeron said. "I didn't get a hit, but a number of people said I needed to come back later when the night shifts come on."

"Well, considering this was supposed to be your day off, I'm surprised you're not hanging around to see if your hunch is right."

"Actually, I was hoping I could talk you into taking over for me this evening," Bergeron said. "I've kind of got a date."

"Kind of got? You don't know if you do or not?"

"It's a date."

"Well far be it for me to stand in the way of your love life. The restaurants probably change at – what – 5:30?"

"They said 6 p.m."

"Then drop off the photo array at the barracks on your way

home. I'll pick it up from there."

"I also promised Mrs. Laconda I'd see what I could do to get her brother's body released sooner."

"That was the right thing to say, Lou. I'll make a couple of calls before I leave here."

* * * * *

After the initial surge of energy when she first realized that there was another scheme to be uncovered at SoftRidge, Lynn's resolve to continue weakened with every encounter with SoftRidge managers. She would watch them in her peripheral vision as they approached the conference room, dragging themselves through the motions of assisting, knowing that this was the final week of their employment and that they were here only because it might extend the paychecks of those who reported to them by a few months.

As they drew nearer to her, they would make an effort to stand erect. They would rap on the metal molding of the conference room door and, when she looked up, they would be smiling and cheerful.

They didn't deserve this. Neither did their families, which had likely learned only this morning that the hoped-for severance would be little or nothing, and that their final check would reflect the pay of someone who flipped hamburgers at a fast-food restaurant.

She was respectful and she tried to show the concern she felt for them. But it was too much. At 4 p.m., she had enough.

"I'm shutting it down for the rest of the weekend," she announced to Deb. "Tell the munchkins to go back to New York. The accountants and attorneys can do what they want, but I'm telling the management team that we've done everything we can do for today and tomorrow, and we'll start fresh on Monday morning for the final push."

Deb looked at her appreciatively. "By God, I think you're going to be management material after all. That's the best decision I've heard anyone make around here for quite a while."

"And Deb, you don't need to come back on Monday," Lynn said. "I can do the rest with these kids. That shoulder of yours deserves some rest."

Deb shook her head. "I'm here as long as you're here. Besides, assuming you're right and there's some other scam in these books, I'd like to be the one who finds it for a change. And someone's got to debrief you after your date with the trooper. Assuming you come up for air."

Lynn smiled. "I doubt he even remembers we were going out tonight. He was driving over to Portsmouth this morning to talk to the sister of the guy whose house burned last night. Some day off."

"Some day off for all of us," Deb said. "What do you say we hit the malls and find you something decent to wear tonight?"

* * * * *

On the 42nd floor of the One International Place office building in Boston occupied by Highsmith & Co., Josh Tilighman, age thirty, flicked a piece of lint off his five hundred dollar autumn-weight Brioni windbreaker as he listened to the fury of his boss wind up like some grossly overweight human nor'easter. Why couldn't this have been done by email? Tilighman could have scrolled through the diatribe on his iPad, composed some sincere-sounding response, and had plenty of time for a set of racquetball. Or, if the blowhard insisted on talking, why not a conference call? Tilighman could do all kinds of enjoyable things with the call on speaker and the mute button engaged. One memorable evening, he had the pleasure of getting head from an eager-to-please summer intern while listening to Ralston talk non-stop for twenty minutes.

No, instead of simply chewing him out electronically, Stewart Ralston, a fat management fossil whose contribution to Highsmith was that he was a four handicap golfer, had roused himself from his Weston home on a Saturday and gone to Nashua to sit in on the SoftRidge Board presentation. Then, he had driven back into Boston and demanded a face-to-face meeting with the three-member team assigned to the sale of SoftRidge.

As a vice president, and as the person who had successfully pitched SoftRidge to use Highsmith as their investment banker,

Tilighman was the guy on the hot seat. It did not stop him from admiring the shine on his Barker Black shoes with the ostrich cap toes.

"You dumb-ass sons of bitches," Ralston was saying as he paced back and forth. "It isn't just turning a two million dollar fee into a one million dollar fee. It's opening Highsmith to what is essentially unlimited liability…"

Yada, yada, yada, Tilighman thought. It wasn't *he* who missed that controller's fictitious shares. It was the accountants. *They* were the ones with the deep pockets. *They* ought to be standing in front of a firing squad. Investment bankers weren't supposed to count shares. That was for dorky accountants with tape around their glasses. Jesus Christ, he had gotten almost ten bucks a share for a company that counted the remaining money on their postage meter as a key component of their cash reserves. SoftRidge's shareholders ought to kiss his ass out of gratitude.

And, how the hell was he supposed to know that the controller was crooked? Had Ralston ever set foot in SoftRidge's crappy headquarters? Not for an instant. Of course, if SoftRidge had a facility in the south of France, Ralston would have invented reasons to go there every few weeks. Or set up shop for the season.

"It's the sort of thing that puts a cloud over careers," Ralston was saying, looking directly at Tilighman. "We market ourselves as the firm that pays attention to the details…"

Yeah, and what the hell were you doing all that time, you pompous smartass? Tilighman thought. Ralston had shown up for the management pitch in the big conference room upstairs. He had glad-handed the pathetic SoftRidge management for two hours, plied them with good Scotch, then begged off to do something really important – like play golf. He had never returned a single iteration of the IM with any comments. Yet he, Tilighman, made a vice president of the firm nine months earlier, was getting called on the carpet in front of his five-months-out-of-B-school subordinates. They'd probably be sneering at him were it not for the likelihood that they probably all had brown stains in their tighty-whitey jockey shorts from being scared they'd get fired for this.

Tilighman stole a glance at his vintage Rolex Oyster Commander, a gift from his grandfather commemorating his graduation from Wharton. Fifteen minutes of this horseshit already.

"...And to have some associate from Clarenden catch the discrepancy..." Ralston continued.

Ralston was really red in the face now. But he had finally touched on a nerve. God damn Lynn Kowalchuk. God damn her and her nerdy clothes and her sexless body. God damn her for staying there night after night on a stupid little deal like this, looking for piss-ant mistakes. Looking for nickels and dimes so that Pericles and its megalomaniac of a CEO, Ross Maynard, could feel like he had Won The Big One. And then finding those shares, which allowed him to squeeze everyone's nuts.

God damn Lynn Kowalchuk.

"We compete against Clarenden every week," Ralston fumed, "and if you think they're not going to put this screw-up into every presentation they do for the next twelve months, you don't understand the investment banking business..."

Somebody ought to take Ralston out to his country club and wrap a nine iron around his neck, Tilighman thought. Jesus Christ, it's a frigging fire sale of a company with management too dumb to know they were bankrupt. It was a beautiful afternoon. He should be tearing through the countryside in his Porsche, feeling the wind in his hair and the warmth of his date's hand as she massaged him between his legs. *We can wrap the sale up by the end of next week*, he thought. *We can collect our fee. We can get the hell on to the next deal and maybe, this time, choose a real client with real assets. And it won't be in some backwater dump of a town where haute cuisine is a pizza with four toppings.*

"If anyone else on the other side catches anything else that lowers the price of this sale," Ralston said, "you gentlemen can consider yourselves free agents. I don't care whose fault it is or who should have flagged the error..."

Free agents? Tilighman thought. *He'd fire us over something that wasn't our fault? Highsmith would can us because our client hired a crook with a mistress? That isn't fair. That's the biggest piece of crap I've ever heard come out of Ralston's mouth. Or is someone threatening to take away his bonus? The guy's an equity partner, for Christ's sake.*

"I suggest you get your asses back up to SoftRidge and plan on staying there until this deal is done," Ralston said. "I further suggest you take this deal apart and question every underlying assumption. In other words, do the job we were paid to do in the first place."

"And Josh, stay behind," Ralston said, motioning the others out of his office.

Jesus Christ, Tilighman thought. *What the hell does he want now?*

Ralston closed the door, giving it an extra hard push to hear the 'click' of the latch mechanism.

"Sit down," Ralston said. He was a big man, probably tipping the scales at close to three hundred pounds. Decades of eating gourmet meals and drinking superb wines on clients' tabs had given him a fifty-inch waist. This afternoon, that girth was covered by what was probably a custom-made sweater. To Tilighman, Ralston looked like an enormous yellow beach ball.

"Josh, you let us down," Ralston said.

The blame has been successfully shifted, Tilighman thought. *Ralston probably called ten senior partners on his way back down here. They've all agreed that I'm the fall guy. Suddenly, this is all my fault. "You" let "us" down.*

"This is your baby. You had direct, management responsibility for the conduct of our due diligence. The buck stops with you."

Am I about to get fired? Tilighman hoped his face betrayed no anxiety.

"I know you're thinking that an investment banker can't be responsible for illegal actions on the part of its client," Ralston said, keeping his tone neutral. "But as any number of civil court cases have proven, it's no defense. When we accept an assignment and agree to a fee, we take on a fiduciary responsibility. And, even if we resign the account, we're still legally culpable. And, if somebody sues, we've got the deepest pockets."

I am going to get fired. Jesus H. Christ…

"Here's what we're going to do, Josh. You're going to get that smug, Darien-bred, Penn-educated ass of yours back up to Nashua. You're going to stay in that building with those two associates, and you're going to take SoftRidge's books apart, ledger page by ledger page. And only when you're ready to lay your career on the line that it's completely clean are you going to bless this deal."

Ralston put his hand on Tilighman's shoulder. "Because if it isn't… if there's anything else in this deal that's rotten and you, personally, didn't find it and bring it to the attention of Ross Maynard, it isn't just that you're going to get bounced out of Highsmith. I'm going to make certain that you never go to work in the investment banking business again. And so you'd better hope that your daddy has put away a boat-load of money to finance your way through three years of law school, because you can kiss Wall Street goodbye."

With that, Ralston rose, walked to the door of his office, opened it, and motioned Tilighman out.

Josh Tilighman had never been invited to say a word. When he was safely out of sight, Tilighman kicked a wall so hard his heel went through the drywall.

Driving back to Nashua, Tilighman fumed. *It isn't my fault. It's Ralston's fault. Hell no, it's that frigging Kowalchuk's fault. If she were out of the picture, all this would go away….*

And that was when the idea occurred to him. Ever since that auto accident Wednesday night, there had been this rumor flying around SoftRidge that it wasn't an accident at all; that someone had deliberately run Kowalchuk and the hot blonde babe off the road. The word around the company – whispered, because no one knew anything for certain – was that someone had tried to break into Kowalchuk's room and stab her, but that police had shot the guy.

Which would explain why someone else had told him a state

police car had brought Kowalchuk to work Thursday and Friday morning. And which would explain why the confidential contact sheet had been updated to show that Kowalchuk was now at the Radisson instead of the Crowne Plaza.

Was it was possible that Griffin had hired some hit man to whack Kowalchuk?

What a surreal opportunity, Tilighman thought. *Griffin is on the hook for anything that happens to the bitch. It's like one of those movies where the contract stays out on someone even though the guy who ordered it got his brains splattered all over the ceiling twenty minutes ago.*

He had another thought. The beginning of a brilliant plan. One that saved his job and got sweet revenge all at the same time.

Tilighman didn't even wait for the next exit. He saw an official-use-only gravel cut-across a hundred yards ahead. He veered onto the shoulder, downshifted, braked, and spewed gravel. He turned his six-month-old, jet black Porsche Boxster around and started heading south. South toward the solution to his Kowalchuk problem.

18.

It was 7 p.m. and Claude Johnson walked the brick-paved arcades of Quincy Market. In his jacket pocket were four photos. While the inexperienced Lou Bergeron had started at one end of the plaza showing photographs and went shop to shop doing so, Johnson applied thirty-plus years of detective experience to the problem. He tried to visualize the market from the perspective of the late Gerald Sullivan, racketeer. Given the number of security cameras in this tourist destination, Sullivan would want to steer any conversation to an area where men congregated and talked without attracting the attention of anyone monitoring the screens. Yet the conversation needed to be private. This severely limited the number of possible rendezvous points.

There was a Harley Davidson showroom. Two men could talk there for several minutes as long as they kept the sales staff at arm's length for the necessary time. A Victoria's Secret also met the description. At this hour, several men were in fact in front of the display window, contemplating the merchandise. These would have been the most likely places where Sullivan met his client and, if he failed to get a hit on any of the photos from store employees, he would review security tapes for those locations.

But, once the conversation was completed – and it would be a short one – money needed to change hands. The exchange needed to be out of view of security cameras and in an area where Sullivan would feel comfortable. He went to the two storefronts and looked for a spot Sullivan would have chosen.

His gaze went immediately to Cheers. A tourist bar, loud and crowded. Anonymous. That would be where Sullivan would have steered his guy.

He went to the bar entrance and visualized a handoff. Sullivan would have sent the guy on ahead. This would give Sullivan the opportunity to see if anyone were watching or if their earlier conversation had attracted any attention. He would go to Cheers via a different route, possibly walking around the central market building.

Thus, the guy he was looking for would have been in Cheers for at least five minutes and possibly ten before Sullivan's arrival. Long enough, perhaps, to have made an impression on a bartender. Sullivan would have wanted his guy to stay as close to the entrance as possible, the better to effect his own quick departure once the money was in hand. Johnson positioned himself at the bar at the most likely spot where Sullivan's client would have stood.

Sullivan would have come up behind the guy and told him to pass back an envelope. Sullivan would have looked at it quickly then told the guy to stay for at least another ten minutes so that there would be no temptation to follow Sullivan or otherwise prolong the conversation. But the guy would likely have nursed a single beer, marking time. It was the sort of behavior that would attract the attention of – and annoy – bartenders.

Johnson nodded at the nearest of the three bartenders. The man walked over, expecting an order.

"Were you working here this past week?" Johnson asked.

The bartender immediately scowled. It was a policeman, not a drink order.

"Couple of nights," the bartender said, the mixologist equivalent of 'let's get this over with quickly.'

Johnson spread out the four photos. "A guy was in here around eight o'clock Wednesday night and probably again on Thursday, a little later. You recognize any of these faces? He would have been standing about where I am now."

The bartender looked quickly. "Naw. I'm usually at the other end of the bar, anyway."

"Then ask your buddies to come over and look."

The bartender gave Johnson a nasty look. Seven o'clock on a Saturday night was prime time at the bar, and prime time for drinking was prime time for tipping.

"Give me a minute."

Two minutes later, a second bartender came over. "You're trying to identify a guy at the bar Wednesday or Thursday night?"

Johnson pushed the four photos forward. "He would have been about where I'm standing."

The bartender pointed at the second photo. "Him. Wednesday night. Drank one lousy beer in half an hour. Left a fifty-cent tip. Asshole."

Right in one, Johnson thought.

He got the bartender's name and home phone number.

He was whistling on his way out of the bar when a man with an Irish accent placed a hand on his shoulder and said, "Excuse me, but I think you have some information that you'd like to share with us."

Johnson knew better than to twist away and run. He cursed himself for not paying closer attention to his surroundings. At a time like this, you cooperated. It's why he was still alive after all these years.

* * * * *

Willie Catalano watched what he assumed was the sun setting through the translucent glass of his hospital room. He had run through all the ideas that might allow him to beat this rap without giving up someone's name. The idea of going back to the guy at SoftRidge and demanding big bucks – fifty thousand was the number he had in mind – was enticing.

But it was one of those chicken-and-egg kind of things. To put on the squeeze, you had to be out on the street. To get out on the street, he had to give up a name. And there was no way in hell he was giving up Gerry Sullivan's name. So, it would be the SoftRidge guy and Willie could squeeze the guy's family as well as him. Maybe he would offer not to testify; have a memory loss when he got onto the stand. That might work.

He had this Claude Johnson guy's card. He fished it out of his pocket. He knocked on the door of his hospital room to get the attention of the guard who patrolled the area.

"I got a cop I want to call," Catalano said. "This is official police business."

Consultations were made. Half an hour later, Catalano was wheeled to a telephone. He dialed the number for Johnson's cell phone.

Six rings later the call went to voice mail. Catalano hung up. No way in hell he was leaving that kind of information on a cop's cell phone. He wanted full credit. He wanted his ticket out of there.

* * * * *

Lynn Kowalchuk and Lou Bergeron lay in the bed in her hotel room, their arms and legs intertwined. He had picked her up at seven and they had gone to a very nice restaurant. Halfway through their entrée, however, it was clear that where they both wanted to be was here. And so they had skipped the obligatory coffee and dessert and drove, several miles above the speed limit, to the Radisson. Lynn's carefully done hair and makeup were still in place, the blue dress she had purchased a few hours earlier was on the floor along with the rest of their clothing.

Lynn felt a contentment she had not experienced in a very long time. It was not just the sex, though the lovemaking was wonderful. It was the comfort of being in loving arms, caressed and held. It was at once peaceful and exhilarating.

She listened to Bergeron's breathing and felt the rhythmic rise and fall of his chest. She could feel his heart beat. *God, this is wonderful*, she thought. *Let this night go on forever.*

* * * * *

Across town, the SoftRidge executive itemized his purchases, laid out on the kitchen counter. Accidents required careful planning and he had always excelled at planning. He had driven to Lowell, Boston, and Cambridge to purchase what he needed. It had been surprisingly easy and the cash outlay was not as onerous as he had feared. Because he had the ten thousand dollar cash 'refund' given to him by G. Sullivan, he was not even especially sensitive to price, and he wondered, as he examined his purchases, how he might best spend the rest of this unexpected windfall.

His only question was one of timing Kowalchuk's accident. While he would have liked to do it on Sunday, it wasn't practical because he needed both to be close to her and part of a crowd around her. He also needed to leave the trail of evidence that would leave no question about it being an accident and that would take a day. So, his big day would be Monday. Bright and early; the sooner the better. After a little preparatory work Sunday morning, it would be his day of rest, and he knew just how he would spend it.

He kept his mind on his ultimate goal. *Ten days,* he thought. *In ten days I'll be able to clean out those accounts and be beyond all of this.* In ten days he would be wealthy and with a guaranteed lifetime income. All that stood between him and his goal was one woman. And now he had the perfect plan to be rid of her, once and for all.

* * * * *

In a nondescript motel that might have once been a Travelodge or other budget chain, but that had fallen below franchise standards and so bore no name except for a legend of 'Rooms $33.95 and up', Tony D'Alessio snored the sleep of a man who had polished off the better part of two bottles of Sambuca.

He had driven across the New Hampshire state line and, while searching for an inexpensive hotel, had stumbled across a New Hampshire State Liquor Authority retail store. Until that moment, he had been unaware that just thirty miles from Boston, a state had granted itself a monopoly on the sale of liquor, priced that liquor so as to attract the maximum number of visitors from out of state, and placed stores within sight of the Massachusetts border.

Inside, he immediately gravitated toward the Italian liqueurs section and had been rewarded with a dazzling array of products. He chose an 84 proof Sambuca di Amore, found it priced under $10 versus half again as much for a less potent product in Boston, and bought two bottles.

D'Alessio was ordinarily far more reliable in such matters but the death of Gerry Sullivan had deeply affected him. He had known and looked up to Gerry since he was a boy. Sullivan had sponsored him to Aidan Parker's organization and made certain he committed no blunders during his probationary period. Though he was now accepted in his own right as the lone non-Irishman in the gang, he had felt slightly disoriented when questioned by Parker. He would never have felt that way had Gerry been present – or Gerry's death not been the subject of the interrogation.

He did not turn off his phone, but neither did its persistent ringing awaken him over the sound of his own snoring.

* * * * *

At a quarter to midnight, Josh Tilighman pushed his Boxter to 85 as he crossed from Connecticut into Rhode Island.

What a hell of an idea, he thought. He had made it from whatever freaking ugly suburb of Boston he had turned around in to Darien in a little over three hours. His parents had, fortunately, not been home so he had nothing to explain and no reason to make nice. It was Saturday night so they'd likely be at the Wee Burn getting sloshed on vodka martinis in the company of other bored, empty-nest couples. He headed straight for his room, went to his closet and found that nothing had changed. His mother kept his room like some kind of goddamn shrine. Keep it just like it was, and Josh will come home for Thanksgiving.

Jesus Christ, he was thirty. *Get over it, Mom, I'm taking a babe to Antigua the last week in November and while you and dad sit down to that sad excuse of a turkey, I'll be getting laid non-stop all afternoon. Think about that with your cranberry sauce, Dad.*

In a trunk in his closet was the prize that brought him home. His dad had bought it for his fourteenth birthday. For six weeks he had shot at paper targets until he could hit the bulls-eye with unerring accuracy. Then he had lost interest and moved onto girls. But you never forget how to use those things, and this time, hitting the bulls-eye was going to save his job. And the sweet part was that the cops would figure it was Griffin's hit man, finishing the job.

Josh Tilighman, rifle man.

He punched on a SiriusXM hard rock station and was rewarded with a thumping beat on his Bose Surround Sound system that took his already terrific mood to a new, higher level. Ninety minutes to his apartment for a few hours of sleep. Then an hour to Nashua to set the trap. Maybe six hours to the perfect solution to the Kolwachuk problem.

As he pushed the accelerator toward 90, Tilighman thought, *somebody should write this up as a B-school case study.*

19.

Sunday, September 23

The morning sunlight streamed through the curtains. It was a bright, clear New England day, the kind that state tourism boards and chambers of commerce promoted in their brochures and videos. There was the start of color in the maples and birch and the crisp breeze underscored that summer was officially over.

"Please tell me you don't have to go to work this morning," Lynn said, tracing her finger on Bergeron's chest as they lay under the sheets.

"I don't have to go to work this morning," he said. "I don't have to be anywhere for another twenty-four hours. We can do anything you like. Go anywhere you like."

"Including stay here?" Lynn amazed herself that she didn't feel embarrassed by being so bold. The phrase *brazen hussy* crossed her mind. She liked it.

"I might start demanding something to eat pretty soon but, yes, we could stay right here." He rolled over and embraced her. "But if you're game, I have something in mind for later on. I'm pretty sure that you've never done anything like it before and that you'll like it."

"Does it involve putting on our clothes?" Again, she wondered that she could be so frank. She had known this man only a few days. She had brought him to her hotel room and enthusiastically made love with him until they had both collapsed from exhaustion. And now, she was still naked in bed with him, her body pressed tightly against his. She was aware of his musky scent and the commingled smell of sex. *How long has it been?* She pushed the thought out of her mind. *Right now is all that counts*, she thought.

"It's something I thought of before I knew how last night was going to turn out," he said. "Let's let it be a surprise. Life needs to have its share of surprises to be interesting."

* * * * *

Claude Johnson awakened in a dimly lit room. There was apparently bright sunshine outside because it filtered through the blackout curtains on the room's two windows. He was surprised that he had slept through the night. But then, the sour taste in his mouth indicated that he may well have been drugged.

It had all been very simple. A man had gripped his arm and began steering him toward the same spot that had been the last one Gerry Sullivan saw before he was pushed under a truck.

"Excuse me, but I think you have some information that you'd like to share with us."

It was all so civilized. He had walked with them – there was another man a few feet away. They were both goons. Irish goons, with not-long-off-the-boat accents. He had been hustled into a Jeep. No one had shown a gun, no one had threatened him. Except that it was clear that if he bolted or fought back, they would beat him up. Not kill him, because he had information they wanted. But they would cause him pain. One of the men relieved him of his wallet, shield, gun, and cell phone.

They blindfolded him and started driving. He had a sense they were driving in circles so that he would not know where they were taking him. Then again, the crazy flow of Boston streets produced much the same, disorienting feeling.

Wordlessly, they had taken him to the second floor of a building and to this room, where his blindfold was removed. In the room was a bed, two chairs, a bucket and a roll of toilet paper.

"Wait here," one of them had said. The door closed behind him.

Five minutes later, the door opened. A burly man in a Red Sox warm-up jacket walked in, holding Johnson's wallet in one hand, slapping it against the other. The man had huge, beefy hands, a pock-marked face and curly brown hair. He was perhaps thirty. Young to be in charge. At thirty, they were usually soldiers.

"Detective Johnson," the man had said. Also Irish, though here for a long time. Perhaps even just an accent acquired by hanging around more recent immigrants.

Johnson had nodded.

"I'm told you're a reasonable man." It was a statement.

Johnson nodded again.

"A young state trooper was asking questions around Quincy Market this afternoon. He didn't get the answers he was looking for. You came back and got answers to those questions."

Johnson said nothing. You didn't get hurt by saying nothing as long as a question was not hanging in the air.

"The man you've now identified is someone of great interest to us," the man in the Red Sox jacket said. "I'd be obliged if you'd share his name with us."

Now was the time to talk. And not to bargain. His life depended upon how he comported himself in the next few minutes.

He gave them the name.

The man nodded. "And who is this man? How did you come to think it might be him?"

He told them.

The man nodded again.

"And where would I find this man?"

He gave them the SoftRidge office address and his home address.

"Good lad," the man said, though Johnson was twice his age.

Johnson was silent.

The man slapped Johnson's wallet in his hands several more times, thinking. He nodded to himself. Still thinking.

"We'll be obliged if you'd stay with us a few hours while we take care of a few things," the man said, making it sound as though it were a favor he were asking. He held up Johnson's wallet. "When I return this to you, it will be a bit fatter. You'll get back your gun and cell phone, too, though your phone's SIM card may have been a bit damaged when one of my boys removed it. We've no cause to harm you. You were just doing your duty." He pronounced it 'dew-tee'.

Very immigrant Irish.

He had closed the door, and Johnson lay back on the bed.

Perhaps twenty minutes went by. The man opened the door again and sat down in the chair opposite Johnson, who now sat on the edge of the bed. The man had a puzzled look on his face.

"My colleague in Nashua doesn't seem to be answering his phone," the man said. "He's usually very reliable. As a result, we're going to have to figure out why he doesn't pick up, and we may have to send up a few people. I'm afraid you're likely to be with us overnight. I'll have some dinner sent in."

"That isn't necessary," Johnson said.

"It's the least we can do for inconveniencing you." The man in the Red Sox warm-up jacket seemed genuinely concerned that he not be thought of as lacking hospitality. "However, for your own safety and as a courtesy to your hosts, I would ask that you make use of that blindfold on the bed when you hear a knock on the door. Some of my boys have an aversion to being known to the boys in blue."

"You needn't wear it when no one's about," the man said. "Just put it on if you hear a tap at the door. It will make them feel more comfortable with you as a guest."

A plate with a lukewarm hamburger and French fries had shown up half an hour later, together with a bottle of beer. Johnson put on the blindfold to accept the meal, took it off as soon as the door closed, had his dinner and used the chamber pot. Shortly thereafter, he fell into a deep sleep.

Now he was awake and wondering what was taking so long.

Johnson knocked on the door and then took several respectful steps back into the center of the room, making certain his blindfold was in place.

The door opened part way and a man – not with the same voice as the one on the Red Sox jacket – asked what Johnson wanted.

"Is everything OK?" Johnson asked. "Your boss said it would be a couple of hours." It was a casual request, given that he was being held captive in this room and had no certainty that he would leave the building alive.

"My orders are to keep you here" the man said. Then he added, "Would you be wanting some breakfast or something?" Another strong Irish accent.

"That would be nice," Johnson said. He went back to the bed, sat, and wondered. *What in the hell is going on out there?*

* * * * *

He drummed his fingers on the steering wheel of his car, trying to relieve the monotony of sitting in the parking lot of the Radisson. He had been here since 7 a.m., watching and waiting. From his observation post, he could see anyone entering or exiting the hotel from either the front or the rear. The hotel catered principally to business travelers on weekdays. The weekend leaf-peeking season was still two or three weeks away so, on a Sunday morning, there were few cars in the parking lot. In the event that Lynn Kowalchuk found some sneaky way out of the building, he would still see her at the hotel's lone vehicle exit.

As he waited for signs of activity, he wondered about Joey Gavrille's sister, Katie. Something about this day reminded him of her. What had ever become of her? After that summer, he had not stayed in touch. Why bother? After all, how much humiliation did one guy need? While one of Joey's tough-guy pals was probably humping Katie five nights a week, on the other two evenings he had meekly put up with Katie removing his hand from any part of her body except her face and arms.

Humiliated him. What a crock. She gets knocked up by somebody else and comes to him for help. And, nice guy that he was, he had helped, even paying part of the fee for the abortion. Yeah, she had cried and thanked him, and at the time he had felt like he was doing the manly thing. But it was clear that Katie wanted it both ways: hot and sexy with the guys with the fast cars and the cool looks, and safe and romantic with someone like him. Someone who drove his father's Olds and spent the summer taking ice cream orders at Friendly's.

She was probably still in town. Probably married with four or five children. If she had gotten pregnant at seventeen, what were the odds she would ever keep her legs together long enough to make it through high school? He imagined her: five kids, fat, her hair graying prematurely. Probably with less than a full set of teeth and no insurance to pay for dentures. She would be dressed in some WalMart dress, shapeless and without style. And to think that he once thought he was in love with her. What a sap he had been.

When I get rich, Katie, I definitely am not going to look you up, he thought.

At 7:45, a black Porsche pulled into the parking lot entrance. He paid it little attention at first but was puzzled that the car went to the far corner of the parking lot instead of one of the multiple spots close by the entrance. A guy got out of the Porsche. At a distance of nearly three hundred feet, he could not say with certainty that he recognized the man, and he certainly didn't know anyone who drove such a car. But what happened next was unmistakable. The guy went to the trunk of the Porsche and took out a rifle.

People with guns in hotel parking lots on Sunday morning are up to no good, he thought.

The man then proceeded to put on a long raincoat and tried to hide the rifle under the coat, Clint Eastwood style.

This can't be happening, he thought. And then it hit him. *The asshole investment banker from Highsmith. It's that cocky prick... Tilighman. What is he doing with a rifle?*

He got out of his own car as quietly as possible and crept into the woods that surrounded the hotel. Tilighman seemed to be looking for a hiding place of his own. A few minutes later, he appeared to find it, a nook within a stand of bright red burning bush. Tilighman went to a prone position and disappeared.

He continued his path through the woods, walking silently and keeping his lowest profile. His watch showed it was a few minutes after eight o'clock, probably too early for Kowalchuk to be leaving the hotel.

Then he was perhaps thirty feet behind Tilighman, who lay like some outlaw in a western movie, feet apart, his rifle trained on the front entrance of the Radisson. Tilighman was apparently intent on getting off a quick shot: he kept his eye trained down the sighting notch of the rifle.

He almost laughed at the spectacle. Here, before him, was some idiot investment banker with a .22 – a gun suitable for annoying rabbits. Tilighman was undoubtedly here to 'assassinate' Kowalchuk. He had decided he was going to pick her off as she came out of the front door. The clown was pathetic. He couldn't kill anyone at that distance with that rifle. A .22 caliber bullet's velocity was such that it would drop a foot or more between here and the door and be traveling at about fifty miles per hour when and if it hit anything.

Obviously, Tilighman was scared of Kowalchuk. He had probably gotten reamed out by his managers over his ineptitude at not spotting Griffin's little stock dividend. But he had picked the most pitiful solution to his problem; one that couldn't work but that could and would upset his own plans. Tilighman needed to be stopped.

He looked around. There was a rock. A little bigger than his fist. It would be close work. Tilighman continued to peer down the barrel of the rifle, oblivious to the rest of the world.

He got to Tilighman's feet. He made certain there was no one at the hotel entrance. He raised the rock over his head, he jumped.

It was over in a second. Tilighman was unconscious, never knowing who or what had hit him. There was a head wound and it would bleed for a while.

He took the .22 from Tilighman's limp hands and crept back into the woods. When he was at a sufficient distance he smashed the rifle into a tree until the barrel was visibly bent. He then wiped it clean of prints and walked back to his car to resume his wait.

At 9:32, his patience was rewarded as Kowalchuk walked out the front entrance. But he froze when he saw who she was with. The damned state trooper. He was sure it was the same guy even though he was not in uniform. He had the same hair color and short cut, and the same athletic build.

Was he her full-time bodyguard? The question was answered when she paused, threw her arms around the trooper, and kissed him.

So there's a little sex going on, too, he thought. *Is he putting in for overtime? Or is this a freebie, off the taxpayer's clock?*

The two got into a light truck and drove away. He wasted no time, getting out of his own car and walking to the lobby. The kid at the reception desk looked to be about nineteen. Sunday morning duty at a lightly populated hotel.

He brandished a large envelope he had retrieved from his office. It bore a Clarenden Brothers logo and its New York address, and contained an unmarked copy of the SoftRidge Information Memorandum.

"I want to leave this for Lynn Kowalchuk," he said, handing over the envelope. The desk clerk nodded and accepted the envelope. He turned to walk away, then stopped. "She is staying here?" he asked the clerk. "There was some confusion about whether she was going home for the weekend." He returned to the reception desk, as if ready to reclaim the envelope if she wasn't a guest.

"I'll check," the kid said. He typed the name into the terminal in front of him. "Yes, she's here."

"Well, make sure that gets to her this morning," he said.

The kid nodded. Saving a step he would otherwise have done a few minutes later, he wrote down the room number on the envelope.

He watched, noted the room number, then gave the kid a tap of the forehead salute. "Thanks."

He went back to his car, retrieved his briefcase, and re-entered the hotel via the rear entrance. Because it was going to be a tragic accident without an investigation, he did not worry about security cameras. On the third floor, he saw a maid's cart near the elevator. He found the maid cleaning one of the rooms.

"I just locked myself out of my room," he said, sheepishly, patting his pockets. "Can you let me back in?"

The maid nodded, walked with him to Lynn's room, and opened the door.

Inside, he worked quickly. He had evidence to plant. Most of it went into Lynn's suitcase, into compartments that she would not ordinarily scrutinize but that the police would subsequently look in as they pieced together her death. Other bits of evidence went into Lynn's toiletries bag and even under the bed, on the theory that the maid's vacuum was unlikely to reach such areas. When the police filed their report, it would be one of those open-and-shut affairs. After ten minutes he was satisfied. He left the room and returned to his car. He had a lot to do today, a full slate of activities.

He noted that Tilighman, in among the burning bush, still had not stirred.

* * * * *

Willie Catalano got the word from the policeman outside his hospital room. "You're on a van to Panther Drive at nine." He was going to the Nashua city jail.

"Call Detective Johnson at the state police," Catalano said. "Tell him I'm ready to talk. And you can cancel that van. I'm staying here. Johnson will tell you so."

That had been an hour earlier. Catalano waited in his room to be summoned to the phone. He was still waiting.

The door opened. The policeman looked at Catalano, who was still in a hospital gown. "You didn't hear right," the policeman said. "We're leaving in fifteen minutes. If you want to go to jail dressed in that thing, it's OK with me, but my advice would be not to lean over."

"Did you call Detective Johnson?"

"Yeah, I called him. I left messages at his office, with the dispatcher, and on his home phone. He ain't responded. So you're going to jail. Now get some clothes on."

* * * * *

At 10 a.m., Tony D'Alessio awakened, his head pounding from too much Sambuca. There were seven voice-mail messages on his cell phone, all from Aidan Parker. He called Parker and said the battery in his phone had died and that he had just now noticed it.

"We got a name and an address," Parker said, ignoring the obvious lie. "He's all yours. Go get him. Just make sure he's still alive when he gets here so I can finish him off with my own hands."

20.

The man behind Lynn gave the order. "Just step off the ledge."

And fall to my death, Lynn thought. *It's amazing. I've come through two attempts on my life in a week, only to die in a way that will be called 'a tragic accident'.*

Lynn looked down. Below her, it was more than forty feet to the ground. She knew her chances of surviving such a fall were nil. At twenty feet, she might survive with some broken bones. At forty feet, the force of impact would be the same as falling from the fourth or fifth floor of a building. These were probably her last moments on earth.

"Don't think about it. Just jump," the man implored, his voice betraying a patience worn thin.

Oh, you're impatient for me to jump? she thought. *Why don't you just push me off this ledge and get it over?*

She turned around and looked at Lou, who was standing next to the man who had told her to jump. He was smiling. She returned his smile and blew him a kiss, closed her eyes and then stepped off the ledge into the abyss.

Lou, I'm doing this for you....

She fell about four feet, then the harness caught, jerking her to a bouncing stop. Slowly, she was lowered along a cable a distance of a few hundred feet, a yellow rope tied to the harness around her to control her descent.

At ground level, another man was there to unhitch the cable from her harness and help her down. "That wasn't so scary, was it?" he said.

They were on the side of Barron Mountain above Lincoln, a village in the White Mountains approximately a hundred miles north of Nashua. Bergeron's 'surprise' was to take her on an alpine zipline.

"Some buddies of mine got the idea from reading about the ones in Central America," he said when he finally revealed their destination. "They opened it about six years ago and, as far as I'm concerned, they've still got the best one in New England."

They had talked throughout the drive up to the White Mountains. Bergeron spoke of growing up in Berlin, a town farther north, a place without tourists, sustained only by a handful of technologically obsolete paper mills.

"It was the region's way of life for a hundred years," he said. "Paper mills are like a coal mine, except that it's cellulose dust instead of coal, and the pay used to be better. Guys took their father's jobs when either the alcohol or the dust got to them."

"But you got out," Lynn said. "You did OK."

Bergeron smiled. "There but for the grace of Uncle Sam go I. Yeah, I got out. Right into the line of fire. Uncle Sam sent me to Afghanistan to get Osama Bin Laden, and then Iraq to get Saddam Hussein, and then back to Afghanistan. If I had been a little greedier or the recruiter had been more persuasive, I would have signed on for the Reserves option for the extra thirty bucks a month. In which case, I'd still be somewhere in the Sandbox right now. As it was, I acquired a whole set of skills that I never thought I'd need. And I hope I never have use for again."

"Like what?"

He squinted as he looked at her. "I did an emergency tracheotomy on a twenty-year-old guy on my patrol after a sniper got him. A medic told me how to do it over the radio. Drugs are a big problem over there. A lot of guys over there were scared they'd fall asleep while they were on watch, and they took speed. A lot of other guys had too much time on their hands and they did opium. I did more than my share of detox work."

"Do you ever go back to Berlin?" Lynn asked.

Bergeron shook his head. "I used to, but there's not much reason to go any more. One brother lives in the old family place. The others all got married and scattered to other towns as soon as they got out of high school. They thought I deserted the family when I joined the Army. It's sad, but we're just not close. My father is a drunk who thinks having a state trooper for a son means he can drive with half a bottle of whiskey in him. I've seen him once in six years."

"I had no idea," Lynn said, softly.

Bergeron looked over at her. "Don't feel sorry for me. I'd have turned out just like him if it hadn't been for my Grandma Doucette. She was my mother's mother. After mom died, Grandma Doucette took on the job of raising five boys with a dad who wasn't much of a role model. I guess I was her favorite. What I know for certain is that I was the only one who went back to visit her regularly after they left school; even my brothers who stayed in Berlin. I'd go up to see her every month and spent every home leave with her."

"Why did you stop?"

"She died in March. A stroke. I had been up there on Sunday, she apparently died on Tuesday. A neighbor found her on Thursday."

"It sounds like you're the only person who cared."

"Sometimes I think I was."

They passed the exit for Plymouth State College. Bergeron pointed at the sign for the school. "I was there for a semester after I got out of the Army," he said. "The whole idea of signing up for the six years was that I'd have a fully paid college education when I got out. What the Army forgot to tell us was that we'd be fish out of water. I was twenty-five, the freshmen around me were eighteen and nineteen. They looked at me like I was either some kind of Neanderthal or some Rambo mercenary because I had been in uniform. Since I didn't know what I wanted to major in, or what I'd do after I graduated, it was easy to leave."

"But you didn't go back to Berlin, either."

Bergeron shook his head. "Wasn't even tempted. What I realized, though, was that I was too old for college and I had no trade. That's when the recruiter says, 'Son, I can see some stripes on those shoulders if you re-up.' A lot of guys go back in. I had no desire to go back to the Sandbox. Then, one morning when I was feeling sorry for myself, I saw a state trooper drive by. I had been assigned to a military police unit for two years and I said, 'Lou, I bet you could do that.' And here I am to prove it."

"Saving lives," Lynn said.

"And handing out fifty speeding tickets a month. Anyone who tells you there isn't a quota doesn't know what they're talking about."

"Is it what you want to keep doing?"

"I take classes – law enforcement and criminal justice stuff, mostly. Uncle Sam foots the bill. I kind of enjoyed being a detective for a few days. That engaged my brain full time. However, I suspect opportunities like that come along to third-year troopers about once every blue moon. Unless I hear otherwise, I'm back on the Everett Turnpike as of tomorrow morning, handing out tickets and directing traffic around little old ladies' cars when they break down."

"How about you?" he added after a moment. "Is this what you want to keep doing?"

Lynn thought before answering. "I'm good at it, and they pay me a lot of money. If I stay with it, they'll pay me really serious money. But there are a couple of problems. The first problem is that, in investment banking, it's up or out. For three years, all I've done is work on other people's deals."

She saw the confusion on Bergeron's face. "At Clarenden Brothers, you're an 'associate' for a maximum of four years," she explained. "You can be asked to leave any time for poor performance, but at the end of those four years, you either get made a vice president or else you get told 'it didn't work out'. That's a legal way of saying, 'you're too expensive to keep on the payroll when we can hire cheaper help right out of college to do what you're doing'."

"So, let's assume that at the end of four years, I get made a vice president. It's a nice title, but all it means is that now I'm part of a team that pitches work to potential clients. And, after a year or two of pitching business as part of that team, I'm expected to start coming up with my own leads using my own network of sources. And those leads had better generate income for the firm. If I generate enough income, I'll get equity and become a partner. If I don't generate enough income, I'll get invited to leave."

"You said there were a couple of problems. Is there something else?" Bergeron asked.

Lynn nodded. "People like Ross Maynard. He's the CEO of Pericles, the company that's buying SoftRidge. He's a mean son of a bitch who uses M&A – mergers and acquisitions – to screw people. And this weekend, I helped him do just that. He's paying the fee, he hired Clarenden, and so I do whatever I'm told."

Lynn continued. "The problem is that after what happened at the meeting yesterday – when Maynard came in and threatened to walk away – I realized I hate the guy and what he stands for. He's a sadist. If I could find a way to screw him without him knowing it, I'd do it."

"Wouldn't that be unethical?" Lou asked.

Lynn shook her head wearily. "Of course it would be unethical. But so is telling managers that they're going to spend the last week of their job working for fast food wages and forego salary continuance. The managers have no choice because, if Maynard made good on his threat, the company would shut down the next day for lack of cash and every employee would be out of a job. And, of course, now Maynard has all the company secrets: the customer names and order amounts, the working drawings, the patent work-arounds. Sure, if you tank the acquisition you're supposed to give back everything. But you can't 'unlearn' what you picked up in final due diligence."

She looked out the window at the passing scenery. "I've been working with these people at SoftRidge for a week. They're decent people trying to save a company, or at least save the jobs of the people who work for them. Ross Maynard can't wait to get rid of everyone on that staff. And when he's done that, he'll use every legal maneuver available to keep those people from competing with him."

"One of those people you like so much wants to kill you,"

Bergeron said.

"That's one person out of hundreds, and you'll catch him," Lynn said. "You and Detective Johnson."

"Whom I haven't heard from today, which is weird," Bergeron said. "I've been expecting the phone to ring all morning with some kind of progress report."

"Don't detectives get a day off?"

"I don't think so, at least not according to Claude. He sleeps, eats, and works – and not necessarily in that order," Bergeron said, then added, "So what do you do about the Ross Maynards of the world?"

"I wish I knew," Lynn said, looking back at Bergeron. "They're not all like him, but I don't get to pick and choose. There's a lot of human damage done in investment banking. Some of it is inevitable: the stronger company takes over the weaker one but the weaker one would have gone by the wayside eventually. But sometimes the damage is unnecessary and personal. My father worked twenty-five years for Allied Department Stores. He started at the bottom but worked his way up into corporate management – territory development. He opened fifteen stores in seventeen years and did an incredible job of it. Then, Federated bought Allied. Six months later, as part of 'eliminating overlapping positions,' he was out of a job. He was supposed to start over again at fifty. Nobody can start over at fifty. Five years later, he's still 'a consultant', which means he hasn't had a steady job since he was let go."

Bergeron said nothing immediately, but nodded. After a few moments, he said, "So maybe you don't want to keep doing this."

"It's not all rape and pillage," Lynn said. "SoftRidge was dying. They apparently had the wrong guy at the top. Had the company not hired a banker, it would have gone under and no one would have gotten anything – employees, shareholders, vendors. So, what I'm doing is beneficial, but sometimes, the Ross Maynards of the world make me a little sick to my stomach."

"Maybe you should start your own investment bank," Bergeron

said. "Ethical bankers for hire – no egomaniac CEOs need call."

Lynn laughed. "Yeah, all I'd need would be about fifty million of start-up capital and a dozen specialists. Plus, I'd have to be out there pitching business, which is why I wonder if I'm going to last in investment banking."

Lynn was keenly aware of how comfortable she felt talking with Lou about her fears, something she had never done with friends at Clarenden Brothers. She knew she was envied for her skill, and that everyone jockeyed with everyone else for the most visible assignments, however subtly. Were she to have had this conversation with another associate, even Deb, it was likely that a less benign version of her qualms would inevitably be told to managers in an effort to sidetrack her career. Lou, though, had no one to tell. And perhaps, she thought, she wanted to convey that her life was not settled. Major changes could perhaps be made under the right circumstances.

"Do you think you'll always want to be in New York?"

Bergeron's question caught her by surprise. She was quiet for a long time. "I'm thinking," she said when she realized it had been nearly a minute since he asked.

"I never had one place that I called home for more than a year and a half," she said. "Dad moved all over the Midwest. I started fifth grade in Urbana, Illinois and finished it in Ladue, Missouri. We were one step up from nomads but with better housing. I did my undergraduate work in California and got my MBA here. New York was just a place we went on vacation until I accepted the offer from Clarenden. So, I'm not tied to New York."

She wanted to say, *'why do you ask?'* She wanted to hear him say, *'Could you be happy here?'* But they reached the exit for Lincoln and, instead, he said, "And now for the surprise."

* * * * *

Tony D'Alessio was perplexed by New Hampshire and its essentially rural nature, even in the locales that were, at least technically, cities. 1062 Leaning Pine Circle was near no discernible landmarks and stops at three service stations had resulted in shrugs. He had finally been forced to purchase, for nearly twenty dollars, an atlas of southern New Hampshire.

Worse, when he finally located the address, there was no one home. He broke into the house to be certain. A consultation with the atlas showed that SoftRidge's offices were a few miles distant. There, he found a half dozen cars in the parking lot. But by six o'clock, they had all departed, none bearing the man he had seen at Quincy Market.

D'Alessio reported his lack of progress and returned to the house to resume his stakeout.

* * * * *

He had spent the morning and afternoon looking at boats. He started in Newburyport, looking at the eighteen- and twenty-footers, then moved up the coast to Portsmouth. Though he had never owned a sailboat, or even sailed, he decided his first important purchase after collecting the money was going to be a boat. There was something about a boat that indicated a man of means. After looking at the people who piloted the smaller craft – ordinary men and their families – he quickly raised his sights to larger vessels.

He admired the wood trims and the catchy names of the large boats that paraded in and out of Portsmouth's harbor. The array of spinning electronics above their cabins spoke of safety and comfort below. He figured something around thirty feet was probably about right.

He had almost $10,000 in cash with him, which he now thought of as 'found' money. He dined at a waterside restaurant, ordered a two-pound lobster and did not flinch at the bill. He went through the little shops of downtown Portsmouth, looking at clothes and artwork.

And he bought clothes. Casual clothes. A pair of slacks, an autumn-weight shirt. Even new shoes. Something he almost never did.

You really screwed me up, old man, he thought. *You and your damned lottery tickets. Sitting there in front of the television in that moth-eaten lounge chair, night after night, staring at your tickets while the drums spun, dreaming of what you were going to buy when you hit it big. And while you were wasting your miserable post office paycheck on the lottery, your family was going hungry. Mom and I ate Vienna sausages and rice and smiled at each other and told one another that winning the lottery was your dream. I wore my cousins' hand-me-downs because there was nothing left for shoes and clothing for your own son.*

So you turned me into this miser who never spent money unless he had to. I choose my hobbies because they're inexpensive. I drive a crappy car and, because you did it when I was a kid, I make a detailed inspection of my car every time I get into it to make certain no one put a scratch or ding on a door or fender. Like father, like son.

Except it's all going to change. I've hit that lottery that you never won, and I did it on my own terms. I'm a few days away from having more money than you ever dreamed of, and I'm not going to be afraid to spend it. I'm going to start with a boat and then the nicest damn car I can find and then I'm going to live it up. I'm going to get so far away from here.

After viewing the boats and buying the clothes, he was antsy to get on with his new life and to leave behind what he now admitted had been a humdrum, miserly existence. *Four point two million*, he kept thinking. *Tax free.* And then he wondered, *why not a few hundred thousand more? Why not round it up to a nice, even four and a half million? Why not enough to pay for that cabin cruiser on day one without having to stint on his other lifestyle changes?*

He had time. The company was still issuing purchase orders. What was the harm of another few hundred thousand, especially since they were to what were now 'established' vendors? The paperwork would be easy.

And, because Lynn Kowalchuk would be dead tomorrow, the chance of discovery would be nil.

Any why go home? Back to his crummy house with its second-hand furniture? It was late afternoon and only a ninety minute drive to Nashua. He could create the invoices in his office in less than an hour tomorrow morning. His route out of the center of town took him by the Sheraton Portsmouth. It looked like a very luxurious hotel. On impulse, he pulled into the driveway and asked if a deluxe executive room was available. He paid cash.

* * * * *

Each successive 'zip' was more exhilarating than the last. The first, training run had allowed her to overcome her fear of stepping off one of the platforms nestled high in the pine trees. The second run, starting at ground level, had taken her a quarter mile over a ravine, with the trees racing by her, close enough to touch.

"Now I know what it's like to be a bird," she said to Bergeron, giving him a hug. "I was flying!"

As she became more comfortable in the tight harness around her, she tested her ability to turn for a better view of the quickly passing scenery. She was focused as much on the natural beauty around her as she was on the runs. Being a hundred miles north of Nashua – and at a higher altitude – autumn's progress was more pronounced, with more color in the trees and brisker temperatures.

It's wonderful, she kept thinking. *And it was Lou's idea. He wanted me to share this.*

The final 'zip' covered nearly a third of a mile and she was warned that her speed could reach forty miles an hour. At her guide's urging, she cannonballed off the platform and then spread her arms as she raced to the bottom of a steep ravine and back up the other side. Just as she thought she would crash into a tree on the other side of the ravine, her forward progress abruptly slowed and stopped, and she began traveling backward toward the base of the ravine. She gave into the rocking motion and closed her eyes, smelling the pine and fir around her.

I could do this every day.

When she came to a rest, she was ten feet above a platform. A ladder was wheeled out, and she descended to the ground. She threw her arms around Bergeron. "I can't remember when I had a more perfect day," she whispered.

"It's not on the original itinerary, but I can take you one more place," Lou said as they walked back toward his truck.

"If you want to take me there, it's fine with me," Lynn said.

"It's an hour from here, and it's a world away," he said. "But if you want to know me, you ought to see it for yourself."

Lynn hugged his waist. "I want to know you," she said simply.

They got in the truck. "Next stop, Berlin," Lou said.

* * * * *

At 10 p.m., Tony D'Alessio, stiff from having sat in the car all day, made a call to Aidan Parker in Boston. He had seen neither movement nor lights in the house all day. He had even broken in a second time, listening for the sound of human occupation and looking for an itinerary or evidence of where the man might have gone. He heard and found nothing.

"He ain't come back," D'Alessio told Parker. "This guy either took it on the lam or else he's gone for the weekend. Either way, we're wasting our time. Instead of sending some guy up here to camp out, why don't you let me pick it up in the morning? I really want to see this job through to the end."

Parker agreed. "Be in place at his office by seven. Snatch him and bring him back alive, that's all I ask. You can hurt him if you want, but leave the best part for me. Gerry was a good man. I owe him to take care of his murderer personally."

21.

Monday, September 24

He was awake before 4 a.m., brimming with energy and eager to get the day underway. He needed to be in the office early in order to get his purchase orders into the system before his presence and movements were noted. *This might well be the most important day of my life*, he thought.

He showered and shaved using the hotel's deluxe amenities kit, ordered a room service breakfast, and reluctantly donned his old clothes. This was indeed his lucky day, but he didn't want to stand out at SoftRidge by being seen in expensive clothing. At five, he was in his car and pulling out of the hotel garage. Before 6:30, he was in his office, logging invoices into the system.

In a little over an hour, he created $273,000 of perfectly reasonable accounts payable and lodged them into the appropriate expense categories. It was, he knew from the sales brochures and his talks with the boat brokers, almost exactly what a new, superbly-equipped 30-foot cabin cruiser would cost.

* * * * *

Bergeron awakened first, the first hint of dawn just starting to redden the eastern sky. He rolled over and kissed Lynn's bare shoulders. She stirred and murmured something, a smile on her face. He kissed her shoulder again and ran his hand down her back until he reached her buttocks, which he rubbed gently.

Lynn raised her head from the pillow, smiled, and rolled over, throwing her arms around him.

"You trying to start something, mister?"

"I wish," he said. "I've got to go home and get a uniform. I'm supposed to be at the barracks at 7:30."

Lynn nodded, wiping the sleep from her eyes. "Damn," she said. "You get a girl used to something, then you change the rules."

He embraced her, feeling the warmth of her body. *It's never been like this*, he thought. *It's never been even remotely like this. It was always the same: I couldn't wait to leave. I didn't have anything to say in the morning. But this is different: I could stay here all morning. All day. If only...*

"Lynn, I've never had such a good weekend," he said. It was simple. It summed up his feelings.

She smiled. "Neither have I."

He felt his heart racing. *Say something now or you'll never have the courage to say it.* "I don't know what's going to happen this week, or after this week. But I want to see you again. I have no idea of how we could work it or..."

She pressed her finger to his lips. "Me, too. I've waited a long time for something like this. We'll figure it out. Right now, you need to get yourself out of here."

He held her tightly. *We'll figure it out*, she had said. *We'll figure it out.*

He had taken her home. Home to where he had been born. A home he had left behind at nineteen, that he had returned to after the Army only out of respect for his grandmother and then only for a day or two each month. He had felt no compunction to return since his grandmother's funeral six months earlier.

It had been a beautiful ride across the mountains. Autumn was in its glory on the mountainsides. But as they dropped from Mount Crescent to the Androscoggin River Valley, the natural riches of the mountains gave way to the hardscrabble reality of a dying region. Boarded-up businesses lined the highway, old houses with peeling paint dotted the side streets. The old paper mills, the last industrial employers, were silent. Some had even been dismantled and carted away for scrap, leaving behind piles of broken concrete and weeds.

They had driven by his old house, now occupied by one of his brothers who found sporadic work as a carpenter. The porch screens were torn and the yard grown up in weeds. Lou slowed but did not stop. The high school was new, a project undertaken more to provide construction employment than because of educational need. The former high school he had attended was now a middle school. The old haunts were gone, their windows streaked, the 'for rent' signs warped and faded. His grandmother's home, old even by Berlin standards, sported a Realtors' sign in the front yard. There had been few lookers and no offers.

"This is why I had to leave," he had told her. "If I stayed, I'd end up like my brothers."

Lynn had squeezed his hand. "It was the right decision," she said. "You made the only sensible decision a smart person could make. You've no cause for regret."

* * * * *

Claude Johnson badly needed a shower, a shave, and a decent meal. The blacked-out windows made it difficult to assess the passage of time, but he sensed that it must be morning and that he had been in this room for nearly thirty-six hours.

He knocked on the door. As he had done each time before, he stepped back as soon as he heard footsteps in the hallway and put on his blindfold. The door opened a crack.

"I think I need to speak to the head guy," Johnson said.

The man who opened the door grunted. "I think so, too," the man said. "We're all getting pretty tired of this."

Johnson parsed what the man had said while he waited for the door to re-open. 'We're getting pretty tired of this' could be interpreted several ways, not all of them benign.

After fifteen minutes, Aidan Parker opened the door and walked in.

"You can take off the blindfold, detective," Parker said. "We're wondering if your friend has flown the coop. Our guy has been up there since Saturday, but there's been no sighting. We started staking out his home and his office yesterday morning. He hasn't been in either place. Do you think he might have discovered someone was onto him and taken it on the lam?"

Johnson shook his head. "He's a business executive. He may have spent the weekend away, but he has to be at work this morning.

I interviewed him at his office last week before I knew what he had done and he was one cool customer. He didn't give away anything. And, with Griffin's arrest, he probably thinks he's gotten away clean."

"But as to running, these guys are under tremendous pressure to get a deal done this week," Johnson added. "Unless he's at the bottom of a chasm, he's going to be at his desk this morning."

Parker nodded.

"Any chance I can get out of here? They're going to miss me at work this morning."

Parker smiled. "You'll leave when I say you can leave. We've treated you well, haven't we?"

"I could use a shower."

Parker smiled again, then spoke to the man outside the door. "This fellow needs a shower. Do you think you could arrange something?"

* * * * *

At 7 a.m., Tony D'Alessio positioned his car outside of SoftRidge's offices to see the faces of people as they went in. He was surprised, however, to see more than a dozen vehicles already in the parking lot with several arriving ahead and behind him. He was used to work beginning at 9 a.m. or later, and had expected to get through the Boston *Herald's* sports section before anyone arrived. Instead, he put aside the paper, and began his watch.

* * * * *

Bergeron arrived at the Bedford barracks at 7:30, and was immediately pulled into Captain Sam Hurley's office.

"Claude has disappeared," Hurley said. "Dropped off the face of the earth, and that's not like him. He's a guy who usually checks in with someone every few hours. We've left a dozen messages on his phones. I even sent a car around yesterday to check on his house. He hasn't been home."

Bergeron explained that he had turned over the photos of the four most likely suspects to Johnson Saturday at about five o'clock

Saturday afternoon. "A couple of high-probability places said I needed to come back when the evening crew was around, sir. Claude said he thought he could short-circuit the process and volunteered to show them around."

Hurley drummed his fingers on his desk and whistled. "We've got a guy who hired someone to run those two women off the road and to attack the one woman in her hotel room. We can be reasonably certain he killed Gavrilles. And he probably was the one who pushed the Boston hood who hired Catalano under that semi."

"More than just probably, sir." Bergeron said. "When I went down to Boston Saturday morning, I tried to link up with the Boston PD. They essentially threw me out. Claude said the reason they did that was because they don't want anything that smacks of multi-state cooperation because it invites the feds to take over. The Feds are already trying to horn in because the Boston guy was organized crime. I asked if they had the personal effects of Gerry Sullivan – that's the guy who got pushed under the truck. They said they did, and I just wanted to know if it included a cell phone and did they know the number. That's when they threw me out. But while I was still in earshot, I called the number. It rang somewhere in the homicide bureau."

"Smart thinking," Hurley said and smiled. "Probably drove the bastards up the wall. But what's to say that our perp didn't follow Claude down to Boston?"

"There are security cameras all over Quincy Market, sir." Bergeron said. "I know he was going to start around seven. I could go over them this morning."

"I've got a fishing buddy who is 'way up there in the chain of command at the Mass State Police," Hurley said. "I can get Claude's photo and the four perps down to them in a couple of minutes. They'll give me a call with any video that shows Claude."

"I'd still like to go," Bergeron said.

Hurley shook his head. "I admire the determination, but you do this: you get back down to that company. You sit, face-to-face with those four guys, and you establish where they were Saturday evening. Then, you call me with anything – and I mean anything – that doesn't smell right. And if my friend comes back with something, you get ready to make an arrest."

Bergeron nodded. "Yes, sir. I'll show you how to pull up the photos of the four men Claude was going to show in Quincy Market."

"One more thing before we do," Hurley said, and Bergeron stopped. "Claude was very impressed with you. Not just guessing that Catalano might be going back to the hotel – which was really good intuition on your part – but your whole effort. He doesn't impress easily, and he said you're wasting your time on patrol."

"That's very kind of him, sir."

"When this is all over, we're going to talk about career moves," Hurley said. "But right now, let's get Claude back safely.

Bergeron showed Hurley the four photographs on the SoftRidge web site. By the time Bergeron left for SoftRidge, Hurley was emailing the material to his fishing buddy.

* * * * *

To Lynn, this Monday morning was like leading a well-tuned and thoroughly rehearsed orchestra. Deb had insisted on staying to the end, efficiently giving a stream of orders to the two associates who fetched, carried, and processed papers as a prodigious rate. Lynn, in turn, kept the three of them busy. Exhibits for the contract grew into coherent piles, and she continually reviewed both newly completed materials and that which had been complied in the previous week. It was an intensely satisfying feeling.

Perhaps because of Lynn's energy, or perhaps because an end was now in sight, the lawyers and accountants were all pitching in with equal fervor. Company management was pushing to get the job done, though their efforts carried the imprint that, should their efforts be less than satisfactory, Ross Maynard might pull the plug. This was Monday. Everyone's goal was to have the exhibits completed and signed off on by Thursday evening. At this morning's rate of work, Thursday might be a leisurely day, making the target of closing the transaction on Friday the 28th or Saturday the 29th an easy-to-meet deadline.

Even SoftRidge's investment bankers, the three-person team from Highsmith & Co., who had spent the previous week drinking coffee, checking email, and telling lewd jokes to one another were engaged. They responded to queries and now seemed to know the company's files as well as management.

"Somebody must have really put the fear of God in them," Deb noted to Lynn at one point as a Highsmith associate rushed off to accommodate a request.

Oddly, the senior-most banker, Josh Tilighman (whom everyone called 'Tillie' in his absence) wore a large bandage on his head. He had sustained it, he said, when someone threw a rock from an overpass as he drove up to Nashua Sunday morning. His attitude was the most changed. He was eager to help, but he also eyed with suspicion everyone with whom he came in contact. Commenting on his odd behavior, Deb said it was as though Tilighman had discovered his wallet missing and was looking for a person with a guilty countenance.

Through all of this, Lynn never lost sight of two things. The first was that one of the members of the SoftRidge management team had tried to arrange to have her killed or at least injured. The second was that somewhere in this great pile of paper was a scam. One of these outwardly friendly and helpful managers had devised a way to illegally siphon several million dollars from the sale. And, thus far, she did not have any idea of who it was or how they intended to carry it off. Every figure had tied properly to financial statements, every contract was in order. Whatever it was, it was extremely well hidden.

Moreover, Ross Maynard kept throwing in new assignments. This morning, he had left a lengthy voice mail message demanding that every name on every patent issued to SoftRidge in the previous decade be annotated. Was the name on any patent that of an employee? Were they still an active employee? And, if they were not, where were they now working?

SoftRidge had over thirty patents that met the ten-year definition, plus three more pending registration. A few patents were to individuals, but most had between three and six names. And, while certain names recurred, Lynn guessed that there were upwards of fifty current or former employees that had to be tracked down. Each would have to be presented with a document asking them to waive any rights under the patent. In theory, the original patents had been assigned to SoftRidge and the employees had already given up such rights. Requesting a waiver letter was just extra, and perhaps pointless, protection along with additional work.

A few minutes after eight, she was surprised to glimpse Lou Bergeron in the lobby. He had said he would be back on patrol today, disappointed that his career as a detective was to be so brief. If he were here today, though, it meant he was being entrusted with additional assignments. She smiled, pleased for him.

But she could not go out to meet him, and the conference room door was kept closed to ensure privacy. Two managers, Frank Kepner and Jeff Wright, were at her side; Deb and two Clarenden associates were at the table, reviewing spreadsheets updated over the weekend. Kepner was responding to questions about manufacturing invoices, Wright was providing employment dates for patent holders. In their zeal to help – prompted by Maynard's threat to walk away from the deal if they did not lend full assistance – and their desire to get the deal done, they were talking over one another, vying for Lynn's attention.

"Lynn, I've done a spreadsheet of the employees whose names are on patents. What kind of contact information do you want for employees who have left the company? Last known addresses and phone numbers as of when they left, or do you want me to try for more current data?"

"Lynn, I've done a chronological listing of outstanding vendor invoices but I've only brought it up to last Friday. Do you want orders done today and through the 30th, or will you do that as a supplemental schedule?"

Lynn waved through the closed door of the conference room glass at Bergeron, who either could not or did not see her. *Well,* she thought, *I'll see you tonight and we will make love until we're both too tired to go on.* That she could have such thoughts was astonishing. That she could have such thoughts about a man whom she had known for less than a week was beyond belief. That she could care so much for a man was thrilling. She listened to the competing requests and answered them calmly. But as she did, she imagined herself, under the duvet in her hotel room with Lou. She could not remember when she had been so happy.

She was sufficiently preoccupied with attempting to catch Bergeron's attention that she did not see the pile of papers slide off the table until the first dozen pages hit the floor. And, while everyone scrambled to their hands and knees to pick them up, she did not notice a powder being poured into the large cup of Dunkin' Donuts coffee in front of her. Nor did she or anyone notice a hand reaching into her purse and placing something in it.

* * * * *

Tony D'Alessio watched the arrival of a state police cruiser in front of SoftRidge's entrance. The trooper who emerged from the vehicle looked young; too young, almost certainly, to have any seniority in the state police organization. In fact, the young man looked like an ordinary traffic cop. Detectives dressed in suits and ties. This man was in the dark green jacket and gray pants uniform and carried his Smokey-the-bear hat under his arm.

If this trooper was here to arrest the same man as D'Alessio sought, the trooper would have to be disabled, even killed if necessary. But Gerry Sullivan's death had taken place in Boston and so would be investigated by Massachusetts police. This man, Tony concluded, was here on some other business. He could be ignored and would likely be gone in a few minutes. Tony went back to watching the passage of people into and out of the front entrance.

His man had still not shown his face.

* * * * *

Bergeron walked briskly to the reception desk, presented his card, and asked to speak to Larry Driscoll. To Driscoll, he said needed to meet with Sandy Calo, Frank Kepner, Paul Fuller and Jeff Wright. He needed to speak with them individually and immediately.

Driscoll saw the look of urgency on Bergeron's face. "Let's use my office," he said.

Paul Fuller, the sales and marketing vice president was the first to come in. Bergeron dismissed him almost immediately. "How old are you, Mr. Fuller?" he asked.

"Thirty-two," was Fuller's reply.

"And where did you grow up?"

"Minneapolis."

"When did you first come to New Hampshire?"

"About five years ago."

Bergeron made the decision that Fuller was not his man. He was too young to have known Joey Gavrilles even if he were lying about having grown up in the Midwest. Bergeron thanked Fuller and said he had no further questions.

Jeff Wright, the head of human resources, was next.

"How old are you, Mr. Wright?" Bergeron asked.

"Forty," Wright said.

The same age as Joey Gavrilles, Bergeron thought. "And where did you grow up?"

"Here in Nashua," Wright said, and grinned. "Local boy makes good."

Bergeron's heart beat faster. "I need to know where you were Friday evening and Saturday evening."

Wright cocked his head. "That seems like a very long time ago. I was here late on Friday, probably until ten."

"And after ten?"

"I went home. I was wiped out. And then Saturday morning, we were all back here before eight to hear the wonderful news that we're all working for minimum wage. I think I was here until four."

"I asked about Saturday evening – say between seven and midnight," Bergeron asked. He studied Wright's reactions carefully, including where he looked as he answered.

Wright crossed his legs and looked up at the ceiling. "Saturday night… let me think… I was very tired and more than a little depressed." Wright's gaze returned directly to Bergeron. "Frankly, I hit the bottle. By the time it got dark, I was out of it. Drunk. Feeling sorry for myself. I awakened with a hell of a hangover on Sunday."

An alibi with no way to prove or disprove its veracity, Bergeron thought.

"Let's go back to Friday evening," Bergeron said. "After you went home, did you do anything in your home? Make a phone call. Use the computer. Anything that would allow us to confirm that you were, in fact, at home."

Wright thought a second, then shook his head. "Not that I can remember. It was late. I had already written all the emails I needed to write here in the office."

"How about Saturday night?"

"I turned on television, but don't ask me what I watched," Wright said. "Does that leave a record?"

"Did you order a pay-per-view movie? Call out for a pizza? Leave the house to get more liquor?"

Wright shook his head rapidly. "No. None of that. I'll be completely honest with you. Look, I drank myself into a stupor. I think anyone here would have done exactly the same thing under the circumstances, and most of us did."

Out of questions and running out of time, Bergeron said he could go.

"You have Bill Griffin," Wright said. "Why are you still questioning us?"

"Because…" And then Bergeron thought of another question. "Where specifically in Nashua did you grow up?"

Wright looked at Bergeron oddly. "What the hell kind of

question is that?"

"Please, Mr. Wright. I don't have time. Where in Nashua did you grow up?"

"On Lock Street. East of Chandler."

Less than a mile from Joey Gavrilles, Bergeron thought.

"If I say the name Joey Gavrilles, does that mean anything to you?"

Wright shook his head. "No. Nothing. Should it?"

"The two of you may have gone to high school together."

Wright shrugged. "I threw away my yearbook a long time ago. That was a different life."

* * * * *

Sandy Calo, SoftRidge's chief financial officer, sat down across from Bergeron. He was fidgeting, looking at his watch.

"I'll try to make this quick," Bergeron said. First, I need your age and I need to know where you grew up."

"I just turned forty-two," Calo said. "I was born in New York and raised on Long Island. What the hell do you need that kind of information for?"

Bergeron ignored the question. "And where were you Saturday night – say from 7 p.m. onward?"

"Listening to my wife scream at me."

"When we talked before, you said she was in Connecticut with some relative," Bergeron said, confused.

"When you call your spouse and tell her that one of your direct reports just tried to embezzle a couple of million dollars from the company and that your career is in jeopardy as a result, it tends to get them headed home in a big hurry."

"So your wife was with you, at home, Saturday evening."

"That's what I said. Can I go now?" Calo stood up.

"That's it for now," Bergeron said.

Calo left without further word.

It was several minutes before Frank Kepner, the head of manufacturing showed up.

"Sorry, it's kind of crazy out there," Kepner said.

"I'll try not to hold you too long," Bergeron said and motioned for Kepner to take a seat.

"How old are you and where did you grow up?"

Kepner laughed. "Man, you guys must have a lot of spare time on your hands."

"Please just answer the question."

"I'm thirty-nine. I grew up here."

"In Nashua?"

"Yeah, in Nashua. Is that all?"

"Where, exactly?" Bergeron pressed.

"You're fooling with me, right?" Kepner uncrossed his legs and leaned forward.

"What street?"

"On Gordon, hard by the cemetery."

Another one very close to Gavrilles, Bergeron thought. *And also the right age.* "I need for you to account for your whereabouts Friday after you left here and Saturday evening – say from 7 p.m. onward."

Kepner loosened and retied his shoes, not looking at Bergeron. "Friday night, I left here so late I stopped and got a pizza, went home and crashed. Saturday, after the workathon, I headed north up to Franconia Notch and camped. I spent all day Sunday hiking and was there until this morning. I just drove back a few hours ago."

"Let's start with the pizza," Bergeron said. "Where did you buy it?"

Kepner looked confused. "Some place on the Daniel Webster Highway. I didn't pay attention. Pizza Hut, Papa John's. They're all alike. It's all pizza."

"Did you charge the pizza? Is there a chance you have a receipt for it?"

Kepner shrugged. "I always pay cash. I just throw away the receipt. It isn't like I need it for my taxes. Can I go now? I've got six people screaming for my attention."

Bergeron gritted his teeth. "You'll go when I say you can go.

Let's talk about Saturday night. You drove up to the mountains. Did you go with anyone?"

Kepner exhaled, a sigh of annoyance. He shook his head. "Hiking and camping are solitary activities for me. Some people need the company. I'm the opposite. I go by myself because I *want* to be by myself."

"You must have bought gas."

"Started with a full tank. It shows about half down. You're welcome to go out and look."

"What about a camping permit? Anything you bought during the day that proves you were up there?"

Kepner looked out the window and squinted. "I don't camp in the campgrounds. It's expensive and it's noisy. I pack along my own stuff. I used a bathroom at a McDonald's on the way up, and also on the way down. I'm not sure which one, though."

"Tolls," Bergeron said. "Do you have EZPass?"

"I'm probably the only guy in New Hampshire who doesn't. I still throw quarters into the basket."

Another guy with an uncheckable alibi, Bergeron thought. *Let's take it down a different path.* "Do you remember a high school classmate named Joey Gavrilles? He lived near you."

"Gavrilles," Kepner said, repeating the name to himself. "No, the name doesn't ring a bell. But then I haven't been exactly the keep-up-with-the-reunion-committee type. Sorry, can't help you on that one."

"May I have permission to go through your car?" Bergeron asked. "I'd be looking for receipts, trash, anything that might establish your alibi." He added, "It's in your best interest."

"Knock yourself out," Kepner said, taking keys out of his pocket.

Bergeron's intended next question was interrupted by shouts coming from the direction of the lobby. He heard 'Help!' and 'Call 911!'

He raced for the lobby.

22.

At first, Lynn had felt euphoric, akin to getting an unexpected second wind. She felt a rush of energy through her, as though she had somehow turbo-charged her entire body. She responded to questions without hesitation and snapped off instructions to Deb and the two associates. Her speech became rapid and everyone around her seemed to move in another, slower, dimension. She drank more coffee and, though it tasted slightly bitter, she put it down to the little containers of half-and-half which had probably soured. She added another packet of sugar.

The heightened sense of awareness lasted perhaps ten minutes. Deb, who had looked at her strangely for several minutes, asked, "Are you OK?"

Suddenly, Lynn did not feel OK. "I don't know," she said. "I think I'm getting a headache." And, in fact, Lynn felt a horrendous headache coming on.

"Lynn, you probably need to lie down," Deb said.

Lynn snapped back. "I don't need to lie down, and I don't need your help!" But she was becoming dizzy and felt hot.

Lynn stood up, holding the table for support, and tried to take a step. The headache was worsening. Suddenly, a wave of nausea overcame her, and she retched onto the papers on the table.

"Oh, crap," Lynn said. And then she collapsed. She lay on the floor, convulsing.

Deb opened the conference room door and screamed at the receptionist, "Call 911!"

One of the associates ran out into the lobby yelling, "We need help!"

A few seconds later, Bergeron ran into the conference room. He was stunned to see that it was Lynn who needed help.

"What happened?" he asked Deb as he turned Lynn over on her

back. He pulled up an eyelid. Her eyes were fully dilated. She skin was almost hot to the touch and her pulse was racing.

"She started acting strange about ten minutes ago, like she was on some incredible high," Deb said. "She was just jabbering away, faster and faster. Then, she said she was getting a headache. And then this."

"Amphetamine poisoning," Bergeron said, taking her pulse, which was racing. "But how?"

Deb shook her head.

"We need to get her to throw up again before she metabolizes any more of the stuff," he said. "Help me."

Together, they got Lynn to her knees and help her up. Bergeron put a finger into her mouth. Lynn retched immediately, then gagged.

"I've called for an ambulance," Deb said.

Lou shook his head. "I can get her to St. Joe's before an ambulance gets here. Let's go."

Bergeron carried her out of the building. He laid Lynn in the back seat of his cruiser with Deb, who held her head up. He squealed out of the parking lot.

"Patch me through to St. Joe's emergency," he told the dispatcher. "I've got an amphetamine poisoning case. I'm taking the victim there."

"St. Joseph's," came a response, almost immediately.

"This is Trooper Lou Bergeron. I'm bringing in a female, late twenties, with amphetamine poisoning. I should be at the ER entrance in about three minutes. I need a gurney and activated charcoal treatment as soon as she gets in."

"Sir, what's the basis of your diagnosis?" the ER operator asked.

"Because I saw it about fifty times while I was in the Army." He threw on his siren to move through a traffic light.

"Deb, has Lynn ever taken speed?"

"No!" Deb said. "I've been with her on lots of these road jobs, and she's never taken anything. Oh, God, she's shaking again."

"Dispatch, you need to get another unit to SoftRidge on Spit

Brook Road. They need to sweep the conference room for anything that might have been a drug delivery system. They also want to search the offices of two employees, Frank Kepner and Jeff Wright, and look for any traces of amphetamines, particularly in their desks or briefcases. If they object, then detain them until we can get a warrant."

Bergeron final call was to Captain Hurley. "Someone fed her a massive dose of speed. Frank Kepner and Jeff Wright are both the right age and grew up in the right neighborhood to have known Gavrilles. It's almost certainly one of those two guys. I've asked dispatch to get someone over to SoftRidge to check out the conference room and the offices of the two guys."

He finished the conversation as he pulled into the ER ambulance area. Three people were standing by with a gurney. Bergeron shouted instructions as the EMTs lifted Lynn out of the police car.

Deb came to his side. "Is she going to be OK?" she asked.

Bergeron put his arm around her. "We got her here the fastest way available and we got as much of the speed out of her stomach as possible before her body could metabolize it. I saw more than my share of this in the service. I never lost one of my guys, I'm not going to lose her."

"I heard you say to someone that it was Kepner or Wright," Deb said. "Both of them were in the conference room with Lynn this morning."

"Anything unusual happen while they were in the room?"

"No," she said, then reconsidered. "Well, one thing. There was a lot of commotion – a lot of people circling around asking questions. A pile of papers went over and onto the floor. We were all scrambling to pick them up."

"Why was that unusual?"

"Because – at least the way I remember it – the papers weren't teetering on the edge of the table or anything. They just fell off the table."

"Were both men in the room?"

Deb thought for a second. "I'm not sure. It wasn't a big deal at the time. Just an example of how much of a circus it was."

"Was Lynn drinking or eating anything?"

"Coffee. Lots of coffee. We stopped and got a couple of those big cups at Dunkin' Donuts."

"Anything to eat?"

"Lynn's been staying away from the food." Deb smiled. "I think you may have had something to do with that."

"So no pastries? No sandwiches in the conference room?"

"There was a big plate of donuts in the room. I think one of the accountants brought them this morning. I'm pretty sure Lynn didn't have one."

Bergeron opened the door of the patrol car and picked up the microphone. "Dispatch, has anyone been sent to SoftRidge?"

There was a silence, then, "Two detectives are in transit now."

"They want to look in the main conference room for a large Dunkin' Donuts coffee cup that Lynn Kowalchuk would have used. They definitely want to bag it and any coffee still in it for evidence."

"I've also got Captain Hurley for you."

The captain was on the radio quickly. "Good news and bad news," he said. "The Mass state police guys found a surveillance video of Claude almost immediately. The time code was a quarter past seven on Saturday night. The bad news is that he was intercepted by two men who the state police say are local hoods – part of some Irish mafia. We're checking, but we think they're associates of the late Gerry Sullivan."

Bergeron's mind raced. "Which means Claude got a hit on the identity somewhere, and these guys wanted the information. Would Claude have given it to them?"

"Lou, that's not the kind of question you ask. Just get back to my office as quickly as you can."

Bergeron slapped his forehead. All of these calls were logged and recorded. And the answer was obvious: if Johnson had withheld the name of the person identified, he might well be dead now. If he surrendered it, he was breaking police policy, though it was unlikely any action would ever be taken against him.

"I'll be there in a few minutes," Bergeron said. Then, to Deb he said, "You've got to stay with her until she's out of danger." He gave her his cell phone number. "Call me as soon as there's any word."

Deb nodded. "This is where I'll be for as long as it takes."

* * * * *

Tony D'Alessio watched the state trooper carry out a woman in his arms. The trooper's face showed considerable fear. It struck D'Alessio as very odd that the trooper had walked in as if on ordinary business but come out carrying someone who had been injured. This was not his concern, however. What he now understood was that employees had stopped coming into the building. The man he sought had apparently arrived as one of those first cars.

Twenty minutes later, D'Alessio watched as a second New Hampshire state trooper car arrived, this one with two men in suits carrying evidence collection equipment. They walked, rather than rushed inside, indicating they were going to a crime scene, but not an ongoing police action. But the man he was after had not come out. This was all that mattered.

D'Alessio had listened carefully to the instructions from Aidan Parker. He was to bring the man back alive. This limited his options. In the best case, the man would come out of the building, on his own, for some reason. Tony would knock him out, put him in the trunk of his car, and take the man to a place where Parker could have his revenge. But there was nothing in Parker's instructions that said the man needed to be completely unharmed. Gerry Sullivan had been his mentor. D'Alessio would get a little revenge of his own.

Two hours passed before the detectives left the building with evidence crates. Tony D'Alessio continued to wait. He was nothing if not a patient man.

* * * * *

It's all going wrong, he thought. *How in the hell could things go so wrong so quickly?*

He had been at the office a few minutes after six. He had processed the invoices. They were safely in the system. He had increased his ultimate take to more than four and a half million dollars without any additional risk.

Lynn and the other woman and their gang of junior woodchucks had shown up around 7:30, and he was ready for her. He had crushed fifteen of the amphetamine tablets into a fine powder while reserving another half dozen to slip into her purse. The powder would go into whatever she was drinking.

In his scenario, he would slip her the lethal dose, then leave the conference room and go back to his office. He would return to the room only when it was clear she was in distress. The medical information he had gathered indicated she could go into cardiac arrest within minutes and be dead before an ambulance arrived. He might even be the one who administered the futile CPR while everyone else stood by, wringing their hands.

It had started well enough. He had ample reasons to go into the conference room and did so with a crowd. Crowds were good because they allowed him free movement without being observed. She was gesturing to someone out in the lobby, trying to attract that person's attention. She had a large cup of coffee in front of her, a perfect delivery vehicle for the amphetamines.

Then, one of the junior woodchucks dropped a couple of sheets of paper on the floor and he had the perfect idea of how to get the speed into her coffee. He nudged a larger pile close to the edge of the table, then gave one more innocuous tap to them and they went flying. It was a wonderful sight as everyone scrambled to pick up paper. The powder was in her coffee in the blink of an eye and he stooped down to help gather papers. The drugs were slipped into her purse easily.

It was easy making these things happen around simpletons. He wondered why he had not done the same with other people who had gotten in his way over the years. He thought of how easily he had knocked out the idiot Tilighman with his pop gun. He smirked that Tilighman was telling everyone this morning that someone had thrown a rock at his car from an overpass. Tilighman would have awakened in the bushes, his head covered in blood, his gun nowhere to be seen. He would have driven himself to a hospital and invented the excuse to cover up what he had really been doing. It would have been delicious to see Tilighman telling his story with its improbable lies.

Once he had administered the drugs, he left the room and went back to his office. He felt exhilarated. He had executed the crime perfectly. In ten or fifteen minutes, she would have consumed the coffee. Before she knew what hit her, she would be in convulsions. And then her heart would stop. Cardiac arrest. The downside of being an investment banker. You take all that speed to get you through these things, and then you get a bad hit or just an overdose.

The police would find speed in her purse. They'd go to her hotel room and fine dozens of tabs in her luggage. *Poor girl,* they'd think. *What a shame. She had such a future.*

Ten minutes after he went back to his office, Larry Driscoll had stood in his doorway, unsmiling, delivering his instructions in something close to a monotone. "That state trooper from last week is back. He specifically wants to talk to you. Drop whatever you're doing and go to my office." The command had been delivered coldly, as though Larry knew what he had been up to.

What the hell was the trooper doing here? And then he realized that it was the trooper that the Polish Princess had seen through the conference room glass. She had seen her boyfriend arrive. That's who she was waving to.

There was still hope. The trooper might panic. The trooper might be inept at first aid. Or, the dosage he had administered might be high enough that she would succumb anyway. His best course of action was to go through the motions of finding out whatever it was that the trooper wanted, and then wait for all hell to break loose.

The disturbing thing about the trooper's interrogation was his desire to know where he had grown up. It was such a bizarre question. He had answered truthfully and noted that the trooper seemed to absorb the information with only a passing degree of interest. The trooper then asked if he had known Joey Gavrilles. Now the question made more sense. He had lied, and very smoothly, he thought. There was no reason why he should have known or remembered Joey. The blank look on his face was very convincing as were his answers about his whereabouts on Friday and Saturday evenings.

Then had come the cries for assistance. He had waited until he was certain there would be a crowd. He watched as the trooper carried the Polish Princess out to his car. The trip to an emergency room would be quicker than he had expected. Hopefully, though, not too much quicker.

Then he went into the conference room. His task was to retrieve the coffee cup, but accomplishing the mission was made more difficult both because of the crowd and the vomit on the floor. He was disturbed that so little coffee was gone from the container and hoped that Kowalchuk had topped up the cup at some point.

He took the cup back to the office's kitchen, threw the container's contents down the sink and washed the cup thoroughly before crumpling it and throwing it the trash receptacle. He then rejoined the crowd in the lobby and listened intently as people speculated on what might have happened to the young investment banker. No one suggested amphetamines. Eventually, he went back to his office and resumed his work.

But not without the feeling that things were going wrong, and that he might yet have to take final, direct and overt action.

* * * * *

"I'm going to make the assumption that you have no previous experience with methamphetamines?"

Lynn blinked her eyes, which at least were no longer so dilated as to make opening them in a lighted room painful. The headache was still there, though it, too, was abating. She looked at the doctor, then over at Deb.

"None," Lynn said.

"You were lucky," the doctor said, allowing a smile. He was an elderly Asian man, not the kind of person Lynn expected to see in an emergency room.

"You apparently lost most of what you ingested before it could metabolize," he said. "That's not uncommon for someone with no history of using speed. Miss Fowler tells me you were drinking coffee in the minutes before your incident and that you said the coffee tasted bitter."

Lynn nodded. Yes, the coffee's taste had been off, and she had added extra sugar.

"Miss Fowler believes you ingested only a few ounces of the coffee, which I'll assume was how the methamphetamines were delivered. She also said that the state trooper who came as soon as you collapsed also induced you to vomit a second time. That was extremely fortunate for you that there was someone assisting you who knew how to handle amphetamine poisoning."

Lynn tried to think. She remembered the sudden onset of the headache. She tried to stand and then she felt sick. After that? Nothing until she had awakened in the emergency room, IVs in her arm, monitors on her chest and a compress on her head.

The state trooper. Lou had been in the lobby. She had tried to get his attention. But he hadn't been there to see her. She looked over at Deb. "Lou found me?"

Deb smiled and nodded. "Your hero. Third time was the charm."

Lynn gave a wan smile and nodded, then closed her eyes. She tried to imagine him there, helping her, but couldn't. The blackout had been total.

"Working on the assumption that the speed was in your coffee and that you did not put it there yourself, there remains the question of how it got there," the doctor said. It wasn't exactly a question, but it seemed that he wanted a response.

"There were a lot of people in the room," Lynn said.

"Which is what Miss Fowler says. It is a police matter at this point. But you need to know that whoever did this did not intend for you to be answering these questions right now." The doctor let the words sink in before continuing. "Based on your reaction to the drug, that coffee cup contained what was probably a lethal dose of methamphetamines. You consumed a small amount and your body reacted quickly. Had you drunk the full cup – and Miss Fowler says it was a very large cup indeed – or if your body had built up a tolerance for the drug through prior use, you would have likely metabolized a lethal amount. I've seen cases where there was permanent brain damage. I've also seen a great many cases where the user's heart stopped."

Lynn heard the words. She was trying to take her mind back to the conference room. It was Deb and the two associates. Jeff Wright and Frank Kepner were there, bringing her papers and answering questions.

"Someone wants you dead, Miss Kowalchuk."

Someone wants you dead. What an incredible thing for someone say to you, she thought. *I've lived my entire life without making a real enemy or a real friend, and in one week, I meet someone whom I can fall in love with, and someone I barely know is trying to kill me.*

"They've tried twice before," Deb said. She pointed to her shoulder. "That's how I got this." Then, to Lynn, she said, "I promised Lou I'd give him a call as soon as I knew anything. I'm going to excuse myself for a few minutes."

When Deb left the room, the doctor continued. "Miss Fowler tells me you're an investment banker and that nothing like this has ever happened to you before. I'm not in the habit of giving this kind of advice to my patients, but I'll make an exception in your case. Miss Kowalchuk, the person who did this has no compunction about killing, and that person is apparently focused on killing you. The police are apparently already aware of this. I would stay as far as possible out of that person's path."

The doctor continued. "The police will catch this person. Miss Fowler seemed to indicate they are already very close. I would give this person the widest possible berth because, having failed, seeing you again could potentially have a catastrophic result."

Lynn looked at the doctor more closely. Fukiyama, the name badge said.

The doctor saw her looking, and smiled. "The light dawns," he said. "No, I'm not an ER doctor. I'm a little old for that and more than a little out of practice. The hospital's policy is that in any methamphetamine or drug-related admission, there's a psych consult requirement. Your friend and I talked for a while and I went over your chart carefully."

"You don't need a psych consultation because those drugs were not self-administered. But you are in need of some good advice. And my advice is this: get away from here. Have your friend take you to the airport and take the first flight home, and don't tell anyone where you're going."

Fukiyama took off his glasses and stared intently at her. "I don't make curbstone diagnoses as a general rule, but it seems to me that the person who did this may well be, at best, borderline psychotic. Seeing you again could possibly push him over the edge. That the person got close enough to you to put a dangerous drug in your coffee tells me that the individual is acting with increasing recklessness and disregard for his personal safety. It wouldn't surprise me to find that the person feels superior to you and to everyone around him. Right now, he thinks he's gotten away with it. He probably thinks you're lying here, now, in a coma or worse."

The doctor looked to see if his words were having the desired effect. Lynn's face showed comprehension, but not fear. "When that person learns that you're still alive, it's entirely possible that he'll panic. In cases like these, the person on whom they're fixated is the primary target, but they may perceive others as equally dangerous to them, and they'll act without regard for their own safety. Miss Fowler said that you've never worked with this company before and did not know anyone from it previously. That leads me to believe that the person who is trying to hurt you was already suffering from some form of mental impairment. You became that person's fixation, possibly the first time he saw you. His psychosis has deepened each time you've 'escaped' unharmed. That's why he's becoming more reckless. The need to act on this fixation is coming to a head."

"The sale of the company is supposed to be wrapped up this week," Lynn said.

"Let them wrap it up without you," the doctor replied, shaking his head. *Wrong response, Lynn.* "Don't give that person the opportunity to hurt you or anyone else. Let the police finish this."

"Could I leave now?" Lynn asked. "I mean, leave to go back to New York?"

The doctor consulted the chart. "I wouldn't drive, but the activated charcoal therapy seems to have neutralized the remaining drugs. The headache should abate over the next few hours. So, yes, you can leave. Provided you're headed for the airport and home."

Lynn nodded. "Thank you for the advice. I think I need to stay here a while longer. At least until my headache clears up."

The doctor smiled and then shook her hand. *Finally, the right response.* "Good luck, Miss Kowalchuk. But then, you seem to be blessed with it."

When Lynn was alone, she tested her ability to stand. There was a small amount of dizziness, but it quickly passed. She put her fingers in front of her eyes and made them meet. They touched the first time she tried. The headache, too, was disappearing much more quickly than she had let on. She reached over and touched her toes. No nausea.

She sat back on the examining table and thought back on her conversation with Fukiyama. *Someone wants you dead. Go home.* That was what it boiled down to.

And I am tired of being a victim, Lynn thought. *I am tired of being passive. I am not going to run away from this. It's one of those two guys. I'm going to nail the bastard and find out what they've done that makes killing me worthwhile.*

Her thoughts were interrupted by Deb, who was holding her cell phone out, trying to hand it to Lynn.

Lynn thought that it would be Lou Bergeron and she said, "Hi! They tell me I'm going to live, thanks to you."

She was not prepared to hear Ross Maynard's voice on the other end of the phone. "I just heard from Miss Fowler what happened," he said. "Thank God you're all right."

Lynn's words stumbled out. "Ummm, thanks for your concern, Mr. Maynard…"

"And I want you to know that we're going to get the depraved bastard who did this," Maynard said. "That company is full of sickos, and I'm going to clean it out, but I'm saving the worst for that bastard. We're going to get him, Lynn. We're going to make the state file every criminal charge that they can, and then we're going to go after him in civil court. By the time we're through with him, he's going to wish he were dead."

"Uhhh, thank you, Mr. Maynard…"

"It's Ross. I'm going to take care of this. That whole gang up there is going to pay for this…"

Lynn handed the phone back to Deb. "Tell him I'm lying down," she whispered. "Tell him anything. I don't want to talk to him."

An idea was forming in her mind. She needed some time to think.

23.

Lou Bergeron looked over Hurley's shoulder. They were in Hurley's office, viewing video on a computer screen as someone from the Mass State Police provided commentary over a conference call phone line.

"This was the camera at Cheers right after 7 p.m.," the voice said "Johnson goes in. He talks to several people. We're getting names of the people who were bartending Saturday evening and we'll go visit them this afternoon."

The video seemed to advance a frame every few seconds. From the left side of the frame, two men joined Johnson. One grabbed Johnson's arm. The other walked a pace behind, scanning the crowds for trouble. The video stream then switched to a new camera and the three men now walked straight on. "This is them about fifteen seconds later." The screen froze.

"This is our best shot of the two men. They're both local hoods, part of a mostly Irish outfit run by a goon named Aidan Parker. Gerry Sullivan was one of Parker's right-hand men. The gang steals anything in the Financial District that isn't welded down. While they're not as gratuitously violent as a lot of what's out there, they're thorough. When someone they're after disappears, the person stays disappeared. No bodies floating to the surface a week later."

"Where would they have taken Claude?" Hurley asked.

"They've got a network of houses and apartments around the city. We've got the two of them we know about staked out, but that's only been an hour or so," the voice on the other end of the phone said.

Hurley said, "So let's assume they got the information from Claude. We now know it's probably one of two guys at SoftRidge. Both of them are still alive and at work this morning. Why hasn't the guy been taken out?"

There was a moment's silence on the line. "Let's say Parker got the information Saturday night. He sent up some guys to watch his house and maybe the office. I've got some photos of the guys he'd likely send up for you to look at, by the way. Whoever they sent, they'd wait for your guy to show. If he didn't show, they'd switch teams and wait some more."

"So our guy may not have been home Saturday night or Sunday?"

"That's one possibility," the voice from Boston said. "The other is that there was a screw-up in communications. These hoods are trained to keep a low profile, strike quickly, and then get out. But, they're not always the smartest guys in the cell block. They're loyal and they're lethal, but some of them are downright stupid. They might have sent up a guy who promptly got lost. Their hit man might have gotten drunk. They might be staking out the wrong house or apartment right now. By the way, here are those photos."

Six photos appeared on the screen, all of them bookings prints. Hurley quickly pushed the computer's 'print screen' button.

Bergeron looked at the height marks for each man. All were in the 5'9" to 5'11" range except one, a bearded man who showed 6'6". "That top right guy would be hard to miss," Bergeron said.

"That's your token Italian," said the voice from Boston. "Anthony D'Alessio. He was supposed to have been with Gerry Sullivan the night he got croaked. A pair of uniformed Boston PDs got a verbal tip he was pickpocketing at Quincy Market. They found a knife on him, but no wallet except his own. The best guess is that Sullivan was going to meet your guy, then have D'Alessio mess with him. The guy saw D'Alessio first, put two and two together, and enlisted the two uniforms to detain him. Pretty smart thinking, actually."

"Would D'Alessio have seen our guy?" Bergeron asked.

"No way to know. The uniforms were walking him over to booking when Sullivan went under the truck. Your guy went back toward Congress Street. If D'Alessio were in the right place, he would have seen your guy go by. In any event, if he's part of the tag team, he's got your guy's full information now."

"What's the prognosis for Claude?" Hurley asked.

"I mentioned Aidan Parker," the voice said. "He's extremely well connected into Boston PD if you get my drift. He always seems to know when someone's looking for him. As a result, I've stayed well away from the department this morning because I don't want to inadvertently give Parker a heads up. From what I know of Parker, he's focused. If Johnson was straight with him, there's a very good chance he'll walk away from there with nothing more serious than a bump on the head – and the bump will be for Johnson's own deniability. If Johnson tries to pull anything, there's an equally good chance you'll never see him again. Parker gets very good legal advice and he understands the meaning of *habeus corpus* and *corpus delecti* very well. That's what I was saying about bodies staying disappeared."

"Claude's no hero," Hurley said. "He's been around too long."

"I hope so for his sake," said the voice.

"What about our guy's contact with Gerry Sullivan Friday night?" Bergeron asked. "Do we have video on that?"

"Boston PD impounded everything they could think of," the voice said. "If I go asking for it, I'm going to start opening cans of worms. You better need that video very badly before you start asking for it from them."

"We've got it down to two suspects," Hurley said. "Something will break."

The call concluded and Hurley asked Bergeron to be seated. "I've got a team over at SoftRidge right now collecting evidence," Hurley said. "But, while I know you asked me to do it, I can't hold the two guys. I even called over to the DA's office just to be certain. I can't get anyone to stretch 'probable cause' to your girl's poisoning based on what we've got right now. All we've got is your word that there was a poisoning attempt and that the drugs weren't self-administered. The two guys have responded thoroughly to your questions, so we have no right to bring them in."

Bergeron felt himself getting angry, his face growing red.

Hurley saw his rising ire. "Calm down," he said. "It's temporary. This is the way the world works. We'll analyze what we get from that conference room. If, as you suspect, it's speed, we'll know in a few hours. If it was in the coffee, that ought to throw out the self-administered accidental overdose argument. The minute I think I can reasonably detain either of those two guys, I'll send you in with full backup."

Bergeron appeared to lose the look of anger.

"I also take it that you know this Kowalchuk girl in more than a casual way?"

Bergeron answered the question with his voice in as much of a neutral tone as possible. "We went out on a date."

Hurley nodded slightly and leaned forward. "There's nothing in the official rule book about that, but I want you to know that, unofficially, it's not a career-building move. You were assigned to make certain no harm came to her and to get her back and forth to that office building."

"I was off duty Saturday and Sunday, sir," Bergeron said.

"You're never really 'off duty' in law enforcement, son," Hurley said. "It's just that sometimes you're in uniform and sometimes you're in civvies. If you like her, you wait until everything is over and done with. Then you ask her out on a date. Cops as ladies' men is something for television, not for real life. Do you understand?"

Bergeron felt his stomach sink. "I understand, sir."

"Lou, last week you proved you have a future here, and I don't mean burning gas on Route 3. A very small number of troopers get the chance to go for their detective shields. It takes experience, it takes test scores, it also takes recommendations. Right now, you're on that track. Keep up the good work. Don't screw it up."

Bergeron bit his lip, then said, "What's my assignment for the rest of the day?"

"Keep an eye on SoftRidge. If either one of your guys leave the building, call it in and follow them, but don't confront them. If you see any of the guys in this photo array hanging around that building, you call me immediately. Is that clear?"

Bergeron said it was clear.

* * * * *

"We're getting out of here," Lynn told Deb. "We need to get back to the hotel and get me into some fresh clothes. I stink."

"Using what for transportation?" Deb asked. "Our car is back at SoftRidge."

"Let's call a cab," Lynn said. "I may even charge it back to Ross Maynard. I think he owes me that much. And I'm starved. I feel like I haven't eaten in a week."

"You kind of left your breakfast on the conference room floor," Deb said. "And then you're going home?"

"And then we'll see," Lynn said. "I have one thing I need to finish up. Then I promise I'll go home."

* * * * *

Katie Laconda slumped in her minivan's front seat. She had driven to Nashua from Portsmouth that morning to make arrangements for her brother's funeral. It had been a horrible, depressing and stressful experience.

There was as yet no body, yet all of the decisions had to be made regarding caskets, liners, burial locations, hearses, flower cars, and a dozen other items. All of those decisions, all falling on her to choose without knowing what Joey would have wanted.

It had been different with her father. He was old and had been sick, and Joey had been there to help. Now, she was making those arrangements for Joey, who was just a year older than she. He was far too young to die, too young to lie beside his parents at Edgewood Cemetery.

Her car was stopped in front of the house she had grown up on Linden Street, the first time she had returned here in over a year. She wasn't prepared for the blackened ruin before her, or the lingering, acrid scent of burnt wood. The outline of the house was there, but the windows had blown out or had been broken as the fireman raced to douse the flames.

This was her house now, she imagined. There was no other family, and Joey had no one to whom he would have left it. The decision of what to do with the property was now also hers, just as she had been left with the responsibility for burying her brother.

She reached into her purse and fished out the state trooper's card. *Call me anytime*, he had said. She fingered the card on which he had written his cell phone number.

It isn't fair. It isn't right that Joey is dead, and it isn't fair that I have to do this on my own. And I have to carry around the guilt that I knew who may have killed him.

She felt the texture on the card, wondering if she was doing the right thing, knowing her husband would not approve. She reached for her phone and, through the tears, dialed the number handwritten on it.

* * * * *

As Bergeron drove down Route 3 from Bedford toward Nashua, his cell phone rang with a number he did not recognize. "Hello?" he said.

"This is Katie Laconda. Are you the trooper who came to see me on Saturday?"

He heard the sobbing through the voice on the other end of the line. "Yes, Mrs. Laconda. That was me."

There was only the sound of breathing on the other end of the phone, and then words choked with tears. "I didn't tell you everything when we talked. I did recognize somebody. I think I know who killed my brother."

"Who?"

"Can we talk? In person?"

Bergeron looked at his watch. It was noon. He had promised Captain Hurley he would keep watch over SoftRidge's office while analysis was done on what the crime scene team found there. Portsmouth was at least an hour away.

"Mrs. Laconda…"

"I'm in Nashua," she said. "I'm at my brother's house."

Jesus Christ, he thought. *She's five minutes away.*

"I'll be there in five minutes, he said.

* * * * *

At noon, a taxi pulled up in front of SoftRidge. Tony D'Alessio watched two women get out. His brow furrowed when he saw that one of the women was the one carried out of the building by the state trooper four hours earlier. The other was the blonde who had driven away with the trooper, caring for the woman in the back seat.

Nice recovery, he thought.

He continued his watch and noted with some satisfaction that people were starting to come out of the building for lunch. Some got into cars, some carried bags to picnic tables under trees at the far end of the building. He began flexing his fingers, getting ready to make his move.

* * * * *

Lynn's phone rang as soon as they were in the lobby. She looked at the phone's caller screen and saw it was Lou. An hour earlier, she would have thrilled at the call, at the attention, and at the voice on the other end of the line. Now, she was on a mission.

I will not be a victim, Lynn repeated to herself. *I will not be passive. I will not run away from this. It's either Wright or Kepner. They were in the conference room with me. Give me fifteen minutes and I can both nail the bastard my way and find out what he did.*

Lynn held out her phone. "You talk to him. I want to get this over with. Tell him I'll see him in a little while, when it's all finished."

Deb gave a look of disapproval but took the call and spoke for a minute.

"He was on his way over here," Deb said. "He's been told by his captain to keep an eye on the place, but he just got a call from some woman who says she recognized one of the managers. He wanted you to know he's 'that close' to having a name. He'll call you as soon as he has it."

Lynn nodded. *Stay close, my love, but let me do this on my own*, she thought.

"I need to speak to Larry Driscoll," Lynn told the receptionist. "It's worth interrupting him."

The SoftRidge chairman was in the lobby in under a minute. The look of concern combined with relief on his face was genuine. "What happened this morning?" he asked.

Lynn gave a dismissive wave of her hand. "Bad Chinese food last night, I'm told. I'm really sorry I made such a mess of the conference room." From the corner of her eye, Lynn saw the look of incredulity on Deb's face.

Driscoll's look turned to one of confusion. "I've had Ross Maynard on the phone screaming that someone was trying to poison you."

Lynn gave a look of exasperation. "I have no idea where he got that information. The emergency room said it was Kung Pao poisoning and told me to stay away from the duck sauce. I'll talk to Ross and let him know. I guess he's being a little over-protective after that incident with Bill Griffin."

"But there were two detectives here going over that conference room with a fine-toothed comb..."

Lynn shook her head. "Lou Bergeron. He's the trooper who was here this morning and took me to the hospital. The police more or less assigned him to me to make certain nothing else happened after the incident at the hotel. He's gotten kind of protective, too. I think it's an over-active imagination on everyone's part. Really, I'm fine."

"He questioned four of my managers this morning..." Driscoll said.

"Then I need to tell him to cut it out, too," Lynn said. "This is getting ridiculous. We all want to get this deal closed and I'm not helping things by barfing all over your conference room. Anyway, I have a great shortcut. If you can get me in front of two computers – Jeff Wright's and Frank Kepner's – I can copy off the files I need, do all of the final analysis tonight, and bless this deal on behalf of Clarenden. I absolutely promise."

Driscoll's face relaxed. "You don't know how glad I am to hear you say that," he said, gratefully.

"One final request," Lynn said. "It may seem strange, but after everything that happened over the weekend, I'd like a few minutes alone just to see which files I need. Your guys can be there when I copy them, of course, but I'd like to look at the big picture, without interruption. Deb also has some wrap-up questions. If she can do those, in your office with you and each of the managers individually, that would be ideal."

"Whatever you want," Driscoll said. "If it gets us to the finish line faster, it's better as far as I'm concerned. Besides, the computers and everything on them are SoftRidge property. You have *my* permission. That's all you need."

* * * * *

Bergeron pulled up to the blackened house, still encircled by yellow tape. A white minivan was parked in front of the home, Kate Laconda in the front seat.

"I had no idea it would be this hard," she said, looking down at her lap.

Bergeron stood by her door, uncertain of a response.

"He grew up a couple of blocks away from us. He and Joey were friends when they were growing up. I even dated him one summer. He was always a nice guy, but there was something about him…"

Don't force it, he thought. *Don't blow it again. Let her tell it at her own pace.*

"Do you know why he might have killed your brother?"

"Joey came for dinner a few weeks ago and said one of my old boyfriends had gotten in touch with him. I didn't ask him who and we let the subject drop. He and Joey were friends, but Joey used to kind of 'use' him. He was the 'good kid' Joey could show off to our parents. But as soon as someone from Joey's gang would show up,

Joey would drop him, just like that. I think he was hurt by that. They'd be playing Monopoly out on the porch and Joey would just get up and leave in the middle of a game. It was pretty rotten of Joey, I guess."

The porch, Bergeron thought. *Claude was right.*

"And now, because of me, I have to bury my brother."

"Why is that, Mrs. Laconda?"

She looked up at him. "Because I got pregnant when I was seventeen. Because of the abortion."

"He was the father?" Lou asked. *Gently*, he thought.

"No, I never slept with him. I wouldn't even... you know. But I turned to him when I found out I was pregnant. He helped me. But I realize that I shamed him. I embarrassed him. He thought I was his girlfriend, and all the time I'm sleeping with someone else. But he was the one who had to get me out of the jam. I never saw him after that. It's taken me all this time to realize why."

Bergeron saw that she was doing something in her lap. Holding something. Turning it over and staring at it.

"I don't think you are in any way responsible for your brother's death, Mrs. Laconda. I think he used Joey to help get someone out of the way. And, when that plan failed, he needed to cover his tracks. He killed Joey just like he had killed someone else earlier that night. He was just getting rid of witnesses."

"I could have trusted Joey," she said. "He wouldn't have told my parents. But I thought if they found out about the abortion and then found out that Joey knew, my dad would have killed Joey. But Jeff was so sweet, and I knew he cared for me."

Jeff, Bergeron thought. *Jeff Wright. I have the name.*

"I'll arrest him, Mrs. Laconda. He murdered two people. Your brother, and a man in Boston. He'll pay for that."

She shook her head. "And then there will be two trials. And I'd have to testify. And some attorney would ask me about the abortion. I know it. So everyone – including my children – will know what kind of a slut I was when I was a teenager."

"No, Mrs. Laconda. If he stands trial, it will be with a mountain of evidence from videotapes from Boston and the testimony of a local hood named Willie Catalano. There's no reason for you ever to appear in a courtroom or even be deposed." Lou did not know if any of this was true, but Katie Laconda was clearly distraught.

"I was going to kill him, you know," she said. "When you said all those photos were men from a company, I used Google Images and found that same photo on the internet. I know where the company is."

"Did you bring a gun, Mrs. Laconda?" *Stay calm. Be her voice of reason.*

"Yes."

Bergeron stood on his toes and looked into the minivan and saw a Glock in Katie Laconda's lap.

"Would you like me to take the gun, Mrs. Laconda?"

She shook her head. "I'm certain my husband will miss it."

"I think your husband is going to be proud of you," Bergeron said softly. "And he'll know it was OK that you gave it to me."

She hesitated a few moments, then, from her lap, picked up and handed him the Glock, barrel first. Bergeron checked the safety and put it in his pants pocket. "There isn't going to be a trial. Your past will stay your private affair. Go home, Mrs. Laconda. Stop at a McDonalds, wash your face, and get something to drink. Your brother deserves a good funeral."

The look of gratitude on Laconda's face caused Bergeron on add, "Everything you've told me says that, while he may have had his problems with the law, he was at heart a good man. That's the way he'll be remembered. If your family doesn't object, I'd like to be there. I think it's going to be a beautiful service."

She nodded, still sobbing, though more with the emotion of a great weight lifted from her.

"I'm going to go arrest Jeff Wright now, Mrs. Laconda."

She nodded. Thirty seconds later, the minivan pulled slowly out of the fire-blackened home's driveway on its journey back to

Portsmouth.

When the minivan was out of sight, Bergeron let out a sigh of relief. He had made up for rushing the first interview. He had prevented Katie Laconda from getting involved in an honor killing that would have found few sympathetic jurors.

He got in his patrol car and looked at his watch. SoftRidge was less than ten minutes away, less if he used his siren. He could be there by 12:15.

Now he knew who he was looking for.

* * * * *

Driscoll, Lynn, and Deb walked to Frank Kepner's office. Driscoll knocked and Kepner looked up. His eyes fell on Lynn and he blinked.

"I didn't think we'd be seeing you the rest of today," Kepner said, staring.

"Nobody wanted to mop up the conference room after me," Lynn said, smiling. "I had to come back and clean it myself."

Kepner kept staring.

"Deb has a few things to go over with you, and Larry asked to sit in. Is that OK?"

Kepner continued to stare. Then he said, "You appeared very ill this morning. I saw you. You were in convulsions."

Lynn shrugged. "Too much Chinese takeout, or at least that's what they told me at the emergency room. I'm fine now."

"Can we get this done, Frank?" Driscoll asked impatiently.

Kepner rose slowly from his desk, still looking at Lynn. He moved slowly to the door.

"Any time today, Frank," Driscoll said.

Lynn walked with them as far as Driscoll's office. "I'll be here if you need me," she said.

When Driscoll's door closed, she walked back to Kepner's office and closed the door behind her. From her purse, she extracted a large-capacity memory stick, a ubiquitous, pack-of-gum-sized tool of the investment banking and computer technology community. She plugged it into a port on the side of Kepner's computer. A moment later, a new folder appeared on the desktop of the computer. Lynn highlighted every folder on the computer desktop and dragged them into the new folder representing the 32 gigabytes of memory on the stick. Thirty seconds later, twelve gigabytes of material representing hundreds of files had been copied onto the memory stick.

Some of the files, she knew, would be password protected. As the files loaded onto the stick, Lynn looked on Kepner's desk, flipped the appointment book on the desk to the back pages and began thumbing forward. A few pages from the end were a series of neatly printed accounts and passwords.

Never underestimate the laziness of mankind, she thought to herself. She made a copy of the page at a nearby Xerox machine. She replaced the appointment book where she had found it, detached her memory stick and returned it to her purse.

In opening her purse she spotted the red pills.

The bastard planted evidence, she thought. *Dead girl on the floor with a load of speed in her purse for the police to find. These I need to get to Lou, just as soon as I'm through here.*

Kepner's office looked exactly as she had found it, and she left the room. Jeff Wright's office was down the corridor and she walked by it hoping he might be elsewhere in the building and she could avoid the subterfuge of having him sit with Deb and Driscoll.

Lynn found the office empty, a laptop computer open and in the middle of a document. She closed his office door behind her, sat down at his desk, and inserted the memory stick. She again copied all desktop files into the folder for the memory device.

As the copying progressed, she looked for something with passwords on it. They were not in Wright's appointment book nor were they in the top desk drawer. She found them under the desk blotter.

Lynn was reading the list of passwords when the office door opened and Jeff Wright walked in.

"What in the hell are you doing in my office?" he screamed.

* * * * *

Tony D'Alessio also studied each person who came out of the building, comparing them both with his memory from Saturday night and the photo in front of him. More than fifty people had come out of the door since noon, but none of them was his man.

But now a new car entered the parking lot. A state police car and, even from the distance where the car parked, it appeared to be the same trooper who had carried out the woman several hours earlier.

The trooper's presence altered the calculus of taking out the man he had been sent to retrieve. Tony had a well-hidden gun in the car but his preferred weapon, when he used one, was his knife. He used a gun only as a last resort. Policemen, on the other hand, knew only guns, which was both their strength and their weakness. Tony did not especially want to kill a state trooper, but neither would he leave without doing his assigned job.

* * * * *

Bergeron was in place. He had been told to wait until the analysis of what was found in the conference room was completed. He contemplated calling Captain Hurley and telling him of the conversation with Katie Laconda identifying Jeff Wright as the likely killer. But if he did that, it would involve her in the chain of evidence. On the drive to SoftRidge he had made the decision that he would avoid acknowledging Katie Laconda as the source of his information unless there was no other option.

But he needed to call Lynn, to let her know that she must take special care with Wright. He called her cell number.

Six rings later, her voice mail kicked in. That wasn't right. She knew it was him and she knew he wouldn't call frivolously. Perhaps she was in a meeting.

He hung up and patted his pockets, feeling for the slip of paper with Deb Fowler's phone number. He found it and called. She picked up immediately.

"Deb, where's Lynn?"

"She's copying some files from some computers. She said she'd just be a few minutes."

"Find her and tell her she needs to stay away from Jeff Wright. He's our guy."

There was a brief silence. "That's one of the two guys whose computer files she was going to copy," Deb said. Then, from somewhere in the building but clearly audible over Deb's phone, Lou could hear the sound of shouting.

Lou dropped his phone and began sprinting for the lobby door.

* * * * *

"I'm looking for some personnel files you promised me earlier," Lynn said, trying to smile and look cheerful. "You weren't here and Larry Driscoll said it was OK to…"

Jeff Wright took in the tableau and focused on the askew blotter and slip of paper in her hand. His face was red and his teeth were bared. "Then what the hell is that in your hand?"

"I thought some of the files might be encrypted and…"

"You have no right to be in this office!" Wright screamed.

"I'm just…"

"You're not supposed to be alive!" he raged.

"Well, I am…" Lynn was still trying to be conciliatory, though it was now apparent that this was the face of the man who had tried to kill her.

"What the hell does it take to get rid of you?" Wright said, his face contorted. "Who the hell are you, you goddamn Polish bitch?"

Lynn's cell phone began to ring.

"Turn that damn thing off!"

"It's just my phone," Lynn said, trying for her calmest voice. She was starting to move around the desk. Inside, she was shaking, and, her eyes darted around the office, looking for anything that might work as a weapon. The phone rang a second time.

"You bitch!" Wright screamed. He took a step toward her, sensing that she was about to attempt to run for safety.

Lynn remembered seeing a pair of scissors in the center desk drawer. Her hand went slowly to the drawer. As it did, the phone rang a third time.

"Turn off that damn phone!" Wright screamed.

"I can't," Lynn said in exasperation, wondering why he was fixated on the phone. Her hand moved to where she could slide open the drawer. She started to do so, and Wright saw the movement.

"The hell you will!" he screamed, spittle flying from his mouth. "You're finally going to die like you should have died!"

The phone rang again.

Wright lunged for the desk. Lynn abandoned her plan to grab the scissors. She grabbed the password list and memory stick from the side of the computer and ran around the desk, toward the door, away from Wright's lunge.

Wright reached out as she passed by, snatching her shirt. Lynn jerked away, hearing the fabric tear on the sleeve of one arm. She ran for the door. Behind her, she heard Wright pull open a drawer.

She ran into the hallway, then turned right toward the lobby, which lay perhaps two hundred feet away through an area of Steelcase partitions and another corridor, along which was Larry Driscoll's office.

She heard footsteps behind her and she shouted for help, but the few people in the open area of the office only looked on in confusion. "Help!" she cried again. The footsteps were gaining on her.

Mentally, she calculated the odds of gaining safety inside Driscoll's office versus the opportunities the lobby would present. Deb, Driscoll and Kepner were inside but, if the door were locked, Wright would have all the time he needed to stab her.

She passed by Driscoll's door, pounded on the wall as she went by, and sprinted down the final short corridor to the lobby. She could hear Wright's footsteps growing louder. She could hear his ragged breathing. She kept the memory stick and password list tightly in her fist.

Lynn burst into the lobby, past the startled receptionist, and ran for the door. As she did, she saw Lou racing for the door from the parking lot.

She pushed on the door, which slowed her slightly and she turned her head to see Wright directly behind her. He raised his arm, the scissors held like a knife. The door opened, and she felt the cool air outside.

Wright's arm came down and she felt the brush of his hand against her back. He had missed her by inches. She went through the door, not looking behind her. In front of her, Lou was less than ten feet away, running hard. She saw him plant his feet and leap, but at a point behind her and slightly to her right. Lynn lurched away from where Bergeron was aimed.

As Lou sailed by her she saw the look of grim determination on his face. There was a 'thump' as two bodies collided. Lynn stopped and turned. Bergeron and Wright were in a writhing pile. Wright raised his arm, the scissors again held as a knife and this time plunged into Lou's bicep. Bergeron yowled in pain but did not stop. His hands were on Wright's neck in a chokehold. Wright's arm went up and the scissors came down again. A fountain of blood sprayed up from Bergeron's arm.

Then Lynn saw the gun on the ground, which had fallen from Lou's pocket in the collision with Wright. She did not hesitate, but rushed forward to pick it up. She was only a few feet from the two of them. Wright lifted his arm again, the scissors ready to do more, possibly fatal, damage.

She positioned herself so that she could shoot Wright without danger of hitting Lou. She pulled the trigger.

The trigger would not budge.

She pulled harder as she saw Wright's arm squeezing on the scissors, preparing for yet another jab.

Then there was a movement behind her.

"Get out of the way!" a man's voice said. A large leg and shoe shot out in front of her and kicked the scissors out of Wright's hand.

Wright screamed in pain. A large bearded man with an ear ring reached down, grabbed Wright's wrist and twisted it more than 180 degrees. Wright screamed again and the man jerked Wright off of the ground with a single pull. Only then did Lynn see the blood pooling on the ground underneath Lou's arm.

"I said, get out of my way," the bearded man said. "This one's mine." Lynn quickly fell to her knees, seeing the look of agony on Bergeron's face. Her hands went instinctively to the wound. Her own shirt was already torn from Wright's lunge back in his office. She tugged at the remnant of her sleeve, desperate to create a tourniquet.

The bearded man grunted slightly as he hefted Wright over his shoulder. Wright screamed yet again and the bearded man did something that caused Wright to scream even more loudly. The bearded man began trotting, Wright over his shoulder, toward a car.

The entire sequence of events outside of the lobby, from the time Lynn burst through the door and Lou had started his flying leap, had taken under twenty seconds. The people at the picnic benches had at first seemed immobilized by the violence taking place in front of the building. As soon as the bearded man began loping toward his car with Wright thrown over his shoulder, those people began to rise and start running toward the point where Lynn now kneeled over Bergeron.

Lynn tore the sleeve of her blouse free and twisted it around Lou's arm, looking up in time to see the bearded man reach his car, open the trunk, and throw Wright in as he would a bale of peat moss. The bearded man scrambled back to the driver's door, opened it, started the engine, and burned rubber tearing out of the driveway.

The tourniquet staunched the bleeding. The pool of blood was large but no longer growing. Lou opened his eyes and looked up at Lynn. In front of her, she saw Deb and Driscoll run out the lobby door, panicked looks on their faces.

"Get rid of the gun," he whispered. "Now. Hide it. No one

should know about it. It'll hurt someone innocent. And don't think this means we're even."

And then he passed out, and Lynn began screaming for help.

24.

The Nashua police arrived, followed closely by the state police and an ambulance. Deb choreographed calls to 911, describing Bergeron's injuries and need for medical attention. The paramedics called the wounds – there had been a third puncture by the scissors Lynn had not seen – 'serious but not life-threatening'.

There were multiple mysteries and Lynn answered all questions carefully.

Why had Wright attacked her? He had apparently snapped under the strain of the acquisition deadline and had come to see Clarenden Brothers as the cause of his life spinning out of control. He was almost certainly behind the earlier attacks on her rather than Bill Griffin, who had only tried to steal money from the company. Why Wright had fixated on her, Lynn had no idea. A doctor at St. Joseph's had thrown out some psychological clues, and Lynn had stupidly chosen to ignore them. The police should speak with Dr. Fukiyama. He had insights into Wright that might offer hints to his motives.

Who was the bearded man? Lynn honestly had no idea. She had been focused on tending to Bergeron. She only knew that he had kicked the scissors out of Wright's hands, immobilized him, and taken him away. She had never seen the man before and did not know he was in the parking lot. She never got a good look at him, didn't see his car, and certainly could not help the police with a license number.

The police repeatedly asked her about the gun that employees on the picnic benches said they saw in her hand. Lynn expressed surprise and said there never was a gun. She had stood over the two of them, trying to find a way to wrestle the scissors out of Wright's hand, and perhaps people mistook that action from a distance of fifty or a hundred feet. Lynn did not know why Lou was so adamant that the gun not be found, but she had acted quickly on his whispered plea. The gun, spirited away under Deb's sweatshirt, was in her briefcase.

Deb was able to add the information that, in the seconds before Wright attacked Lynn and Bergeron, Bergeron had called Deb to warn Lynn that Wright was behind the other attacks. He did not explain how he knew; the call had lasted only a few seconds. Captain Hurley was able to confirm that Trooper Bergeron had been told to watch for and follow the two suspects, should either one leave the building. He had been told not to approach either man, but such instructions would not apply if someone's life were in danger, as Lynn Kowalchuk's definitely was when she came running out the door followed by a man with a pair of scissors.

Lynn was an object of sympathy as well as of admiration. Her blue, Oxford-cloth shirt was spattered with blood and had only one sleeve. But everyone knew that she had torn off the other sleeve to make the tourniquet that had saved the state trooper's life. What they did not know was that, lodged in the pocket of her slacks, was a full, 32-gigabyte memory stick and a piece of paper containing passwords for files from Jeff Wright's computer.

* * * * *

At three o'clock that afternoon, police in Boston's Kenmore Square found a man in a gray suit, badly disoriented, and with a goose-egg sized bump on his head. His identification said he was Claude Johnson, a detective with the New Hampshire State Police. Detective Johnson said he had been taken captive Saturday evening by persons unknown. The abduction was confirmed by video surveillance cameras at Quincy Market. His abductors had demanded information from him and he had refused to cooperate. He had been taken, blindfolded, to a room somewhere in the area and held against his will for forty hours. He did not know why he had been released and he was somewhat surprised that he was still alive. Shortly before being found, he had been struck on the head, had passed out, and found himself wandering Commonwealth Avenue.

* * * * *

Lou Bergeron was kept overnight in the hospital recuperating from multiple stab wounds and loss of blood. His first visitor was Captain Hurley. Bergeron told Hurley that, while driving from the state police barracks in Bedford to take up his position at SoftRidge, he had received a call from Katie Laconda. Laconda told him she had remembered that Jeff Wright had been friends with her brother. Bergeron made no mention that he had met with Katie Laconda at her brother's house.

Bergeron said he never saw the face of the man who had abducted Wright and so could not say if he was the same man whose photo they had viewed in Hurley's office. He had called Lynn to tell her to be cautious around Wright and got no answer. He had then called Deb Fowler and been told that Lynn was likely in Wright's office. However, Bergeron said he left his vehicle only when he heard the sound of screaming in the background as he spoke with Deb.

"Your instincts were perfect," Hurley said, "and you did exactly what I told you to do. Everything was by the book. I've put out what little description we've got of the guy, but nothing's come back. I'm not pressing hard on it for two reasons: first, he may have saved your life and that counts for a lot. Second, assuming it was this Anthony D'Alessio guy, it's a matter of underworld justice. Wright killed Gerry Sullivan trying to cover his tracks. Aidan Parker sent his goons to get Wright. We're never going to find Wright's body, and I'll bet D'Alessio has six witnesses who will swear he was in an all-day poker game somewhere in Boston. In the great scheme of things, Wright got what was coming to him and, unless someone steps forward with something solid on who stuffed Wright into the trunk of that car, the case is going to get cold in a hurry."

"But we need to talk about the gun," Hurley said. "Three people saw the Kowalchuk woman with a gun in her hand, apparently trying to shoot Wright."

"How far away were they?" Bergeron asked. "Fifty feet? A hundred feet? And how many of them have ever seen a gun except on television?"

"There was a gun," Hurley said firmly.

"Then why didn't two police crews find a gun? And, why didn't she use it?"

"My guess is that the safety was on and she didn't know how to flip it off," Hurley said.

"Then maybe she was using my gun. I was otherwise engaged."

"Your gun was in your holster."

"Then I really have no idea," Bergeron said, adding a touch of exasperation to his voice. "No one fired a gun. No one found a gun. Lynn says there was no gun."

"You see, I can fit almost everything else into this neat theory I have," Hurley said. "Last Monday, Wright contacted his old school buddy Joey Gavrilles to get the Kowalchuk woman out of the picture. Joey called Gerry Sullivan. Sullivan met with Wright, collected a fee, and then hired Slick Willie Catalano as the local talent. Catalano did his job, but Kowalchuk bounced back with nothing more on her that a couple of bruises. So Wright went back to Sullivan and demanded that Catalano do the job right, and he probably handed over more money. Catalano went to Kowalchuk's hotel – most likely with the idea of killing her – but you got the inspired idea that he was going to be there. Claude took Catalano out of the picture with one clean shot."

"Wright, however, felt both that he was being cheated and that Sullivan was incompetent to do a simple job. Not knowing how these things work, he was also fearful that when everyone got to court, Catalano would roll on Sullivan and that Sullivan would roll on Wright. So, he set up another meeting – probably saying he wanted to get his money back. Sullivan was no fool, and he probably had other plans for Wright, but Wright spotted the set-up and got lucky. Sullivan went under a truck. Wright was so happy with what he had done that he decided to close the loop and take out Joey Gavrilles. He killed Gavrilles and tried to torch the house. What he didn't count on was that Sullivan worked for Aidan Parker, and Parker doesn't stand by when someone kills one of his boys."

Hurley paused, looking for a reaction from Bergeron. He saw only keen interest. He continued, "The Boston PD, faced with a homicide, started tracing Sullivan's movements using surveillance camera tapes. Parker was looking over their shoulder, trying to get the same information. Then you showed up with a photo array asking exactly the right questions and having narrowed the field to just a handful of finalists, which definitely caught their interest. When Claude went back Saturday night and asked the questions again – this time of the right people – Parker's guys were there."

"Claude's statement is that he declined to tell them anything, and that's the way the official record is going to stand. But what I think happened is that Claude, being no fool, gave them the name, and they stashed him somewhere until the job was done. I'm told that Aidan Parker can be brutal, but he's not dumb, and killing a detective would be an act of manifest stupidity."

"Wright did something that kept him out of everyone's sight until Monday morning. He had to be somewhere other than Nashua; otherwise Parker's man would have snatched Wright from his home. He thought he was home free. He went into work with a great new plan to get rid of Kowalchuk once and for all, his way. He laced her coffee with speed. The problem was, you showed up. You've treated guys in the Army with amphetamine poisoning. Lynn was back in action in a couple of hours. That, by the way, is going to earn you an additional commendation."

Hurley paused. "This is where the theory needs some work: I talked with the psychiatrist who evaluated Kowalchuk. He told her, in no uncertain terms, to stay away from SoftRidge. Yet that's exactly where Kowalchuk went. She confronted the two guys, one of whom is the guy who has been trying to kill her. Probably rubbed their noses in the fact that she was alive and well. Next thing you know, Wright is trying to stab her with scissors. But you're there and so is D'Alessio. You get Wright off of Kowalchuk, D'Alessio finishes the job."

"So, what about the gun?" Hurley asked. "If it was Wright's gun, he would have used it on Kowalchuk instead of a pair of scissors. If Kowalchuk had the gun all along, she wouldn't have waited for Wright to try to stab her. If D'Alessio had brought the gun, he would have used it. Plus, people say Kowalchuk already had the gun in her hand when D'Alessio showed up. Which means you must have had the gun – a second gun. Except that you didn't have a holster for it and a gun isn't exactly the kind of thing you carry around in your pocket unless you don't care about losing valuable body parts."

Hurley looked again for a reaction from Bergeron. There was still no hint of an impending confession. Hurley continued, "The other part of the theory that needs an answer is what Wright was trying to hide. The guy at St. Joe's said Wright may have been basically unstable and cracked under the pressure. I'm not buying that. You don't put out a contract on someone because you're distressed that some investment banker is going to put you out of a job."

"I think Wright had something big going on. He perceived Kowalchuk was the only person with the brains to figure out what it was. We're not the IRS or the state department of revenue. It's not our job to figure it out. But, if Kowalchuk found something, it would be nice to know it. You apparently got very close to Miss Kowalchuk. And there's still the question of where the gun came from."

Hurley leaned back in his chair and studied Bergeron's face, waiting for a response.

"Captain, if Lynn found something, she never told me, and that's the God's-honest truth," Bergeron said. "And if she did find something, I think she'd immediately notify the companies that are paying her. That's her job. She blew the whistle on that Griffin guy in about thirty seconds. I'd say that, if Wright had some scam going, it died with him and we'll never know what it was. And, as to the gun, I never saw it. I don't think there was a gun. I think people sitting fifty or a hundred feet away watch '*CSI*' too much."

Hurley said nothing for a moment, then, "Katie Laconda – whose husband is about as well connected in crime circles as anyone can be in New Hampshire – did call you shortly after you left my office, which was roughly fifteen minutes before you called the two women. Both your and Laconda's cell phone records show that. But it was a short call. The interesting part was that she used a cell phone. So, why did she use a cell phone? Why not call from her home phone?"

"She said she was making arrangements for her brother's funeral," Lou said. "I didn't ask her where she was."

"Maybe she wasn't in Portsmouth," Hurley said. "Maybe, just maybe, she was here in Nashua. And, with her husband's connections, maybe she had a gun."

"There was no gun," Bergeron said adamantly.

They stared at each other for more than a minute, neither saying a word.

"You've made quite a splash, Lou," Hurley said. "Claude says you're a natural detective. I agree. You've got at least a week's paid leave to get healed. When you come back, you're going to start with some classes up in Concord. They're the ones that detective candidates take. On paper, you don't have nearly enough years on the job to qualify to take the exam, but that MP stint in the Army counts for something, and the state tries to keep good talent. So, figure two or three days a week for the foreseeable future, you're going to be in class."

Hurley watched the grin creep across Bergeron's face.

"You can also kiss your days off goodbye, too, because Claude is taking you under his wing. It's possible that, two years from now, New Hampshire may have its youngest Detective."

"That would be an honor, sir," Bergeron said.

"Then get healthy and then get back to work," Hurley said and shook Bergeron's uninjured hand.

* * * * *

Lynn visited Bergeron that evening.

"I don't think I've ever seen the inside of a hospital more than I have this one," she said. "First me – twice – then you."

"You saved my life," Bergeron said.

"I'd still be there squeezing that trigger and getting nowhere if it weren't for the guy with the beard," Lynn said. "Some lifesaver I am."

"Remind me to show you how to take off the safety on a Glock sometime. You still saved my life." Bergeron squeezed her hand.

Lynn smiled.

"My captain was here to see me a little earlier," Bergeron said. "As far as I'm concerned, there never was a gun. Just get rid of it when you can. It belonged to Katie Laconda, who brought it with her to Nashua with some idea of shooting Wright for killing her brother. She recognized his name when I gave her the names of the executives at SoftRidge and, like a dummy, I told her what they all had in common. She was going to avenge his death. Fortunately, at the last minute, she called me. I took the gun and told her to go home."

"You're a sweet guy," Lynn said. "She trusted you. You kept her out of it."

"And my captain is content to leave Anthony D'Alessio out of it unless something happens that brings him back into the story. Claude Johnson spent the weekend as the guest of the Irish mafia in Boston but showed up this afternoon uninjured. Something about 'underworld justice'. It looks like all the cases either get closed or marked, 'unsolvable'."

"Anthony D'Alessio was the guy with the beard?" Lynn asked.

"Almost certainly. His assignment was to snatch Wright. No one will ever see Wright again alive or dead."

"Well, Wright or no Wright, we think we can close up SoftRidge by Wednesday," Lynn said. "My boss – Andy Greenglass – is back up here with two more associates. They've told me I can stay or go home. My work is done."

"Which are you going to do?" Bergeron asked.

"They're going to release you tomorrow, aren't they?"

"That's what I hear."

"Then you'll need someone to take care of you for a few days," Lynn said. "I'm a lousy housekeeper, but I can change your dressings."

"What about whatever Wright was stealing?" Bergeron asked.

Lynn shrugged. "There are six people from Clarenden there now, plus two accountants and two lawyers, all from our side. SoftRidge's side has another ten people on the case, all of them having had the fear of God put in them that if anything else gets found, their jobs are history. If twenty people can't find it, chances are it was something Wright was going to pull at the very end of the sale, and now it will never happen."

"Which doesn't explain why you went back to SoftRidge this morning," Bergeron said.

Lynn gave Bergeron a light kiss on the forehead. "I decided I wasn't going to be pushed around anymore. I was tired of being a victim."

Epilogue

Final due diligence was completed on SoftRidge on September 27. The formal sale of SoftRidge to Pericles closed two days later. On the announcement, Pericles' shares rose a little less than one percent. On October 3, shareholders, vendors, and employees of SoftRidge received all payments due to them.

As expected, SoftRidge customers were informed the same week that Pericles would cease production of all SoftRidge products effective with the end of the year and that comparable, albeit higher-priced Pericles products would be substituted on orders with delivery times beyond December 31. Immediately after the closing, requests from current and prospective customers for quotes on Pericles products that had previously overlapped SoftRidge's offerings began coming back uniformly twelve percent higher in price. In the absence of an alternative supplier of comparable quality or technology, customers complained but nevertheless paid the higher prices. Due in large part to higher gross margins resulting from price increases on product lines no longer impacted by SoftRidge competition, Pericles reported record profits in the quarter ended December 31 of that year.

All SoftRidge managers were immediately laid off. In exact conformance with the requirements of the WARN Act, one third of remaining SoftRidge employees were also let go. Additional employees were laid off as soon as subsequent trigger dates were reached. By the end of March, the SoftRidge facility was vacant and all former employees had been dismissed. In the words of one Pericles executive, "It was as though SoftRidge had never existed."

In its annual report, Pericles Chairman and CEO Ross Maynard attributed his company's record performance to 'superior people offering superior products' and lumped the acquisition of SoftRidge in among six other companies purchased during the year. "We will continue to aggressively pursue the acquisition of weaker market participants when it suits our long-term interests and where it helps clarify customer choices," Mr. Maynard said in his letter to shareholders.

In early October, Lynn Kowalchuk received a one-time performance bonus of $50,000 from Clarenden Brothers for her work on the SoftRidge project. The partner who presented the check to Lynn at the closing dinner made it clear that the check was in addition to what was likely to be a substantial year-end bonus for overall excellence and contribution to the firm. He intimated that Lynn's performance was such that a vice presidency was all but assured within the next year and that she was well established on an equity partner track.

In mid-October, Lynn was offered, but turned down, an offer from Pericles to become that company's Vice President – Mergers and Acquisitions. Despite Lynn's turndown, or perhaps because of it, Clarenden's success on the SoftRidge assignment led to the investment banking firm being given three additional M&A projects by Pericles.

In mid-November, Charles Li, formerly the vice president of engineering for SoftRidge and now unemployed, received a call from a Bay Area venture capitalist representing a pool that, the caller said, specialized in funding start-ups by UC-Berkeley alumni. The venture capitalist said that he could advance up to four and a half million dollars to any group of ex-SoftRidge engineers that Li could assemble.

"It's a generous offer," Li told the caller, "but I signed a non-compete agreement and so did everyone else on the engineering staff. Our hands are tied."

"We've had considerable experience with overturning unenforceable non-competes," the venture capitalist said. "In California, they're already considered illegal restraint of trade, and that thinking is making rapid headway on the east coast as well. And, given the treatment your team got —salary reductions for managers and not even a payout for unused vacation days — I'd bet that a lot of judges in New Hampshire would be itching to take that case under advisement."

"I can't use any technology that I developed at SoftRidge," Li warned.

"It's our experience that bright technologists have work-arounds for technology owned by others, and that it's frequently cheaper and more elegant," the venture capitalist said. "We're willing to roll the dice if you are."

Li and a group of twelve engineers formed a company in the following weeks. As predicted by the venture capitalist, the non-compete agreements signed by each of them was held to be unenforceable by reason of hardship and undue broadness.

Frank Kepner kept his vow to start hiking the White Mountains on October 1. By the middle of November, during which it rained or snowed 24 of the 45 days he had camped, he remembered his mother's advice to 'be careful what you wish for'. Maybe going back to work wouldn't be so bad. Among the messages awaiting him upon his return home was one from Li. He became the fourteenth member of the venture-capital-backed company.

The following May, Pericles issued a press release acknowledging that the Securities and Exchange Commission had launched an inquiry into the company's pricing of stock options, and the possible backdating of those options to benefit selected company executives. Ross Maynard was quoted in the company statement as saying he was confident that Pericles' practices were in keeping with those of the industry and that everything the company's Board had done had been specifically blessed by the company's accounting firm. A month later, Maynard and two Board members resigned, and Pericles restated three years' worth of earnings sharply downward. The company's independent auditors also resigned. In six weeks, the stock fell by half. In July, Clarenden Brothers received its third and final assignment from Pericles; this one to find a merger partner for the beleaguered company.

* * * * *

Throughout this period, Lynn visited Nashua monthly, and Bergeron made several trips to New York.

Lynn's feelers to investment banking firms in the Boston area produced multiple offers. She accepted one from Highsmith & Co., which offered her a vice presidency and an equity track. Upon learning that Lynn Kowalchuk had been offered a position with the firm, Josh Tilighman threatened to resign. He was told, bluntly, that his services would not be missed. He left Highsmith & Co. two months later.

In her discussions with each firm with which she interviewed, however, all made it clear that Lynn's future lay in her ability to begin attracting business, which meant an end to due diligence and an emphasis on pitching the firm's services.

"I don't know if I'm ready to grow up," Lynn said to Bergeron one weekend in June. They were at his apartment, the makings of brunch spread out on a sunny breakfast table. "I wish I had more time."

"You grew up when you and Deb took the cab back to SoftRidge," Bergeron said. "You told me you were tired of being pushed around. I don't think it was just Jeff Wright you were talking about. I think you took control of your life that day."

"Maybe," Lynn said. "I don't regret anything I did that day, or for the rest of that week."

"The rest of the week?" Bergeron said. "You took me home, bathed me, fed me, and then worked every night until three in the morning on that damn computer of yours. There's not a lot to regret there."

"You're absolutely right," Lynn said. "I have nothing to regret."

Acknowledgements

My usual practice in writing acknowledgements is to first thank those individuals who helped me learn about the subjects that form the background of my mysteries. Through them, I have become an instant (albeit shallow) expert on topics ranging from modular housing and vernal pools to garden club meeting procedure.

For *Deal Killer's* portrayal of the world of investment banking and mergers and acquisitions, I have no one onto whom I can shift the blame if something isn't right. Until I started writing, I had spent my life in the corporate world and came to know it well. The final two decades of my career were spent around investment bankers and I came to know them, also, quite well. Perhaps *too* well. I have met and worked with real-life counterparts to every one of the bankers portrayed in the book. Fortunately, there are far more Lynn Kowalchuks than there are Josh Tilighmans.

Deal Killer came about because I wanted to write a work of suspense set inside a corporation in the midst of being acquired. I wanted a credible plot and a plausible crime. Sadly, it is my observation that most novels, films and television series that attempt to weave plots around corporate intrigue are, well, not very believable. To be blunt, most of those plots are so far into make-believe that I think the writers aren't even trying. You can take my word that what happens in *Deal Killer* is entirely credible. In fact, I would be surprised if it hasn't happened.

I also wanted to create a compelling protagonist; not a superman who instantly sees the Big Picture but, rather, someone who starts with the uncomfortable feeling that 'something isn't right' and works it out from there. Lynn is such a character. I have sat across the table from young investment bankers like her many times. I also wanted a law enforcement officer who is just learning the ropes; who will make – and recover – from mistakes. Lou Bergeron is such a cop. Every good rookie cop needs a mentor who has seen too much. Claude Johnson fits that description. And, I wanted a villain who could exist in the real world: someone who thinks they're smarter than everyone in the room and who finds out that such assumptions can have disastrous results. I've worked around such people more than I care to admit.

It takes a village to turn a manuscript into something that is actually readable. Connie Stolow, Faith Clunie and Susan Hammond provided the proofreading skills that I so obviously lack and I am grateful for their perseverance and sharp eyes. Ms. Hammond, a trained emergency responder, also allowed me to write accurately about Lynn's car crash. Diane Cullen shared her memories of growing up in Lou Bergeron's hometown of Berlin, New Hampshire.

Writers thrive on appreciative audiences and I want to express my thanks to the book clubs, libraries, senior centers – and now garden clubs – that have hosted me in recent months. Please keep the offers coming. And a special 'thank you' to the staff of BookEnds in Winchester, Massachusetts, for being the truest of true believers in my fiction.

And, as always, I thank my wife, Betty, for peering over my shoulder to offer cogent comments, for not getting miffed when I get a great idea at 4:30 a.m., and for encouraging me to keep coming up with interesting ways to kill people.

Made in the USA
Charleston, SC
09 July 2015